GRACE IN THE DESERT

CHRISTINE DILLON

LINKS IN THE CHAIN PRESS

www.storytellerchristine.com

Grace in the Desert

Cover Design: Lankshear Design

ISBN: 978-0-6485890-5-1

For those who have poured prayer over my life. Your ministry is often hidden but I look forward to one day 'seeing behind the scenes' and understanding your part in what God has brought about.

And for my nieces: Isabella, Jemimah, Hannah, Heidi, and Harmony. I love you so much and am proud of the choices you are making.

May you all, "Trust in the Lord with all your heart and lean not on your own understanding. In all your ways acknowledge Him and He will direct your paths."
Proverbs 3:5-6

NOTES TO READERS

* All books are written from a worldview, be it secular, communist or New Age. This book is unashamedly Christian. If you're not a Christian, the views expressed by the characters might appear strange BUT it's a great opportunity. Why? Because this story allows you, if you're not yet a follower of Jesus, to see things from a perspective totally different to your own. Are the character's views consistent and does their worldview make sense of the challenges in their lives?

* This is an Australian story and thus uses Australian spelling, grammar, punctuation, and word usage.

* This series highlights different parts of Australia in each book. Most of this book is set in Sydney but there are scenes in Kangaroo Valley (New South Wales) and, Perth and Mandurah (Western Australia).

PROLOGUE

*H*e'd always considered himself a strong man. Physically strong. Emotionally strong. Spiritually strong.

But he'd been naïve. Proud. Never considering that some things are capable of overwhelming even the strongest men.

Like the accident that day. A drawn-out spinning, screeching, crashing, and then silence.

Silence.

Silence, except for the sound of his own laboured breaths. Laboured breaths, that ever since had formed the backing track to his nightmares.

Silence. The silence that meant an absence of life.

There were many days in the weeks following the accident when he'd have welcomed death. But somehow his heart went on beating. Laughing at him. Torturing him with its robust health. His body went on waking each morning, regardless of how much or how little sleep he'd had the night before.

Work gave him a full month off. For recovery. Recuperation. The funeral. Perhaps he should have gone back to work immediately, because home had become an empty shell, echoing with loneliness. Populated with ghosts and memories of ghosts.

He'd closed the doors on most of the rooms. Anything to avoid the cheerful clutter of their contents. Anything to avoid sorting and giving away possessions that had been bought with such delight and expectation. A pair of tiny shoes, a handmade dress, a book to be read over and over.

He'd reached into his wardrobe, dragged out his clothes, and transferred everything to the spare room. He couldn't sleep in the master bedroom. The bed was too big, too cold, too wide. And he could still hear his wife's giggle in the darkness. Feel the warmth of her breath on his cheek.

Days passed without his noting the precise time or day of the week. Food had no taste. He chewed it out of habit and shed eight kilos in a month. Weight he couldn't afford to lose.

Thirty days, and he was still living the event daily—and nightly. No drugs in the world could obliterate the squeal of brakes and the shriek of twisting metal. Or worse, the silence that had followed.

He shook his head. *God, can you not give me rest? Peace?*

There was no answer, as there had been none for the last thirty days. Thirty days he never wanted to endure again. Thirty days of grey nothingness. Thirty days of emotional wipeout.

God?

The doorbell rang, jerking him back to life in an ordinary suburban house. They'd moved to Fremantle to have more peace, but the doorbell hadn't rung in two weeks. No phone calls, no visitors, no invitations.

In the first two weeks, various friends and church folk had dropped in with fruit and meals. They'd shuffled their feet and ummed and aahed and offered him platitudes he hadn't heard.

Once his parents went home after the funeral, he'd erected a personal Berlin Wall, bristling with barbed wire and threatening warning notices. Soon, no one had been determined enough to scale the necessary heights, and he'd been too tired to care.

The bell rang again. Whoever they were, they were persistent.

He staggered to his feet, slapped his face to wake himself, and ran his hand through his dishevelled hair. Not worth the effort if it were only someone trying to sell him an overpriced vacuum cleaner.

He walked down the hall, his bare feet slapping against the floorboards. The door stuck, and he pulled it hard. It bounced off his shin, and his eyes watered.

Standing on the front step was the last person he expected to see. His mouth dropped open, but only a strangled sound emerged.

"Son," the man standing outside said. "I've lost the rest of my family. I'm not going to lose you too."

CHAPTER 1

*H*er mother was making a major mistake.

Rachel pulled the suitcase off the bed and stood it upright near the door. She dropped to her knees and looked under the bed for anything that might have rolled there, then checked all the cupboards. Not that it mattered if anything was left. Her mother would only be a few kilometres down the road.

She didn't want to accuse her own mother of being delusional, but her parents had been separated for six months. After that long, anyone but her mother would have given up on their marriage. Especially marriage to William, a man who Rachel could no longer think of as father, not after he didn't turn up to his own daughter's funeral.

Rachel snorted as she hefted the suitcase in her left hand. Esther's cancer had merely shown everyone William's true colours. And now her mother wanted to move back in with him?

Rachel jerked the door closed behind her and turned down the hallway towards the front door. At some point, though she could not say when, she had made the mental shift to calling her father by his name. The thought of calling him 'father' now made her feel queasy. He didn't deserve the title of 'father', let alone something as friendly as 'Dad'. Not after his treatment of her. She hadn't seen him since she was fifteen and never wanted to see him again.

Rachel rolled her eyes. Of course, he probably thought she didn't deserve the title of 'daughter' either. Not that it mattered. She had no desire to regain his good opinion. No desire to reconcile.

Rachel opened the front door and the screen. The light and scent of an early spring morning poured in. Her mother had already backed her car up the drive and was waiting for the suitcase to go in first and before adding the boxes of craft supplies and assorted odds and ends.

Rachel put the suitcase in the boot and left her mother to fuss with everything else. She went to join her grandmother next to the car.

Her mother was glowing. Anyone would think she was going to her wedding. Rachel bit her lip to prevent any more snorts or eye rolls. She'd give it a week before the glow was rubbed off her mother's face. Mum believed God had done a mighty miracle and now William would be a completely different person.

As if.

It wasn't that Rachel denied God could work a miracle. He could. After all, she'd seen more than a few in her own life. But William? That would be a miracle of gargantuan proportions.

She was going to wait and see. Mum might be going off all starry-eyed but then her mother was an optimistic woman who had long proven blind to her husband's failures.

"Okay, I'm off." Her mother shut the car boot and moved around to the driver's side. "Pray for us."

"Of course, dearie." Naomi leaned in to kiss her daughter-in-law's cheek. "Come back soon and visit."

Rachel hugged her mother too, then stood back to let the car drive off.

Naomi put her bony arm around Rachel's waist, and they stood at the gate and waved until the car turned the corner and disappeared from sight.

Naomi wiped the corner of her eye. "It's just you and me now."

"Do you think Mum is going to be okay?" Rachel asked.

"It's certainly not going to be easy. I can't imagine William will cope well with unemployment."

Rachel raised her eyebrows. "Yeah, well, it was the resignation that changed Mum's mind."

Rachel had thought William would rather die than leave Victory Church. Once her mother heard his resignation speech, she'd come rushing home, eyes all sparkly, and started packing.

Her mother might be convinced, but Rachel would reserve judgment. Leopards didn't change their spots and all that.

From her earliest years, William's claws had torn her life apart. No child ever had a hope of meeting his standards. And for what? To protect his precious reputation.

She shook her head. Her mother and grandmother were sweet women, always believing the best and always quick to forgive. Naomi had spent decades praying. Now she was rejoicing at the answers, but maybe old age had left her a little credulous. Not that anyone could blame an old woman for wanting all her prayers answered while she was still around to see the results.

Rachel squeezed her grandmother's waist. Gently, so she wouldn't snap in half. Her sister, Esther, had once described their grandmother as an energetic sparrow before Naomi had fallen and broken her hip. Gran was nothing remotely like a sparrow now.

Sometimes Rachel was fine when she thought of Esther. Other times, a tear sprang to her eye, unwanted and inconvenient, as much for Esther as for her own regret at wasting so many of their last days together. The tear was there now. She blinked it away. Stupid. Now all she had left were her memories, and a pile of Esther's diaries—diaries she hadn't yet had the heart to open.

"You're quiet, Rachel," Naomi said.

"Just thinking."

"You're not worrying about your mother, are you?"

"Not really. She's a grown woman," Rachel said.

Naomi stopped and turned to Rachel. "But you don't approve of her going back to your father?"

Rachel swallowed the bile in her throat. This wasn't a discussion she wanted to have. Not with her grandmother. After all, she was William's mother. "Shall we walk around the garden?" she asked.

Naomi let Rachel lead her across the lawn and over to the rockery. "You didn't answer my question." Naomi turned to look at her.

Rachel avoided her grandmother's gaze. "I don't want to see Mum getting hurt again."

"Your mother and I have been praying William would face up to his issues. Now the process has started, she wants to support him." Naomi reached out a hand and deadheaded a rose. "She thinks if your father is walking away from his job, it's a good time for them to make a fresh start together."

Rachel's stomach soured. "Please, Gran, don't call him my father."

Naomi raised an eyebrow.

Rachel cleared her throat. "I know you want me to forgive him, but I can't even contemplate such a thing. Not at the moment."

Naomi smiled and kept quiet. Rachel knew what the little smile meant. Naomi would keep praying. Well, she was welcome to do so. Rachel wouldn't stop her, but she wouldn't hold her breath about answers either. After all, William hadn't talked to his mother for forty years, and his slanderous lies had prevented the rest of the family from looking for Naomi for far too long. At least he'd finally failed in that.

Rachel took Naomi's arm and assisted her up the back stairs onto the verandah. Her life—and Esther's and Mum's too—had been all the better for reconnecting with Naomi.

"Now Mum's gone, are you sure you don't want me to move out?" Rachel winked. "You know, get back some of that peace and quiet you had before we all turned up."

Naomi gave her a 'don't be silly' look. "As if I could manage without you."

CHAPTER 2

*P*ete Klopper reached into the tray of his work truck and grabbed the first of many dead branches from the back. He'd spent a glorious Sunday afternoon at a friend's property out in the bush, collecting as many twisty branches as he could find, hoping Rachel would find them as full of character as he did.

This was his first year to act as host at the annual work dinner at Klopper's nursery. His dad had been doing them forever, and Pete wanted to get it right. Rachel had been the obvious choice to do the decorating, as her front foyer displays had been generating compliments from day one. He certainly wasn't volunteering. It had been obvious to everyone since he was in pre-school that he didn't have a single design gene in his body.

It was much safer if he stuck with the organisational and business side of things and lent a hand when needed.

Rachel was moving pot plants around from one side of the display area to another.

"What do you want done with all these branches?" Pete asked.

"Josh and I set up a rope down on the back fence." She put down the pot she was holding. "I'll grab a few branches and show you what we're doing."

She was back soon, holding three branches taller than she was. The corner of his mouth curved up. She couldn't blame him—she was the one who'd requested three-metre branches.

"These are perfect," Rachel said. "I'll spray them silver, add some sparkles, and put strands of blue lights between them."

A picture swam into his mind, a vague memory of branches and lights—something similar to what Rachel was describing. A friend's wedding, perhaps, not long after his own? Whatever it was, he'd had Mai by his side. He sucked in a breath.

"Are you okay?" Rachel asked with a frown.

"Yes," he said, controlling his voice. He never knew what would trigger his memories. Sometimes it was someone who looked like one of his family members. Sometimes it was a line of a song, or the smell of a barbecue, or cut grass. Anything really. And it wasn't consistent. Something would bother him one day, yet be fine on another day.

He was like a boxer with his hands permanently up to protect his face and chest. But every so often the hits would come from elsewhere and slam into places he'd failed to protect.

There were ropes strung up between some trees. Rachel hooked her three branches over a rope, and he followed suit.

She licked her finger and held it up. "No wind today. It's a perfect day for spray painting."

Pete headed back for another load. By the time he got back, Rachel had already painted the first branch and was starting on the second.

"Don't feel you need to do all the carrying," Rachel said. "I can easily send Josh to get the rest."

"I enjoy the change from paperwork," he said.

Rachel stopped what she was doing. "Do you like the business side of things?"

"The accounting side is easy enough." He'd told Rachel he was an accountant but not much else. His father had told the staff that Mai had died in an accident. Thankfully, no one had pried any deeper.

Rachel wasn't the only one avoiding asking personal questions. He didn't know how she was coping with the loss of her sister. She seemed okay, but he knew from personal experience that it was possible to look completely normal on the outside, yet be dying on the inside.

"But there's more than just accounting, isn't there?" Rachel's question jerked him back to their conversation.

"Yes, lots of ordering, but Dad still handles that."

Rachel put down the spray canister. "That's a big job. Especially for someone after a heart attack. Do you think it's too much for him?"

"Has he said anything to you?" Pete asked. Rachel and his father seemed close. She dropped in on his parents at least once a week. Said she appreciated his dad's wisdom.

Rachel shook her head. "He was talking about ordering the Australian native plants the other day. I guess it occurred to me that there might not be anyone else who knows how to do the job." She paused. "Dirk is the only one with the connections to the wholesale nurseries, and relationships like that take time to build."

Pete had been on maintenance mode for so long he'd barely noticed how much his father was still doing. "What are you suggesting?"

Rachel picked up the canister and sprayed another few branches, moving around them to coat all the surfaces. "Oh, I don't know. It might be good to talk with Dirk about it. At the very least, someone else could be meeting some of the suppliers and whole-salers and networking with them." Rachel's voice was tinged with enthusiasm and her eyes sparkled. She sprayed another branch.

In the months since Pete had stepped in to help his father and then to take over the business, he'd never stopped to think about what the staff wanted from their jobs. He should have been paying attention instead of letting things continue on cruise control.

"Let me think about it. I'll fetch the last loads of branches and let you get on with things." He turned to go, then surprised himself with his next words. "And when you're ready to put the branches in the pots, let me know. I should have time to help with getting them set up."

She grinned. "Thanks, and please let me know if there is anything else I can help with. We want to make this a success."

He suspected she could probably run the whole show. He'd been guilty of underestimating her. Who knew what other talents she had hidden beneath her blonde hair and dirty fingernails? His father had said she used to work at one of the high-end cosmetics counters at David Jones. Looking at her now, he couldn't picture it. Presumably his father knew the reason for her move, but Dad was famous for keeping confidences. There were times when such reticence was frustrating.

This was one of them.

CHAPTER 3

s Rachel parked the car, a frisson of excitement danced down her spine. It had been ages since she'd attended a party. She twisted the rear-view mirror and used it to put on her lipstick.

"You look beautiful," her grandmother said. "They won't know what hit them."

"It's mostly people from work." Rachel spread her lips to check she had no lipstick on her teeth. Makeup didn't suit her new job, and she hadn't had a social life to speak of in well over a year. She occasionally missed the glamour of her old life. Very occasionally. Most of it had been cheap glitz. Nowadays, she preferred quality conversations and curling up with a good book after a day of physical work over smiling to attract customers. She'd read more books in the last year than the previous twenty.

"Ready?" she asked Gran.

Rachel got out of the car and went around to help her grandmother. She remembered to bend her knees as Esther always told her to do, and hauled Gran upright. Once she'd made sure her grandmother was steady, walking stick in hand, she locked the car and walked arm in arm with Gran towards the main entrance.

Pinpoints of electric blue shone through the plate glass windows. Rachel glanced towards the café, being used tonight as a sit-down dinner space, with crisp white tablecloths, blue serviettes, and blue candles in the centre of each table.

Pete waved from across the foyer. Rachel waved back before looking around. The silver trees with their tracery of blue lights looked as magical as she'd intended. In half an hour, when it was even darker, they'd look spectacular. The sound of the small water-fall in her foyer display blended with the background music. Spanish guitar. Whose taste was that? Pete's, perhaps? Or Dirk's? She didn't know them well enough to guess.

"Why don't you take me over to say hello to that nice young man," her grandmother said.

Rachel raised her eyebrows. "Do you mean Pete?"

"I certainly do," Gran said with more animation in her tone than Rachel had heard all week. She must make an effort to take her grandmother out more often.

Rachel supported Gran's arm and took her over to where Pete was standing next to the drinks table.

Pete stepped forward with a broad smile. "How are you, Mrs Macdonald? Good to see you again."

He was totally focused on Gran. Surely there wasn't any reason for ignoring her.

"Please call me Naomi."

He dipped his head. "Naomi it is. Can I get you a seat so you can watch people arriving?"

Gran's eyes twinkled. "How did you know I like people watching?"

"I guessed you might." He fetched a seat and fussed about, putting it in the right position and making sure she was settled before pouring her a drink.

Rachel moved directly into Pete's line of sight. "Is there anywhere I can help out?"

"We're okay here, but Mum might need some help with the salads. She's in the kitchen."

Once again, Pete avoided her eyes. The man had barely looked at her. Weird. She'd go to the café via the bathroom and see if she'd somehow got lipstick on her teeth or put on mismatched earrings. She'd done that once as a teenager, to the amusement of every customer at the fish and chips shop.

She headed for the bathroom and peered in the mirror. No. Nothing wrong. She looked rather nice for someone who'd spent the day working with compost.

In the kitchen, Norma was putting salads on the main serving tables.

"I'm here to help if I'm needed," Rachel said.

Norma looked over the tables. "Judging by what you've done with the decorating, I couldn't do better than put you to work making things look their best." She gestured towards the main serving tables. "If you'd do something with the cutlery and glasses, that would be great."

It didn't take Rachel long to finish the task. She had just found a basket to put the cutlery in when she heard a distinctive flat voice behind her.

"Miss Rachel, Miss Rachel, you're here. Come and meet my mum and dad."

She turned. Josh's smile beamed as he bounced across the room and gave her a big hug. He was rather like an overenthusiastic Great Dane puppy, all large paws and playful clumsiness.

She hugged him back. "I'd be delighted to meet your parents. Come and introduce me."

He grabbed her hand and dragged her towards the couple standing near the wall. Josh's mother looked relaxed in jeans and an Oxford shirt matched with pearls. "We're Lyn and Ian," she said with a warm smile. "Great to finally meet someone Josh has talked so much about. Thanks for being a friend to our Josh."

"And Josh has been a great friend to me." Rachel grinned and punched Josh gently on his shoulder. "Taught me everything I know about gardening."

He stood up straight and put out his chest, and Josh's dad looked pleased.

"Do you live close by, Ian?" Rachel asked.

"Fairly close, but we're thinking of downsizing soon. Josh has an older brother and two older sisters, but they've already flown the nest." He winked at his son. "Josh was a surprise at the end of the family."

"A good surprise, Dad?"

Ian put his arm around Josh's shoulder. "The best kind of surprise, son."

A series of lumps clumped in Rachel's throat. "Why don't we go and get this party started?" Rachel said. "The drinks and appetisers are at the back of the foyer."

"Come and see the pretty branches. I helped put them up." Josh pulled his parents out of the café.

Guests kept arriving. Many Rachel didn't know, but she greeted the other workers. Colin, who worked on the main sales counter, was accompanied by his girlfriend, whom Rachel had met a few times. Sam and Dave, the other men with Down Syndrome, also arrived with their parents. They did most of the heavy lifting and carrying around the nursery.

Dirk and Pete concentrated on talking with the various guests from outside the nursery—people whose companies supplied specialty plants, fertilisers, pots, or gardening tools.

Rachel helped Norma by circulating and offering food to the guests. Josh soon came over and asked if he could help. She handed him a basket of crackers and dip, and followed him with the cabanossi and cheese.

She met everyone as she did the rounds. Two people, who knew she'd designed the foyer displays, offered her jobs. She turned them down with a pleased laugh.

The smell of barbecued steak, sausages, and lamb kebabs drifted in from outside.

Pete turned down the music and nodded at his father. Dirk clapped his hands for attention.

Rachel moved to stand next to her grandmother.

"We're just about ready to go into the café area for the main meal. Pete is actually in charge this year, but he likes to let an old man feel useful."

"The place wouldn't run without you and well you know it, Dad," Pete said.

"It's been a bit of a tough year with me out of action for months," Dirk said. "When my doctor said he wouldn't let me work full-time anymore, Pete jumped to the rescue, and I'm relieved to say he's going to stay on."

Everyone clapped. Josh and some of the others hooted and stamped their feet.

"It's self-service as usual, and feel free to sit wherever you want. First, I'm going to pray. It's a habit I have, to remind me of all the gifts God has given me." Dirk looked around the foyer and chuckled. "Even if you think praying is a superstitious waste of time, thanks for humouring me once a year."

Rachel glanced around the group to see how they reacted to Dirk's words. A few looked nervous but most seemed relaxed. Esther used to talk a lot about Jesus, and Gran did too. How did someone learn to talk naturally about such topics? Was it a talent, or the result of much practise, or some mysterious combination of factors?

Dirk closed his eyes and projected his voice into the farthest corner. "Dear Creator of All, thank you for all the beauty you have created. Thank you for all the beautiful trees and flowers and fruit that we get to enjoy every day. Thank you for the uniqueness of every person you create, all of whom are precious in your sight."

Dirk had probably thought carefully through every line of his prayer. He lived in a way that showed he truly believed everybody was precious to God. As Josh had once pointed out to her, Dirk hired people with broken wings.

"Thank you, Jesus, for caring for us for another year, for allowing the doctors to patch me up, and for allowing Pete to come and keep this place open. Thank you for the happy family we have here. Thank you for all our friends and colleagues who come to our annual dinner. Bless them, so that they too find the true purpose and joy and peace that you pour into our lives. Thank you, Jesus, for all you did that makes it possible for us to become part of God's family. You are a generous and loving God. In the name of Jesus, Amen."

Someone blew their nose in the silence.

***

Fifteen minutes later, Rachel was seated with her grandmother and Josh's parents.

"Is your son here?" Gran asked Lyn. "I've heard so much about him."

Lyn gestured towards the far corner of the room. "He likes to be with Pete and Dirk, because they treat him as though he's one of them."

"Hmm," Gran said. "Is that rare?"

"Sadly, yes." Ian shook his head. "People speak extra loud and slowly, as though he's deaf or stupid. Or they ignore him and talk about him to us as though he can't hear them."

"Not easy," Gran said as she took a mouthful of sausage.

"It hurts us to see his frustration." Lyn poured herself some water. "But Josh doesn't let them get away with it. He used to peer right into their faces and say, 'I'm right here. You can talk to me.'"

Rachel choked on her steak.

"Although we thought it rather amusing, we had to stop him doing it before it became a habit," Ian said. "We also persuaded him that hitting people or saying 'duh' wasn't the best response either."

"I'd have loved to see him do that." The corner of Rachel's mouth twitched. "How did you teach him to respond?"

"The same way we taught all our children. Most people get the point if Josh tells them politely that he loves answering questions about himself," Ian said.

Rachel had once wondered why a guy like Josh was at the nursery, but Josh had soon put her firmly in her place.

$\mathcal{T}$he annual party had been a terrific success. Good food, loads of laughter, and a warmth that cemented Rachel's loyalty to the business.

Her only issue was that Pete seemed to have avoided her all night. Maybe it was her imagination. She would try to catch his eye at the end and thank him for the help he'd given her with the decorations.

Pete, Dirk, and Norma had just said goodbye to the last of the outside guests when Pete came back into the centre of the foyer and held up his hand.

"Thank you, everyone, for all the hard work and pitching in to help tonight. Hugely appreciated. We need some helpers to take the food home."

"Me!" Josh said, shooting up his arm and waving it.

The group laughed.

"And a little help with chairs and tables. Then we'll be done for the evening."

Some volunteers stepped forward and were quickly organised. Pete picked up a pile of chairs and passed close to Rachel.

"We'll leave the decorations up for a few days. The customers will love them."

Rachel's neck warmed. Okay, maybe she'd been mistaken about Pete ignoring her.

"But there's no need for you to stay," he said, his voice concerned. "Your grandmother looks exhausted."

Rachel looked over her shoulder to where Gran was waiting on a chair. Rachel's breath caught in her throat. Gran was pale, with silvery-grey bags under her eyes. She'd looked like that at Esther's funeral. Rachel must pay more attention to her grandmother's needs and not forget her, just because someone—a man with a kind smile—had given her a compliment about her decorations.

CHAPTER 4

A whole fortnight had gone by since Rachel's mother had left Gran's place, and now she was back to visit. Rachel opened the front door and enveloped her mother in a hug. Who'd have thought someone her age would miss her mother so much?

"I've missed you too." Her mother pulled out of the hug and held Rachel at arm's length. "You're looking more tanned and rested than when I last saw you."

The corner of Rachel's mouth twitched. "Apart from last night's work party, it's not as though I have much of a social life."

"We'll have to see what can be done about that."

Rachel didn't say anything. There was no point. She worked. She went to church. She went for a solitary run twice a week. The rest of the time she spent with her grandmother. Gran was already alone all day, so Rachel needed to be home in the evenings as much as possible. She usually rang Gran during her lunch break, just to check that she was okay.

Her mother and grandmother went and sat down while Rachel finished putting the meal into serving dishes. She'd chosen to go more formal tonight—a decision she might regret, since she already felt uptight.

It was wonderful to see Mum again, but what were they going to talk about? It had been easy enough when she was living here, but not now. William's presence wouldn't disappear just because he wasn't physically here. It would be normal for Mum to talk about him, but to be reminded of his existence was the last thing Rachel wanted.

Her mother caught up with Naomi's doings and then Rachel's. All too soon, she began to talk about what she'd been up to. It only took a few sentences before she said, "William and I are doing some major sorting."

Rachel pasted on a smile, gritted her teeth, and soldiered on with her meal.

"And then William said ..."

Rachel stared at her plate. She didn't want to hurt her mother, but really, was it necessary to mention William in every other sentence?

It was a relief to get up, take their dirty plates out to the kitchen, and bring in the dessert. Rachel dished the stewed pears and cream and handed them around.

"William and I have been having some serious talks about the future." Her mother took a mouthful of dessert.

Rachel clenched her teeth. William, William, and more William. A dull stomach ache radiated all the way around to her back. Please, no more William. She concentrated on her dessert.

"What about?" Gran asked.

"William thinks we should sell the house," her mother said.

Rachel's head jerked up. Sell the house! That house, and what it represented, was William's pride and joy. He'd loved it more than he'd loved his family, if the amount of money he wasted on it was any indication.

"And what do you think?" Naomi asked, her gaze focused on her daughter-in-law.

"I think it makes a whole lot of sense. Of course, I loved the place because it was home, but it is too big for two people." Her mother took another mouthful of her pears. "It costs a fortune to run, and William no longer feels we can justify spending that amount of money."

"Because he's out of work?" Naomi asked.

"No." Her mother shook her head. "I think he'd move whether he had a salary or not. He says the house was a symptom of his ego. Looking successful is no longer his priority." Her face flushed pink. "He feels he should simplify his life and free up money for more important things."

"And what does he now consider more important?" Rachel asked, trying to mask her scepticism.

"We think we'd like to give some of it away. We don't know where yet." Her mother's voice trailed off. "Something, you know, really significant. Maybe the Bible Society, or Scripture in schools."

"That's hugely encouraging," Naomi said. "I've been praying that William's decision on Lord Howe Island would have profound effects."

Her mother brushed the corner of her eye. "Your prayers are being answered. I'm having to get to know my husband all over again."

Her mother was so gullible. William was a chameleon, changing to suit whatever his audience wanted to hear. Now he was out to impress his wife. Her mother would be devastated when this whole life transformation thing turned out to be a cheap imitation.

"Are you planning to put the house on the market soon?" Naomi dabbed the corner of her mouth with her serviette.

"Yes, fairly soon. There are no major repairs to do."

Yes, William had ensured the house was in perfect condition. Rachel hid her eye roll. But he'd also had a wife who had slaved over the interior decorating and cleaning. Perhaps if he'd invested a similar amount of time and effort in his family, they would also be in better condition.

"Where would you go if you sell?" The question spilled out of Rachel before she could stuff it back inside.

"We don't know, but William is considering returning to Lord Howe Island if they'll have us. They still don't have a permanent pastor."

That idea had merit. Rachel considered it for a moment. If they stayed in the local area while the house sold, her mother would be subjected to gossip—and there was bound to be a heap. No one left a radio programme and resigned from a church the size of Victory without creating waves. Her mother had courage, even if her loyalty was misguided.

"And how is William coping?" Gran asked.

Rachel didn't pretend to understand her grandmother's relentless forty years of prayer for her son. Rachel put her head down and kept eating. In a few minutes, she could get up and do the dishes—and leave this awkward conversation.

"He's doing surprisingly well. We're spending a lot of time reading the Bible and praying."

Enough. More than enough. "Are you still working, Mum?" The question burst out of her.

Her grandmother's spoon clattered in her bowl, but her mother answered.

"I certainly am—an extra ten hours a week on top of the original fifteen."

Rachel raised her eyebrows. That was a surprise. With William such a traditionalist, she'd assumed he'd veto her mother's job without discussion. Maybe even he was smart enough to realise that some income was better than none. He wasn't the sort of man to apply for unemployment benefits.

William. She was done having him intrude into her evening.

Rachel stood abruptly and gathered the dessert bowls, almost dropping them in her haste, then shot off towards the kitchen.

Maybe washing the dishes would calm her down.

She took her time. When she was done, she leaned forward on the edge of the sink.

At least it shouldn't be too hard to avoid seeing William. He'd never have the guts to come and beg their forgiveness. Hers and Gran's.

CHAPTER 5

$\mathcal{O}$n Sunday afternoon, Pete loped across several empty football fields.

A whistle gave a long blast. He was late. He jogged the last two hundred metres and looked up into the stands for Josh's parents. There they were. They waved.

He glanced towards the seat beyond them. Rachel. Classy, despite her casual wear. He swallowed.

So she'd been invited too. Not unexpected. Josh had been jumping up and down with excitement that his soccer team had made the semi-final. He'd probably invited everyone.

Pete averted his gaze. It was easier if Rachel was just an employee in work clothes and covered in dirt. An image of her at the annual work party flashed through his mind. His face warmed and he concentrated on his feet as he climbed the stairs.

There was an empty seat waiting for him next to Ian. Much better that he sat there and not next to Rachel.

"Mr Pete, Mr Pete," Josh shouted. He jumped up and down, waving. The ball shot by his foot without him noticing.

Ian grinned, his eyes twinkling. "That's why we have to be early. The players get distracted easily."

"I'll make sure not to be late next time." Pete shifted in the hard seat. "I did want to ask you about Josh's calling me 'Mr Pete' rather than just Pete. He doesn't have to."

"It's a hangover from his childhood." Ian chuckled. "We didn't want him calling people by their first name, but he'd get confused if he heard some people do it while he was calling them by title and surname. Does it bother you?"

"Not at all. I rather like it."

The field was half the regulation size, and there were six players plus a goalie on each side. Josh had the ball and was dribbling it down the field. He evaded the opposing player's foot and kept going.

"Go, son," Ian muttered.

Josh was close enough to the goal. "Shoot," his team members yelled, and Josh gave the ball a powerful kick. It missed.

"Next time, Josh. Next time," Ian said, not nearly loud enough for Josh to hear.

Rachel leaned forward and twisted to look down the row. "How long has Josh been playing?"

"Ever since school," Lyn said.

What kind of school had Josh attended? Pete had friends back in Fremantle who'd wanted their son with Down Syndrome to go to their local school, but it hadn't worked out. Something about not having enough teachers' assistants. He seemed to remember the boy ended up at a special school, even though that wasn't his parents' first choice.

"Josh did play in an ordinary competition for a while," Ian said. "The team loved him, but eventually he couldn't keep up, and some of the parents complained."

"I'm sorry," Pete said. His brow furrowed. "It's … disappointing that people would do that."

"His coach cried when he told us." Lyn wrapped her arms around her waist. "Josh just wants to participate, and he can't figure out why he isn't always welcomed."

Pete could still remember the sharp sting of being rebuffed as a seven-year-old when he'd wanted to play with the older children next door. And that was only one rejection. A lifetime of it would hurt.

There was a cheer. A woman on Josh's team concentrated on the ball in front of her. She managed to dodge past two opponents, then gave the ball a mighty thump, and it flew into the corner of the goal. The whole team rushed together, hugged, and jumped up and down. Josh was whooping and cheering.

It took a while to get the game moving again. Now the player opposite Josh had the ball. Josh moved backwards, keeping his body between the player and the goal, but he stumbled. He tried to keep his balance, then sat down hard, a look of shock on his face. The opposing player kicked, and the ball screamed past the goalie and into the corner.

Josh started laughing, then clambered to his feet and ran to congratulate the boy. "So funny, did you see? I fell over." His voice easily carried up to his cheer squad as he pumped the man's arm vigorously up and down.

After a quick drink and an orange for half time, the game started again. Lyn dug into her bag and pulled out a container of homemade dip, along with carrots, celery and cucumber sticks. A second container held cubes of cheese. She grinned apologetically. "If Josh has to eat healthily, we do too."

"Oh, he's healthy," Pete said. "And very fit."

"His fitness has improved so much since he's worked at the nursery," Ian said.

Rachel laughed. "It makes all of us fit. The first month nearly killed me."

They turned their heads back to the game to see that Josh had the ball and was heading towards the goal.

"Go, Josh, go," Ian muttered again.

"Why don't you yell?" Pete asked, curious. Every soccer game he'd ever been to, the onlookers had yelled and cheered loudly.

"He gets distracted by outside noise. If he's making the noise, he's fine."

At the last moment, Josh saw one of his teammates in a better position. He shouted and passed the ball. She flapped her arms in the air and kicked hard but the ball drifted wide of the goal mouth. Josh dashed in and gave the ball a casual touch, just enough so it was redirected into the goal.

"You did it, Sue," he yelled, running to hug her. She thumped him on the back and the two of them did their little bob-and-dance routine.

"Well done, Josh." Lyn dabbed her eye.

Rachel turned to look at Lyn.

"Josh has been determined to help her score a goal," Lyn said. "She'll bask in the glory of that for weeks."

Rachel continued talking to Lyn, but Pete couldn't hear clearly. He leaned forward to hear better.

"I've been thinking a lot about what we talked about at the party," Rachel said. "I wanted to ask you a question, but you might find it too intrusive. Feel free not to answer."

Pete had noticed Rachel and Naomi had a long conversation with Ian and Lyn at the party. He hadn't dared to join them, much as he'd been tempted to. There had been too many watching eyes.

"We don't find your interest intrusive, do we, Ian?" Lyn said. "There are lots of people who are idly curious, but we don't feel you're one of those."

Rachel's cheeks flushed. "I wanted to ask you ... what's the hardest thing about being a parent of a son with Down Syndrome?"

Lyn squeezed Ian's hand. Pete tried not to notice the intimacy. It got him every time.

"When Josh was born," Ian said, "you could see that people …" He shook his head. "Some of our family and friends pitied us. "

Lyn took out a tissue and blew her nose.

"Nowadays, the pressure is even greater because many people already know during the pregnancy that they're expecting a baby with Down Syndrome. It's often assumed that people will abort the baby. We've known people who've given in, unable to stand against the riptide of society expectations." Ian gave a grim laugh. "No one came out and said anything directly, but even in church it was obvious some people wondered what we'd done to deserve a child like Josh."

"That makes me so mad," Rachel said. "My sister had to deal with the same thing after she was diagnosed with cancer. People implied she must have sinned to get cancer so young."

It was the first time Pete had heard Rachel mention Esther since the funeral. Not that he was any better. He seldom mentioned his grief either.

He hadn't intended to go to Esther's funeral—funerals were too much of a reminder of the worst day of his life. But his parents always attended weddings and funerals to support their workers. He'd sat at the back and got through it better than he'd expected. Probably because he'd barely known Esther.

As far as funerals go, it had been a good one. No one could have left the church without hearing how to get right with God.

"Somehow, when faced with this sort of trial, people revert to being like Job's friends." Ian's fingers made air quotes. "Bad things have happened; therefore you must have sinned for them to fall on your head."

Pete clenched his jaw. Few people came out and said this directly about his tragedy, but their questions and comments had suggested it. He'd thought it enough himself when he was buried under the crushing weight of the *whys*. *Whys* that had almost overwhelmed him. Without the support of his parents and his father-in-law, who could say whether he'd have made it?

Josh's hoot of laughter broke into his thoughts.

"Not that we were exactly thrilled with the situation at the beginning. It was hard not to see Josh as a burden. That he wasn't what we'd have chosen." Lyn laughed shakily. "But we soon worked out God had given us a gift. God knew we needed Josh. Yes, his stubbornness tries our patience sometimes, but everyone has their faults."

Rachel reached out a hand and touched Lyn's arm. "Thanks for sharing."

Lyn blew her nose again. "We did get upset when people used to meet Josh and say, 'You are such wonderful people …' then there'd be this awkward pause, and we'd know what they were trying to say was '… for loving someone like him.'"

Pete blinked. "People actually say things like that?"

"Unbelievable, isn't it?" Ian said. "We've had to bite our tongues and work out how to say something helpful."

"What do you say when people are so insensitive?" Rachel asked.

Lyn shrugged. "Something along the lines of, 'We're not wonderful people for loving our son.' Or 'It's normal for parents to love their children. What would be terrible is if we didn't.'"

Ian squeezed Lyn's hand. "And you usually add in a few reasons why you think Josh is terrific."

"And pray Josh never overhears the conversation."

A whistle blew. Josh's cheering could be heard above everyone else's. Now the game was over, Ian and Lyn cheered loudly. Josh looked up at them, raised his arms above his head, and then ran around in a small, excited circle.

"They're through to the final. He'll be hard to calm down," Ian said. "Now if only they can find a new coach."

Pete stood and stretched. "Is their coach leaving?"

"At the end of the season. That's him over there—he's almost eighty."

The man looked closer to ninety. The exuberance of the team nearly knocked him over.

"Special Olympics is always looking for coaches," Lyn said. "And lots of other volunteers. Neither of us is any good at the sports side of things, but we raise money. Provide snacks. That sort of thing."

Now that was an idea. Pete followed the Smiths down the stairs. He used to play soccer in high school. Maybe this was something he could do. Something to help others, instead of sitting at home alone.

CHAPTER 6

$\mathcal{R}$achel parked in the carport and clambered out of her car. Her grandmother was hovering on the back verandah, face alight and quivering with some sort of emotion.

Naomi wasn't the excitable kind. Rachel went up the back steps and pecked her grandmother on her cheek. "What's up?"

"Have I got news," Gran said, eyes wide.

Work had been particularly draining, and Rachel usually showered before doing anything else, but the table beyond them was already laid with a teapot, cups, and saucers. It would have taken her grandmother twice as long to prepare as normal, because she only had one hand available to carry things. "Gran, I can see you're dying to tell me. As long as you can bear me in this state, let's sit down and you can tell me what you're excited about."

Rachel poured each of them some tea, but her grandmother didn't touch it.

"You'll never guess what happened this morning." Gran paused for a long moment. "William came to visit."

Rachel felt her skin around her eyes stretch as she widened her eyes. William. The name sent a stab through her stomach. No way! Making up with Mum was one thing, but coming to see Naomi after pretending she didn't exist for forty years. How dare he!

Her grandmother should have slammed the door in his face, but Naomi's radiant face showed she'd done no such thing. Naomi was one vast beating heart of love. Rachel wanted to bolt for the shower, but it wouldn't be right. She'd have no qualms about hurting William, but hurting her grandmother was an entirely different thing. It was impossible. Quite impossible. She'd have to hear this out.

Rachel settled herself back in her seat, stripped off her shoes and socks, and wriggled her toes. Her feet probably stank but it was a relief to free them.

"Well, tell me," she said, struggling to keep the disgust and bitterness out of her voice.

"I'd just finished my prayer time when the doorbell rang." Gran looked across at Rachel. "You know how long it takes me to reach the front door nowadays, but he waited. He was just standing there, looking around the garden."

Rachel had to ask some questions or her grandmother would think she wasn't interested. Which she wasn't, but her grandmother didn't need to know that. Gran's cheeks were flushed pink.

"Well what did he say?" Rachel winced at the fake interest in her tone. Hopefully her grandmother didn't notice.

Gran closed her eyes. "'Mother,' he said, 'I've come to try and undo the mess I've made of four decades of your life.'" Gran pulled a pale blue lace handkerchief out of her pocket and blew her nose. "Of course, I got that door open as fast as I could."

Of course.

Rachel hadn't expected any other reaction. Gran had done the same when Esther turned up on her doorstep, a granddaughter she'd never even met. She'd done the same when Rachel arrived as a fifteen-year-old runaway. And she hadn't subjected her to a barrage of prying questions. All she'd done was wrap her in armfuls of warm hugs.

Too bad Rachel hadn't appreciated what her grandmother offered at the time.

Gran's warm hugs and acceptance had still been waiting twenty-five years later when Rachel had lain on the same front doorstep, too broken to do anything more.

So of course Naomi would welcome her son. It made Rachel want to puke. How dare William receive forgiveness with a few words? They were sure to have been flowery and well-polished. After all, William was a wordsmith from way back.

But words were cheap.

"He didn't even let me get him a cup of tea. Just fell on his knees, clutching my feet, and wept." Her grandmother gulped and swiped at a few tears channelling down the wrinkles near her nose. "It took a while until we could sit and talk normally. We never did get that cup of tea."

Rachel snorted. Softly, so her grandmother couldn't hear—one small advantage of Naomi's progressive hearing loss.

"And now I'm not drinking the one you poured me either." Gran picked up her cup, took a sip, and stared over the back garden. "I don't remember everything William said, but his sorrow and repentance were clear."

William might not have done much repenting during his lifetime, but he'd have made sure he studied and got it just right. Probably practised it in front of his mirror.

"I asked him about what happened on Lord Howe Island. I wanted to hear everything in his own words." Her grandmother shook her head. "Amazing to think that while he was heading out to sea to end his life, God woke me up with an urgent desire to pray for his salvation."

Rachel bit the inside of her cheek. Yes, God was a God of miracles, and she was glad, for Gran's sake, that William hadn't succeeded in drowning himself. But it didn't change things for her.

"Rachel, I know you're still angry at your father."

Angry didn't quite cover the range of emotions, but it was a start, with a good dose of disappointment and disgust thrown in.

"At some point you need to forgive him," Gran said.

Rachel's whole body tensed, as if she'd been snap-frozen. Why? Why was forgiving William a necessity? It wasn't fair that a few carefully chosen words should cover a multitude of hurts and years of consequences. If she'd had a normal upbringing, she might have been a wife and mother. Mere words couldn't wipe out all the wrongs of the past.

Her grandmother stood up, taking a moment to straighten herself before coming over and putting her hand on Rachel's shoulder. "I know forgiveness is the hardest thing in the world, but we forgive not just because God forgave us but also for our own sakes. Not forgiving will cost you more than it will cost anyone else."

Rachel squeezed her eyes shut. She was not going to listen. Not going to downplay what William had done. Not going to forgive.

CHAPTER 7

*P*ete had dinner with his parents once a week. His mother made a roast dinner—chicken or lamb or beef, and crunchy potatoes, just the way he loved them. It wasn't the kind of meal to make for one person, or even two. In fact, there'd be plenty for a few other guests. Maybe one day he'd have someone he'd want to invite, instead of living like a hermit.

He admired the yard as he walked up the path to his parents' front door. His father was getting back into gardening, and it showed. Tonight's vegetables would all be home-grown.

"I'm here," he called as he opened the front door. His mother came out of the kitchen, cheeks rosy, and stood on tiptoes to kiss his cheek.

"Hope you've had a good week. Your father's in the garden, picking the first of the snow peas. There should be just enough for dinner."

He went out to help. "They're looking good, Dad."

"Yes—this year hasn't been windy so they haven't blown over." Dirk reached over and snapped off a few more peas to drop in his container.

38

"Your lettuce is looking good." Pete reached down to stroke a seedling.

Dirk stretched his back. "The nursery used to consume all my time. No time for growing vegetables. But this year, I'll have four different varieties of tomato."

"You'll soon get to enjoy them." Pete looked up at the sky. "It's getting warmer." His words came out more enthusiastically than he'd intended, and his father raised an eyebrow.

"You sound happy."

"I guess I am." Pete rubbed his chin. "Been so long, I barely recognise the emotion." He pulled up a weed. "I even went to a soccer game the other day."

"Good to hear."

"Josh invited me, and I was there with his parents."

His father looked at him for a long moment. "Anyone else?"

"Why do you think there was someone else?"

Dirk winked. "A little bird told me."

"Yes, Rachel was there." Pete shrugged, perhaps too casually. His father wasn't stupid. "But I didn't know she'd been invited."

Dirk handed him the container of peas. "Can you take those to your mother, then come and help me with the watering?"

Pete was back in two minutes. The smell of roasted beef wafted out the back windows and his stomach rumbled. He filled a bucket with the water from the tank and carted it out to the furthest plants. His father followed.

"I water half the garden each evening," Dirk said. "Gives me time for thinking and praying."

Pete's own prayer life was coming alive in step with the season. The grey might not have lifted entirely but there were more frequent shafts of light.

"What do you pray for, Dad?"

Unbelievable he'd never asked this, but Dad's heart attack had been a wake-up call. One never knew when it would be too late.

Dirk looked up. "Apart from you and your mother, you mean?"
Pete nodded.

"I have different topics each day, I find it keeps me motivated. Monday is my day to pray for missionaries. Tuesday is teachers' day." Dirk scooped water to pour at the base of each plant. "I pray for all those who teach God's word at the church and in local Scripture classes at the school."

Pete chuckled. "Do you match all the days to first letters?"

His father grinned. "Wednesday is for the workers. I pray for everyone at the nursery and some of the people I order from."

Pete would ask for more details later.

"Saturday and Sunday are for people's spiritual lives. Mine, and those around me."

"You missed Thursday and Friday."

Dirk slapped at a mosquito. "Didn't want to bore you. Thursday is for those going through tough times, and Friday is for family and friends."

"I might pinch some of your topics," Pete said.

He and Mai used to finish every day with prayer for their little family. Somehow holding hands and praying in bed had been as intimate as a kiss. Pete blew out a gusty breath and busied himself fetching more water.

Once Mai died, he hadn't prayed properly for a long time. The Bible said God could interpret his wordless moans. He hoped so because there had been a whole pile of them.

Pete hauled the next bucket over to his father. "You know, if Binh hadn't started coming over to pray with me …" Pete put his hands in his pockets. "Well, I don't know what would have happened."

Dirk paused a moment. "God gave you a great gift in your father-in-law." He shook out the final drops of water over the lettuce seedlings.

Pete nodded. "You know, he still phones me every week to talk and pray together. I couldn't have asked for a better friend."

And Binh was the one person with the most reason to have hated him for all eternity.

CHAPTER 8

*R*achel went in to work with a skip in her step. Today was one of her favourite tasks, grafting citrus. And as a bonus, she'd be working with Dirk for several days. He was always worth talking to.

She checked in and headed for the back shed.

"Good morning, Miss Rachel." Josh gave her his customary grin as he high-fived the hand she held ready.

"What are you doing today, Josh?"

"Repotting."

He said it as though this was a new, exciting task. It was his usual job and one he did with ruthless efficiency, singing as he went.

"Mr Pete is coming to help me."

Dirk was already inside the shed. Not surprising, after a lifetime of starting work soon after dawn. The tools, grafting tape, rootstock, and cuttings were already on the bench. Last year, she hadn't a clue about grafting, but Dirk had patiently taught her. She washed her hands and they set to work.

Rachel inserted the first graft and wrapped the join in grafting tape. It didn't take long to settle back into the routine.

"Good to be doing this job again with you ... not that Pete isn't a good boss." Rachel's face warmed. "When you were in hospital, I was worried the nursery might have to close, and I'd lose my job." She inserted another graft. "Or that you'd be forced to sell, and we'd end up with another boss who didn't understand all you'd done here."

"I wouldn't have handed the place over to someone who didn't understand its values," Dirk said. "Although, I wouldn't have been surprised if Pete had gone back to his accounting job and life in Western Australia."

She broke off a piece of grafting tape with a snap. Thank goodness he hadn't.

"Whatever happened, we didn't want to lose you," Dirk said, with a grin.

"I think you're stuck with me now." Rachel glanced up at Dirk as she reached for another lime twig to graft into the lemon rootstock. Those job offers at the party had shown her how committed she was to this place.

"Pete is beginning to rely on you too," Dirk said.

Rachel flushed. Only yesterday Pete had asked her if she was interested in learning from Dirk how to do the ordering. She was considering it. None of the other workers were really suitable.

They worked until it was time for a cup of tea, then went outside and sat on two stools in the sun.

Although there was a café at the nursery, Rachel never took the time to buy there. Much cheaper and easier to bring food from home.

Dirk took a sip of his tea. "Ah, that's better."

A couple of sparrows flew close and sat waiting for stray crumbs.

"I know we often talk," Dirk said. "But I haven't asked how you've been going since your baptism."

She wouldn't have found it easy to discuss such things with most people, but Dirk wasn't most people. He was the one she'd asked to baptise her, and he knew her better than anyone else outside her family. Dirk wasn't prying. He was caring for what he considered the most important aspect of her life.

Rachel put her head on one side. "I haven't had much time to think about it. Esther died too soon after my decision to accept Jesus. The first few months I just aimed to get through each day."

"And now?"

"I've been thinking quite a bit this last week." Rachel held her cup in two hands.

Dirk kept silent.

Rachel took a deep breath. This was a bit embarrassing. "It's occurred to me ..." She paused and shrugged. "I don't have any real friends. Ever since I was fifteen, I've built walls around my heart."

The only one who'd attempted to scale them was Alice, from their days at David Jones. Rachel must contact her and let her know she was okay. Poor Alice. She probably thought Rachel had vanished off the face of the earth.

Dirk smiled across at her. "Have you ever had any real friendships?"

"Most of the friendships I had were the wrong kind." Rachel's cheeks heated. "And Esther was gone before we got much below the surface."

"Are you attending a church?"

"Yes." Rachel took another sip of her drink. "But I spend most of my time keeping an eye on my grandmother. There isn't really anyone else my age."

"That can be tough," Dirk said. "It's nice to have people you can relate to."

"Yeah, I have found it hard."

"Have you had any thoughts about what to do about it?"

"Not really. Maybe I'll go to another church for a bit. Take Gran to the morning service, then go somewhere else in the evening."

Dirk finished his tea and shook his cup out over the nearest plant. "That might work. Or perhaps thinking of church more like a family would also help."

A family. That was a helpful analogy. Maybe she had been expecting church to be more like a club. The three generations of women in her family hadn't had much in common, yet they'd managed to connect. Eventually. She'd even talked about spiritual things with the disparate group that included Gran, her mother, and some of Esther's friends. Although neither Joy nor Gina was near her age.

"You mean it's okay, even if there is no one my own age? I can enjoy being around uncles and aunts and nephews and nieces without having to have a best friend?"

"Exactly." Dirk peeled a tangerine. Its tart sweetness scented the air.

She'd been worried that hanging around with her grandmother was odd. Yet Naomi was still fun, and always had worthwhile things to say.

"It was obvious at the party that you're close to your grand-mother," Dirk said.

"I'm the only grandchild left. And Gran needs someone around since she's had her hip surgery. Various friends drop in during the day, but I like to be around in the evenings."

They chatted a few minutes about Naomi, then Dirk laid the tangerine peels aside. "Rachel, before we get back to work, could I pray for some of the things you mentioned?"

"Sure," she said, voice cracking. Dirk treated her far better than her own father ever had. Pete was great, but she missed having Dirk as her boss. He'd prayed for her before at work, and she knew she was on his prayer list because he'd told her about it.

They bowed their heads.

"Gracious Father and King, thank you for bringing Rachel home to you. Like most of us who become Christians as adults, there's a lot to learn."

"And unlearn," Rachel muttered under her breath.

"You've enabled Rachel to see she needs some new friends. We thank you that, like Timothy, she is blessed with a godly mother and grandmother."

Rachel's chest tightened. She was so thankful for her mother and grandmother. How had she survived twenty-five years without them in her life?

"Please help Rachel's relationships with her family to continue to improve, but also give her some new friends."

Yes, Lord, Rachel added.

"And Lord, we dare to pray for William."

Rachel fisted her hands. Why could no one leave William out of things? She didn't need him. Didn't want him anywhere near her life. He'd trampled over enough of it already.

"You've brought him to yourself—"

Dirk wouldn't be bringing William up if she hadn't mentioned him on one of her regular visits to Dirk and Norma's.

Dirk took a breath. "Now help him to put all his relationships right."

Rachel sat rigid as a board. *Lord, restoring his relationship with Gran is more than enough.*

"Father, you give us a church family so we can be nurtured and encouraged to follow you. Please provide Rachel with the encouragement she needs."

Rachel didn't hear the rest of what Dirk prayed. His deep voice wrapped her in a blanket of care. She'd been merely surviving for too long. Maybe now was the time to start looking beyond herself. Time to learn to serve others. Time to pray about what she could do.

An idea flashed into her mind. She blinked. The idea, did she have the guts and perseverance needed to follow through with it?

CHAPTER 9

*P*ete had blocked out the whole day to work with Rachel to prepare the new display for the foyer. She'd told him she had grand plans to change the displays to show off each season's plants. His stomach danced in anticipation. Hopefully, working with her all day wouldn't provoke any winks or uncalled-for comments from any of the other workers. Rachel struck him as a woman who might gallop over the horizon if people teased her about him.

Seeing Rachel arrive, he waved, logged off the computer, and did a few quick stretches as he waited for her. He'd swum yesterday for the first time in two years, and he was a little stiff. Rachel had requested a longer lunch break once a week so she could fit in a swim. He'd agreed as long as she returned the favour.

By the time he finished his stretches, Rachel had the plans spread out on a table. They were rough sketches, but the overall scheme was clear. She was leaving the miniature waterfall and using pavers to make a winding path.

"Have you thought about how to place the pavers to stop them grinding on the floor?"

"Not really. I thought you might have some ideas."

He put his head to the side. Newspaper would be too slippery. Some kid would be sure to have an accident. "What about the old carpet underlay I spotted in the shed? That should work."

Rachel nodded and checked her sketches.

They set to work, Rachel laying out the structure while he made sure it was safe. Changing the display once a quarter was hard work, but it was worth it. Some people came especially to see the display, and they invariably spent some money on plants and at the café.

Rachel placed the last paver on top of the matting he'd laid. "Do you mind if I ask you a personal question?"

Pete's whole body tensed. "Try me."

"I've only been a Christian a short time." She bit her lip. "Esther left me her Bible, and I've enjoyed reading the comments she wrote in the margin, but I've finished it and am not sure what to do next. What do you do?"

No one had asked him a question like this in ages. He regularly went to church, but lately he'd merely been sitting on the pew. "I usually aim to read through the whole Bible once a year. In between, I do other things. Mix it up a bit."

"For example?" Rachel's voice wobbled.

"I might follow a theme." He strained as he moved a heavy pot out of their immediate work area. "Like God's care for the outsider. Sometimes I look up all the verses on a topic like peace, or love, or forgiveness."

Rachel turned partially away from him. Had he hit a nerve?

"Another thing I did once was look up all the references to prayer and the actual prayers in the Bible to learn how to improve my prayer life."

He found it much harder to pray since he'd moved to Sydney and lived on the nursery site. He used to pray as he cycled, nearly two hours a day. Lately, he'd felt an internal tug to get back to the way things were. To focus both upwards and outwards again.

"Praying is hard work," Rachel said.

"Working out what to pray, or concentrating?" he asked.

Rachel laughed. "Both."

"I don't know anyone who finds praying easy. It's a matter of trying lots of different methods and working out what suits your personality."

Rachel pushed a few of the pavers to adjust their position.

Did she still want other ideas? He hadn't learned to read her body language. He cleared his throat. "I do find I can concentrate best if I have a notebook and jot down someone's name or a topic. Then I pray for that before I jot down another."

"I'll give that a go." She pointed towards the trolleys packed with plants in pots. "Are you ready to start laying those out?"

"We'll have to put each pot on a saucer, and maybe add gravel. Otherwise we'll turn the foyer into a flood plain whenever we water the plants."

"Good point. How about putting that plant over there?"

He followed her directions for where to place the bigger pots. She took her time getting things right. Something about shapes and colours, she said. They both filled in the spaces with the smaller plants. They'd have to rotate some of the plants out of the display and into the sun in a couple of weeks.

Pete stretched his back and looked at what they'd done. It looked impressive, which he'd come to expect. Rachel had based this design around bright yellow. It would lift people's spirits to look at it. Then they'd reach for their wallets. He grinned. Rachel was good for business.

"Could you take down the branches and lights from the party while I keep fiddling with the smaller pots?" she asked. "The lights aren't much use at the moment because the days are longer, but they'll show up nicely in next winter's display."

"That makes sense." He reached up to start unwinding the first string of lights.

"Talking about the party—was the music that night your choice? The Spanish guitar?"

Pete nodded. Had she liked it? "I used to play." He winced. He and Mai used to play together at church, her hands a ballet of grace moving over the piano keyboard.

"Not now?" Rachel asked, voice brightening.

"No." The denial came out more strongly than he'd meant it to. "I still have the guitar, but haven't much felt like playing it for three years."

"Music does tug the heartstrings." The little tilt of her mouth as she said the last word suggested the pun was intended. "I still can't manage to get through the singing at church without tearing up."

"Because of Esther?" Pete dared ask.

Rachel bit her lip and turned her head away. He knew how she felt. Although maybe that was presumptuous. Maybe losing a sister wasn't at all similar to his experience. Especially when Esther and Rachel had been estranged for so long.

"I'm sorry I haven't asked you how you've been going. I should have," Pete said.

Rachel bent to place another few pots. Had he offended her?

"I appreciate your asking," Rachel said. "I think I'm doing as well as can be expected."

Rachel stepped back to inspect the corner she'd completed. Her tongue poked from the corner of her mouth, something he'd noticed she did when she was concentrating.

"I'd have been a mess without Gran and Mum." Rachel turned another plant around. "Mum came up with the idea of making a quilt in memory of Esther, with each panel commemorating something about her." Her voice held an intriguing mix of sadness and enthusiasm.

"The best part was that Mum found a list of Esther's favourite verses tucked away in her Bible. We each chose a few and we made each verse a separate square and scattered them over the quilt in between the picture squares." Rachel blushed. "Sorry. You don't want to hear all this."

He didn't know anything about quilts, but he did enjoy hearing her talk. He'd love to tell her that, but didn't want her to get the wrong idea. It was rare for her to open up.

"Somehow, doing the project together helped us grieve." Rachel straightened up and massaged the small of her back.

"You sound like you did a better job of grieving than I did." He squatted to tie his shoelace. "I was on my own too much."

There'd been days when he couldn't even remember if he'd had anything to eat.

Rachel grimaced. "I used work as an escape."

He matched her expression. "Yeah, me too. It's a good thing and a bad thing. I was in a much worse state when I had nothing to do. Work got me out of bed and gave me something I could achieve. Housework doesn't do that for me."

"Me neither. Thankfully, housework was Mum's thing. We almost had to wear sunglasses to cope with the reflective surfaces."

He chuckled. "Better than the dump my place became."

"Talking of work ..." She pointed at the last of the lights and branches. "We'd better get moving if we're to finish this today."

They worked steadily on, listening to his choice of guitar music and her choice of eighties pop and—to his surprise—jazz piano. He'd almost asked her not to choose the piano, but he couldn't avoid it for the rest of his life.

Every now and then Pete would hear Rachel humming along, and catch himself smiling.

It only took them half the afternoon to complete the job.

"Thanks, Pete. I can finish the rest."

He looked over what they'd done. "It looks fantastic. I think we'd better raise your salary, or you might be tempted to accept offers from my competitors."

She pushed back her fringe. "They already offered, and I turned them down."

"Glad to hear it," Pete blurted. He'd been joking about her being poached. Thank goodness Dad had agreed to train her to do the ordering. He suspected Rachel would rise to any challenge they threw at her.

CHAPTER 10

*T*he doorbell rang on Saturday afternoon, jerking Rachel out of the thriller holding her in its tight grip.

"What a pain," Rachel muttered as she put down her book. Gran had gone out with a friend, and Rachel had planned a lazy few hours. If it was the Jehovah's Witnesses again, she'd turn them away.

She frowned as she walked down the hall towards the front door. Perhaps she'd been too polite last time. *Firm, Rachel. Be firm.*

She swung open the door, choked back a curse, and took an abrupt step backwards. William.

Her knees were as weak as wet cardboard and a pulse throbbed in her neck.

"Rachel," he said.

She clutched the door handle, struggling to breathe. Last time she'd seen him, he'd loomed like a menacing black thundercloud.

"I'm glad you're home. I didn't mean to give you a fright." His voice was thin and scratchy. Where was the booming confidence she remembered?

"I'm not home now. I'll never be home for you. Go away." The harshness, the finality of the words frightened her.

He flinched as if she'd struck him. "I guess I deserve that." He took a deep breath but didn't turn to leave.

Why didn't he go away? Why didn't he just leave her alone? She'd lived the last twenty-five years without him. He didn't belong in her life. Never had. Never would. "I don't want to see you," she said, her words tight.

"I can understand your anger."

"Can you?" Her hand trembled on the door, ready to slam it. "Can you?" Her voice rose. "Have you got any idea what you did to me? To Esther?" Hot tears stung her eyes. "I was a little girl. All I needed was your love." She rubbed her hand across her face and smeared snot across the back of it. She didn't care. "Instead, I got pressure to look perfect and behave like you thought a pastor's kid should. If you wanted that, why didn't you buy a life-sized doll?" She took a ragged, gasping breath. "All you cared about was your precious reputation."

He looked at her through the locked screen door. "Yes, you're right."

Her shoulders slumped as her lungs deflated. She hadn't expected him to admit his failure. Not William. William never admitted he was wrong. Never admitted he could be wrong.

"I had all my priorities messed up and I'm sorry." His voice was so threadbare she had to lean forward to hear his words. Sorry? Could a word be cheaper? The word was useless and empty.

"Sorry? I don't want your sorrys." She clenched her jaw. He was silent, and stared at her with wide eyes.

She looked over his head and straightened her spine. "What can 'sorry' change? It can't erase the destruction your behaviour and words did to all our lives."

"I know," he whispered. "I know. Nothing can erase what I've done. I only wish it could."

She was hurting him. Good. He deserved it.

But what about me?

She pounded her hand on the door frame. She hadn't heard that gentle voice echoing in her heart for a while. A stab of pain spread across the back of her head. One hard mental stamp on her conscience and it shut up with barely a squeal.

"Well, it can't," Rachel said.

She'd never forgive him. She'd never forgive him for forcing her to flee. For the choices she'd made to survive so she wouldn't end up on the street. She'd never forgive him for the life she'd destroyed so she could keep her job, pay rent, buy food. The tiny child who haunted her memories flitted into her mind. Dancing in pink ballet shoes. The child who wasn't. Her breath came out in gasps as though she'd been chased.

"I know what I did can't be erased." He rubbed his ear. "I know better than anyone. It tortured me on Lord Howe Island. It tortures me now."

It had tortured him enough to make him swim several kilometres away from shore. She shivered. She didn't want him dead. Dead was too easy. Dead, and he couldn't suffer the way he ought to suffer.

My child.

If only the warning in that internal whisper would shut up. She refused to listen. This man didn't deserve her forgiveness.

He didn't deserve mine either.

You're Jesus. You're superhuman. You're supposed to forgive.

William watched her, pain and sadness etched in the lines of his face.

"Rachel. I know I have totally failed you as a father." His shoulders slumped. "But I want to make things right more than anything in this world."

She hated the tremble in his voice. Hated it more than his past arrogance. Hated that he had the audacity to come to her looking weak, looking needy, wanting things she couldn't give.

"Well, you can't." The words shot out her mouth like bullets, leaving a scorched trail of bitterness.

He turned to go, and her shoulders relaxed. He took one step away and then turned again. "Your mother and I are going back to Lord Howe Island next week."

That was a mercy. Six hundred kilometres, give or take, would be just perfect.

"Your mother wanted you to know she'd write." He took another step away from the door. "Thanks for talking to me."

How dare he thank her? She hadn't intended to say anything. She'd intended to slam the door in his face. He could never claim she hadn't aired her grievances. She'd spewed them all over him. Just like he'd spewed them over Esther and even Mum in the past.

"And you're right. I don't deserve your forgiveness." His Adam's apple jerked. "I treated everyone abominably. My mother. Blanche. Esther. You." He took a quivering breath. "I was an arrogant idiot who couldn't see I was destroying all that was most precious. I am more sorry than I can say."

He shook his head slowly. Like a wounded bull.

She hardened her heart.

"You're giving me what I deserve." Tears ran down his face. "But I'm going to be pleading with God to give us—all of us—what we don't deserve."

Hot tears burned her eyes as his words slid in under her anger and stabbed her hard in the heart. Not fair. Couldn't he leave God out of it? She'd spent their whole conversation ruthlessly stamping on any twinges of conscience.

She leaned against the door frame, knees weak, as William walked along the driveway towards the front gate. Hunched and somehow dishevelled. No blood visible, yet she'd stabbed him many times. Stabbed him as he'd so often stabbed her.

But there was no satisfaction in her heart. No victory.

Only the dryness of defeat.

CHAPTER 11

$\mathscr{T}$he floodlights were on as Pete jogged across the field in shorts and T-shirt, not at all sure he was ready for this. About fifteen people were clustered together on the soccer field, wearing a variety of shorts and tracksuits. Probably parents or grandparents.

He crossed over to the man with the whistle and clipboard. "Pieter Klopper with Pieter spelled P-i-e-t-e-r and Klopper with a K and two P's, but everyone calls me Pete."

"I didn't know your name was spelled with an 'i.'" The familiar female voice came from behind him.

Rachel. He turned to face her. "My parents used the Afrikaans spelling."

Rachel looked lithe and trim and ready for action. Someone else came to get their name checked off the list and he stepped to the side.

"Signed up to coach soccer too?" Rachel said.

He nodded. He'd been surprised to discover soccer wasn't a winter sport in Special Olympics. They played all year and alternated three months of friendly games with three months of competitions with other clubs.

"Ian and Lyn challenged me to consider helping."

Rachel laughed. "They did the same for me. Probably hoped that if they suggested it to ten people, they might get one response."

She turned and gave her name to the man he presumed would be training them. Then she came back to stand next to him. "Have you ever coached anything before?"

His jaw tightened and he shook his head. Coaching had been one of the things he'd looked forward to. One of the many things snatched away in his millisecond of wrong choice.

Rachel didn't seem to notice anything amiss.

"Me neither," she said. "I was too busy working and going to the gym."

She had the look of someone who might have been a gym addict, but she was much more relaxed now than the first time he'd met her. Perhaps she was dealing with whatever issues would have led his father to hire her. Not alcohol or drugs, he guessed. She cared too much about her body for that. What then? Mental health issues?

The man with the clipboard looked at his watch. "If you'll gather in a circle, we'll get started."

They all moved closer together.

"I'm Bill. Welcome to Special Olympics." He looked at each individual and smiled like a car salesman. "I've been coaching soccer for twenty years. Started when my second son wanted to continue to play sport, but was struggling to keep up with others his age."

Various people in the group nodded, as if they'd had similar experiences. Were Pete and Rachel the only ones here who weren't parents?

They introduced themselves around the circle, and Bill spent a couple of minutes going over the differences between coaching a regular team and a Special Olympics team. Pete had read the information he'd been sent and nodded along. It was more about participation than winning. More about improving the abilities of each individual player. It all made sense.

Bill tugged on his Special Olympics shirt. "Those of us wearing these shirts have already coached for some years. All of you will be paired with someone more experienced."

So he'd be unlikely to be with Rachel. Pity.

Bill looked around the group. "Okay, we're going to put two or three of you with each coach. Just talk amongst yourselves while we divide you up."

Pete turned to Rachel. "When did you last play soccer?"

She made a wry face. "Not since I was fourteen, but I did play quite a lot for two years. What about you?"

"I played the final two years in high school."

"Well, that should help. Surely we can remember something about how we were coached."

The huddle off to the side broke apart. Bill looked at his clipboard and called out two names and the name of one of the coaches. They moved off to one side.

"Okay, Pete and Rachel, you go with Ryan."

Pete schooled his face to neutral rather than letting his pleasure show.

An older, fit-looking man stepped forward and handed a pile of small cones to Rachel and a ball to Pete, keeping one for himself. They followed him as he headed towards the far end of the field.

"How long have you been coaching?" Rachel asked as they walked.

"Eight years. Ever since my grandson turned twelve."

They reached their corner. Ryan put his ball down and gestured for them to do the same.

"Most of our players appreciate routines," Ryan said. "So we stick with the pattern of general warm-up and then drills to work on specific skills. The last half of each session we spend playing."

"Sounds similar to what I remember from school," Rachel said. "But school was a long time ago."

"Speak for yourself," Pete said.

She raised an eyebrow. "You're not that much younger than me."

How much younger was he? Young enough for it to matter?

"The key thing is that you need to be patient," Ryan said. "Most skills will take longer to teach than you expect."

"We're used to that from work," Pete said.

"I'll show you how to do each of the exercise and drills and then give each of you a printed list." Ryan moved across the field, bending one knee and pulling his foot towards his backside. "Follow me," he called over his shoulder.

Pete looked at Rachel, grinned, and set off. Ryan moved through his list, expecting them to follow like children playing Simon Says. With much laughter, they did.

"A couple of laps around the field never hurts either," Ryan said after they'd completed the warm-up exercises.

They helped Ryan set out cones.

"What if a player can't do the drills?" Rachel asked, hands on her hips.

"One of the advantages of two coaches is that one can work separately with someone who is struggling." Ryan paused. "Remember, we don't exclude people because they don't make the grade."

Rachel smiled. "I love that."

Rachel should smile more often. It lit her up from the inside. Pete averted his eyes. *Keep your mind on the job, Pete.*

Ryan demonstrated various drills, working through trapping and controlling the ball, dribbling the ball, and passing the ball while running forward.

As Pete ran, he felt more light-hearted than he had for years. What he'd started so that he could 'do the right thing' might turn out to be fun. And if it also gave him time to get to know Rachel better, there was nothing wrong with that.

Just because they were paired up today didn't mean they would coach together. They'd almost certainly be assistant coaches on different teams.

Would she have welcomed being with him, or would she have run a mile?

CHAPTER 12

*T*he following Saturday, Rachel and Naomi waited at the gate with lunch, a picnic blanket, and a fold-up chair. Five pink and grey galahs nibbled grass seeds on the front lawn, keeping a wary eye on them.

"It's kind of Pete to include me on this excursion," Gran said.

Rachel put her arm around her grandmother's frail shoulders. "I told him we were a package deal."

When Rachel had mentioned that she didn't want to leave her grandmother alone yet again, Pete had come up with the idea of parking Gran and a good book in a café overlooking the harbour. Once Gran agreed, he'd rung ahead and booked the best table.

"You don't need me to cramp your style," Gran said.

Rachel looked sideways. "It's not a date."

"You sure about that?" her grandmother asked.

Rachel had wondered too, but she doubted it. Most guys his age would be looking for a younger woman. Someone who could have children. Her chest tightened. It was less and less likely she'd ever have that privilege. "Pete is bringing Josh. He asked the other guys too, but they aren't coming."

"I like this boss of yours. He cares about people." Her grandmother stepped forward to peer towards the corner. "And he loves Jesus, which is even more important."

Rachel chuckled and gave her grandmother's shoulders a squeeze. Gran couldn't last a minute without popping Jesus into the conversation. A year ago, Rachel would have scoffed.

But a lot of things had been different a year ago. Back then, she'd never have believed Jesus would ever matter to her.

Pete's blue car turned into their street. As it drew closer, she could see Josh's frantically waving hand at the window. She waved back. He'd been over the moon since she'd told him they'd be coaching his soccer team. After their second training session, Bill and Ryan had admitted there weren't enough coaches to spread around and asked if she and Pete would be willing to work together with Josh's team on their own. She'd looked at Pete to check what he thought about it. He'd given her a lopsided grin and a thumbs up. They'd start on Tuesday evening.

Pete leapt out of the car to help her grandmother into the front and popped open the boot for Rachel to stow their gear. "Off we go. Next stop, Bradleys Head."

Josh was bouncing on his seat. "Miss Rachel, Miss Rachel. God gave us a sunny day."

"He certainly did, Josh. But even if it rained, we'd still have fun." Rachel and Pete were taking Josh on a short hike. Pete had some scheme about using this as a test run to prepare Josh for a longer trip.

He shook his head vigorously. "I get hot in a raincoat."

"And what are your parents doing today, Joshua?" her grandmother asked.

"They said having a date." His forehead wrinkled. "But that seems funny as Dad doesn't like dates. Says they're too sweet."

Rachel's lips twitched. "They're not going to eat dates. They're going out on a date, which means they're spending time together."

"Like us!" Josh said.

"Sort of," Gran said, her laughter just beneath the surface. "Friends like to go out together."

"I don't go out much," Josh said, his mouth drooping. Rachel squeezed his hand and he brightened. "But today I am. Are we nearly there, Mr Pete?"

"Soon, buddy. Soon."

---

*O*nce Gran was comfortably seated at her table and the waiter had brought scones with jam and cream and a pot of tea, Rachel kissed her on the forehead.

"We'd better get moving if we're going to be back by midday."

Gran fluttered her hand. "Toodle-oo, dear. Off you go and enjoy your walk."

Josh set off at a lope. "Come on, slowpokes."

"Slow down, buddy. We're putting sunscreen on first. You need some too."

Josh slid to a stop and walked back towards them, muttering under his breath.

When they were finally ready, Pete led off. "We'll do the Taylors Bay section first and save the best views for later."

Someone—or lots of someones—had put months of hard work into the path, which was a mixture of straight stretches and cut stone steps. Josh shot ahead of them.

"Come on," Pete said, taking big strides. "We'd better keep up."

They set off at a brisk pace, but it didn't last long. Almost immediately, Josh pointed out some twisty trees. To Rachel they looked like severely arthritic fingers. Then he found a dead bug being held aloft by a line of marching ants.

The sand on the path crunched underfoot, and glimpses of

green-blue water glinted between the trees. Her spirits lifted. This was something she needed to do more often.

"What are you thinking about?" Pete asked.

"Just that I needed an expedition like this. My life is back to being work, exercise, church, and housework."

"Yes, your grandmother is looking more and more frail."

"She's still able to manage the dusting and dishes, but I need to do everything else." Rachel shrugged. "Makes me miss my tiny apartment. It only took an hour to clean it completely."

"Where did you live before?"

"Near Chatswood. Close to the train station and a short trip to work."

"If you're finding things a bit much, have you considered getting extra help? Mum did that for her parents and it made things far less stressful."

He slowed down to let Rachel lead the way down some rough steps.

"Yeah, I have thought about it," she said. "I hadn't realised how much Mum was doing."

"Have you heard from your parents?"

A quiver of nerves rippled through her stomach. "I'm expecting a letter from Mum any day now."

He stepped over a big root snaking across the path. "Dad not much of a writer?"

She shook her head. Pete had a fantastic relationship with his parents and often mentioned his father-in-law. How could he understand an estrangement like hers? Her face warmed. He'd be shocked at how she'd spoken to William the other day. She'd been shocked herself. Hadn't expected such raw rage.

She turned her head away so Pete couldn't see her face and pretended to be interested in the jumbled pile of rock next to her. Her mind shied away from the memory of the look in William's eyes as she'd lashed out at him. That man had expected too much of her. Although that was nothing new. He'd expected too much since she'd learned to walk.

Josh called out to her, and she seized the chance to scurry forward and avoid more questions. He'd found a cicada case discarded on a tree trunk. Pete came over and gently disengaged it from the tree. "Would you like me to keep it for you?"

"Yes, please," Josh said, already looking further down the path.

---

*R*achel would have preferred a much longer hike, but what with Gran and Josh, she'd have to be content with a hike that was short on distance but long on views. Bradleys Head certainly had those.

They returned to the café and collected Naomi. It didn't take long to settle her into a camp chair with the rest of them on a picnic blanket.

"The queen with her willing slaves," Pete said.

Her grandmother immediately stretched her neck and put her nose in the air. "My food may now be served," she said in her best regal voice.

Pete chuckled. Rachel handed him a plate holding a chicken salad wrap, which he passed to Gran.

The harbour lay at their feet. To their left was the jagged skyline of the city. Further right, the white sails of the Opera House rose from the water and then the arch of the Sydney Harbour Bridge. A ferry ploughed a foamy furrow right in front of where they sat.

"Is there anything you don't want in your wrap, Josh?" Rachel asked.

"Everything, please."

Rachel spread mayonnaise and laid strips of chicken. Then she added lettuce, tomato, grated cucumber and carrot and wrapped it for Josh.

"Do I get the same service?" Pete asked with a wink.

"Nope." Rachel handed him a plate and a wrap. "You and I have to make our own."

"How about we pray, so the others can start."

She'd never heard him pray. His taking the lead warmed her heart in a way she wasn't prepared to analyse.

Pete bowed his head. "Our amazing Creator. Thank you for this beautiful weather, beautiful views, good food and good company. Amen."

Those with their food already prepared started eating, whilst Pete and Rachel quickly made their own wraps and soon joined them.

Nearby, a group of two-man sailboats zipped to and fro, driven by the gusty breeze that threatened to whip off her grandmother's hat.

Something about the view reduced them all to silence for several minutes.

"Miss Rachel, can I have a biscuit?"

Well, almost all of them. She picked up the container, took off the lid, and handed one to Josh.

He took a big bite and waved his hands around. "Yum. You're a good cook."

There was a flash of movement, a blur of wings, and a yell from Josh. "He took my biscuit!" He glared towards the closest tree. Rachel could see the culprit, who still had the biscuit in his beak.

"Look. That naughty kookaburra took my biscuit."

Pete spluttered. "You shouldn't have told him it was so good."

Josh scowled. "I didn't know kookaburras would take my food."

Rachel wouldn't have expected it either. "Maybe they've gotten used to thieving from careless picnickers." She picked up the container. "Here, have another. This time, perhaps less of the hand waving. That was putting temptation right in front of Mr Kookaburra."

"If there aren't extras, you can have mine," Pete said.

"There's plenty. You don't have to miss out," Rachel said.

Pete rubbed his hands together before reaching for one. He took a mouthful and gave her a thumbs up. "That kookaburra has good taste."

Rachel covered her embarrassment at his praise by leaning across and offering her grandmother some fruit. She'd be in trouble if she hung around with Pete much more. He was too nice a Christian guy to pay her any attention. Why should he even look at someone with her history? She wouldn't if she were in his place.

CHAPTER 13

The following Wednesday evening, Pete had completed his twice-weekly run and had finished showering when the phone rang. Binh. He rang at exactly the same time each week.

Pete reached for the phone. "Hello, son," his father-in-law said.

Son. The word in Binh's broad accent brought a lump to Pete's throat every single time. How little he deserved the title. How much he craved it.

They chatted for a few minutes.

"What are you thankful for this week?" Binh asked. The first few times Binh asked this question Pete had struggled to see anything good in his life. But the more Binh asked, the more evidence Pete saw of God still being present in the day to day. In beauty, in just-in-time encouragements, in little kindnesses like cartons of eggs or fruit left on his doorstep. Finally, even in the good memories. He and Mai had often had minor arguments, especially in the second year of their marriage, but there'd been deep love, respect, and friendship at the core of their relationship, for which he was thankful.

Pete settled down in the comfiest chair in the living room and put his feet up on the footrest. "Best week in a long time."

"What made it the best?" Binh asked.

Pete told him about the trip out with Josh, Naomi, and Rachel to Bradleys Head. "And we had the first coaching session with Josh's team on Tuesday."

"And how did that go?"

"Surprisingly well."

The best part of the night had been watching Rachel's patience with the player who needed the most help. She'd run beside the woman on the field and cheered her on.

"Did you ever play soccer, Binh?"

"We played in the village, back before the war." Binh paused as though remembering. "Barefoot and with a ball that was seldom pumped up hard enough. It hurt to kick, but the bruises were worth it. And, of course, we played in the refugee camp. There wasn't much else to do."

A sliver of guilt lodged in Pete's throat. There couldn't be a bigger contrast to Binh's upbringing and Pete's idyllic childhood in the semi-rural suburbs of northern Sydney.

Binh nearly always asked the questions in their calls. Poor guy. He'd had the far-from-easy task of wringing conversation out of someone who hadn't had the energy to talk. It was way past time to change things.

"Binh, could I ask you something personal?"

"Of course."

"Did you ever consider remarrying?"

Binh laughed. "The first five years, I was too busy surviving. After that Mai needed my full attention." He sighed. "I did ask a lawyer at church what happened in situations like mine. He said that no country on earth would prevent me marrying since it had been over a decade with no news."

"But?" There'd obviously been a but.

"But no matter how much I prayed, I still considered myself married."

Pete's eyes opened wide. If anyone deserved to be happily married, it was Binh. He'd been an amazing father, adjusting his work to fit around Mai's life, and working extra hours so Mai could have the music lessons she'd craved. Music that had resulted in a scholarship to a private girls' school and eventually studying music at university. Before the children arrived, Mai would sit and play just for him at least once a week. Magical, romantic evenings.

Pete cleared his throat. "Have you ever heard any news about your wife?"

"No, nothing."

The sadness in Binh's voice reverberated down the phone line. "No one in the village has ever heard anything about her."

The last time Binh had visited Vietnam, Pete hadn't been up to asking anything about anyone else's tragedies.

"I thought long and hard about how to find her, to find any news of her."

Binh didn't add, 'if she's still alive'. Did he still keep hope, after all these years?

"Years ago—" Binh spoke so quietly, Pete had to clamp the phone against his ear and put his hand over the other ear to block the sound of the watering systems outside. "Women in our village had to collect water from the river. My wife used to wish for a well, right in the centre of the village, so I paid for one on my last trip."

What was the likelihood of Binh's wife returning to the village after so long and working out he had dug the well for her?

"I had a plaque attached to the seat next to it."

That made sense. "What did it say?"

Binh swallowed noisily.

"In memory of my beloved wife." His wife's Vietnamese name

rolled off his tongue. "And the sacrifice she made so her family could be safe."

Pete sniffed, not knowing what to say.

"And I added the verse, 'Greater love has no one than this: to lay down one's life for one's friends' with the full Bible reference, my name, and Mandurah, Western Australia."

"Did anyone in the village still remember you?"

"One or two. I left a Bible and letter with each one, so that if my wife returned, she'd know how to contact me."

It was a tiny chance, but if Binh's wife was still alive, then God was more than capable of helping them find each other.

They talked for another fifteen minutes. "Nearly bedtime for you over there," Binh said. "Time to pray and let you go. I know you get up early."

As it neared summer, the light woke Pete up ever earlier.

"Dear King of All—" Binh always prayed first. He'd been the only one to pray for months, because Pete couldn't even stumble through a short prayer. Not just because of the surface pain, but because Pete had feared what would erupt from deep down once he opened his mouth.

"We praise you that you are a great God who also cares about the tiny details of our lives." Binh praised God as though nothing delighted him more. Sentence after sentence of gratefulness. "Thank you for providing the soccer team to get Pete out of the too-quiet place he's living. Thank you that he has the energy to make friends and get back into exercise."

After his father-in-law finished, Pete prayed. He especially prayed for Binh's wife, that she might still be alive and return to her own village. Binh had suffered more grief than most people did in five lifetimes. He deserved a happily-ever-after ending. If only Pete could believe that one day such happiness could also be his again. But no. He'd had his chance, and he'd blown it. In novels, second chances were as common as dirt, but they weren't so common in real life.

An image of Rachel running down the soccer field flashed into his head. What a futile thought. Once she knew his story, she'd run as fast as possible in the opposite direction.

CHAPTER 14

*R*achel's back had been aching all day.

"Are you okay, Miss Rachel? You keep making funny faces like this." Josh screwed his face up in a grimace.

Rachel laughed. If she looked that bad, she'd scare the customers. "I must have hurt my back at soccer yesterday," she said.

"You'll come next week, won't you?" Josh stopped work on the plant he was transferring to a larger pot.

"It's not that bad. Some of those kicks you sent my way might have been a little hard."

He came over to her and patted her shoulder. "I'll be gentle next time. Mum tells me I need to be gentle with girls."

Josh had taken care of her from the first day she'd arrived at the nursery.

"You weren't rough. It's just been a long time since I've played soccer. I need to get used to it again."

"You and Mr Pete did a good job," Josh said, returning to work.

"Did we? That's kind of you to say so."

They repotted a few more plants.

"You've changed since you came here," Josh said.

"Changed?" she said, looking up at him. "How?"

"You're softer." He put his head to one side in his thinking posture. "And you laugh more."

Josh had a razor-sharp eye. Her former shiny Easter egg exterior hadn't fooled him. He'd had no problem seeing that her inside was hollow.

"You didn't want to talk to anyone. You talked to me because you had to."

Ouch. "I'm sorry if I hurt you."

"It's okay, Miss Rachel. I knew you were sad." Josh rubbed his sleeve across his sweaty forehead.

There was so much she didn't know about him. She'd come to admire his patience and cheery perseverance, but what really went on in his heart?

"You can ask me questions, Miss Rachel."

She blinked. "How did you know I wanted to ask more questions?"

He giggled. "You went all quiet and nibbled your lip. I know people want to ask me questions. Little kids are best. They just ask instead of getting all nervous and uncomfortable."

"I guess I wanted to know what you find hard about ..." She shifted her feet. "You know ..."

"Having Down Syndrome, you mean?" He rubbed his upper lip. "That's easy. When people talk about me as though I'm not there." He sniffed. "I have feelings the same as anyone else. I used to hate going out."

"Why?" Rachel asked.

He frowned. "People stared and said mean things."

"Were your mum and dad able to help you?"

He grinned. "Mum and Dad are the best. They kept telling me that Jesus loved me and I'm special. They told me God had special things for me to do." He puffed out his chest. "Things only Joshua Smith could do."

Rachel's hands were covered in dirt, so she used her upper arm to wipe her eye. "Like introducing me to Jesus."

"Yes. That's the best kind of thing to do. I can't explain things well, but Jesus helps me say the right words."

"You say the right words more often than you realise. I think you're amazing. Last year, I was so angry at God. I wasn't able to listen to other people, so he sent you. You made me listen."

"Really? You're saying that to be nice."

She took two steps around their work bench and side-hugged him. "Not at all. You're one of my spiritual fathers."

He frowned.

"Do you know what I mean?"

He shook his head.

She needed to make things simpler. "You know how dads have children?"

He narrowed his eyes at her. She'd just insulted him by making the first step too simple. "When we tell people about Jesus and someone becomes a Christian, then we're like their spiritual mum or dad."

"Oh." He gave a lighthouse-bright smile. "I like that."

Joy Wong had been Esther's spiritual mother. Esther had led an acquaintance in palliative care to Jesus and become that woman's spiritual mother. Even if Rachel might never be a normal kind of parent, maybe she could follow their lead.

Last night, she'd finally cracked open Esther's diaries. They'd started the year Esther turned eighteen and were all neatly labelled by date. It hadn't taken long to sort them into chronological order. She'd flicked through the first. Nothing startling. Mostly an account of what Esther had done that day at university and veiled references to her latest love interest. Rachel would get around to the diaries from Esther's early twenties someday but she was most interested in the entries from the day Esther discovered she had cancer.

She'd flicked backwards through the last few diaries. If she remembered rightly, Esther had become engaged a short while before her cancer diagnosis.

She'd found the references, and read all the way from the first mention of Nick through to the end of Esther's first round of chemo and radiation. The basic points were familiar, but Esther's diaries were the raw, on-the-spot emotion. All Esther's fears and growing isolation from both Nick and her parents were detailed on the page in black ink. Stark and painful. Rachel had cried for her sister, wanting to comfort her.

Rachel's hands kept moving through the repetitive task of repotting. Slicing off the roots on the bottom of the old pot, putting new soil in the bottom of the new, bigger pot, transferring the plant across, then adding more soil down the sides.

"Miss Rachel, are you thinking too much?" Josh interrupted her thoughts.

She jumped and turned towards him. "Probably. And it's time for a drink."

"I already had one."

Had she been that deep in thought?

"I pushed the trolley out for Sam and Dave."

She had been too distracted. Josh had also collected up all the dirty pots, ready for them to be thoroughly cleaned and reused when they did the next lot of lemon graftings.

"You were thinking for ages. What were you thinking about?"

"About the things Esther left to me when she died." Rachel took a big swig from her water bottle.

"Like your car?" he said.

The car had been transferred to her ownership a month before Esther died. "Yes, and all her clothes and books and photos."

Her mother had done most of the sorting. All that was left were some favourite books, the photos—which Rachel hadn't yet had the time or emotional energy to face—and the diaries. The most complicated part was Esther's investment apartment. They'd probably sell it. The apartment was mortgaged, and Esther had wanted twenty percent of the money to go to the Bible Society. Anything left would be Rachel's. She clenched her teeth to prevent herself crying, as she did whenever she thought about Esther's will.

"You miss your sister," Josh said, staring at her.

Her eyes stung and she nodded.

Josh came over to her and gave her a bear hug. She relaxed into it. He smelled of sweat and earth, but that didn't matter. He was warm and kind, the little brother she'd never had. "I'm going to get your shirt wet," she mumbled.

"It'll dry." He chortled and patted her on the back.

Most of her grief for Esther was complicated by regret. Too many years wasted. Too many years apart. Reading Esther's diaries had more than reminded her of all she'd missed. Reading them had been like a slap in the face.

Josh's heart thudded away, next to hers. Like Josh himself, steady and reliable. Someone who didn't have ulterior motives. How she'd valued his friendship over the last year.

She drew back out of his hug.

"Better?" he said.

"Yes. You're a tremendous guy, Josh, I hope people tell you that often."

He shook his head. His voice was low and sad. "Nope. Most people make me feel I'm not good enough."

"Then they're fools. To me, you're solid gold."

He beamed. "I like you, Miss Rachel. I wish there were more people like you."

CHAPTER 15

*G*ran waved a letter at Rachel as she walked in the back door. "Your mother's written us a letter."

It was disciplined of her grandmother not to have opened it. Gran's days were much more restricted now. A little light housework, hosting a few visitors, and prayer. Loads of prayer. Gran said prayer enabled her to roam the world and impact it for eternity. Rachel had a long way to go in the prayer department, but Pete's notebook idea was proving helpful.

Rachel kissed her grandmother. "Is this a can't-wait-until-after-a-shower letter?"

Her grandmother laughed. "I can wait another half hour, so go ahead and have your shower. I know you like to feel clean before you do anything else."

Rachel showered and then they read the letter together while Rachel prepared the evening meal. She dug around in the vegetable drawer for broccoli, capsicum, carrot, and anything that would accompany the chicken stir-fry she was making.

"Dearest Naomi and Rachel," her grandmother read.

I APOLOGISE FOR THE DELAY IN WRITING. WE WERE MORE EXHAUSTED THAN WE REALISED GETTING THE HOUSE READY FOR SALE, AND ONCE WE ARRIVED HERE, THE ISLAND WORKED ITS MAGIC. THE MINUTE WE SET FOOT IN OUR HOUSE, WE COLLAPSED. WE'VE DONE LITTLE MORE THAN SLEEP AND TODDLE TO AND FROM THE BEACH.

"Weren't they going there to work?" Rachel asked, as she finished slicing the first carrot.

"Your mother mentioned they were going to have two weeks' holiday first."

Her mother hadn't said anything to her, but maybe she'd been inhibited by the state of affairs between herself and William. Rachel's chest tightened. In closing the door to him, she'd also subtly changed her relationship with her mother. Her mother's first loyalty was back with her husband.

WILLIAM WAS RIGHT. THIS PLACE IS SPECTACULAR. EVERY TIME WE SNORKEL, WE SEE DIFFERENT FISH. WILLIAM IS SO EXCITED TO SHARE HIS NEW HOBBY, AND YOUNG DAVY OFTEN JOINS US. DAVY HASN'T MANAGED TO CONVINCE ME TO GO HIKING YET. AT THE MOMENT IT IS MORE THAN ENOUGH TO DO ONE SNORKEL A DAY. THE REST OF THE TIME, I LIE IN THE SHADE ON THE BEACH OR SIT IN THE GARDEN AND READ.

Her grandmother looked up. "I'm glad they're getting some rest. Your mother hasn't had much downtime since well before Esther died."

Rachel minced the garlic. Her mother probably hadn't had any respite since her honeymoon. At least, Rachel assumed they'd had a honeymoon. It was equally possible that William had preached wherever they'd gone.

Gran kept reading. The letter was mostly descriptions of the scenery and the domestic arrangements. It was hard for Rachel to be enthusiastic when every mention of William irritated her like a stone in her shoe. With William conveniently hundreds of kilometres away, she could forget him most of the time.

This letter reminded her of the appeal in his eyes as he pleaded for forgiveness.

She pounded the garlic. Oops. It was now mushed rather than minced. William had always been eloquent. His words—dredged up from a heart she'd never been sure existed—had been unforgettable. She sucked in a sharp breath.

"What was that, dear?" her grandmother said, looking up.

"Nothing, Gran. Nothing."

"Your mother seems to have taken to Reg and Ivy, the couple who were a big part of your father's story."

Rachel bit down a retort. "Good thing too, if they're the closest neighbours."

REG AND IVY REGULARLY INVITE US OVER OR DROP IN. I NEVER REALISED HOW ISOLATED WE WERE IN SYDNEY. HERE, IVY COMES OVER IF SHE'S HEADING TO THE SHOPS TO ASK ME IF I WANT ANYTHING. I CAN POP OVER AND GET SOME EGGS OR FLOUR AND REPAY HER NEXT TIME. BAKING AND HOSPITALITY WILL BE A BIG PART OF THE MINISTRY HERE.

"Mum will be in her element. Hospitality is one thing I didn't inherit from her and wish I had."

Gran looked at Rachel over her glasses. "It might be a lack of practice. Please do feel free to ask people over. This is your home as much as mine." She finished the letter and folded it up. "And why do you conclude you're no good at hospitality? That sounds like one of Satan's lies, another one of those thoughts to be taken captive."

When Rachel had first heard her grandmother talk about Satan, she'd had to stifle a mocking comment. A ridiculous image leapt to her mind—a man in a skintight black suit and red horns, grinning impishly and threatening her with a red pitchfork.

Her grandmother had seemed to read her mind and speared her with her gaze. "Mocking Satan reduces him to a joke, and no one is more pleased about that than he is. If no one takes him seriously, then he's able to work unhindered."

Gran slid the letter back into the envelope and laid it on the table next to her. "Did you ever finish that book I recommended?"

"Screwtape Letters, you mean?"

Her grandmother nodded.

She'd expected Gran to give her non-fiction, but instead she'd given her a thought-provoking novel by C. S. Lewis in which a senior demon instructed a junior colleague how to tempt his human. As she'd laughed, Rachel had absorbed the serious lessons under the humorous surface.

"I finished it last week. You were right—it's brilliant. The sort of book to reread every year. I have been allowing Satan to bury me under a mound of lies."

"How are you going with taking every thought captive, dear?"

"I've a long way to go to reach Olympic standard."

Church on Sunday was the time for the major spiritual battle of each week. All those squeaky-clean people. If they could see the slime in Rachel's past, they'd wrinkle their noses in disgust and carefully step around her. She squirmed at the thought.

Not that they knew her past. Perhaps her assumptions about them were as wrong as theirs about her. After all, she looked as though she had things under control. Humans were masters at covering up pain. Look at Pete. His wife had died, yet he was functioning day by day. Although he did go silent and sad every so often, revealing there was something bubbling away beneath his hazel-eyed handsomeness.

She blinked. She did not just think that.

Pete would never look her way. He was too young and too … too wholesome. Not the sort who would fall head over heels for someone like her.

Unclean. Soiled.

"Are you learning to listen to God's truth?" Her grandmother asked as she massaged her arthritic knee.

Rachel wished.

The condemnation in her heart was loud. Louder than any other voice by far. Like the difference between a mosquito's whine and an elephant's trumpet.

Gran glanced at Rachel. "Keep reading those calligraphies your mother did before she left."

Rachel had intended to, but so often she rushed right on past the cupboard where they were stuck up.

"'As far as the east is from the west, so far does God remove our sin from us,'" her grandmother recited. "And chapter five of Romans: 'Whoever hears my word and believes him who sent me has eternal life and will not be condemned; he has crossed over from death to life.'"

The Romans verses had lassoed Rachel's heart the night God reached down and saved her. Saved her from her past, from her bitterness, from herself.

Gran smiled. "The more you read and meditate on the truths in those verses, the more their truth will migrate from your head to your heart."

Rachel would do it, starting tomorrow. "Thanks for the

reminder, Gran. I haven't been consistent enough. I often feel condemned, even if my head knows God has forgiven me."

"It takes time, dear. Sometimes it takes a long time, but you're moving in the right direction."

Gran didn't need to say any more. Gran would never give up praying for Rachel, for her struggle with condemnation and for the God-given strength to forgive William.

Deep down, Rachel knew forgiving William was the right thing to do. But she had no forgiveness to give. There was only a fire pit of rage.

Jesus forgave his enemies, but he was God. Couldn't she just be human?

CHAPTER 16

*P*ete blew his whistle for the end of the final drill. "You've got ten minutes for snacks," he called. "Then Simon's team is going to come and play against us."

He grinned as a chorus of cheers erupted. The players liked the drills, but he didn't blame them for preferring the games.

Josh's mum was on the sideline with two containers. She made the team line up, then doled out portions of orange, apple, and popcorn. When Josh received his snack, he leaned over and planted a sloppy kiss on Lyn's cheek.

Pete strolled over to Lyn. "Any left for us?"

Lyn drew out two more small containers. "I made sure of it."

He took some fruit, drank from his water bottle that he'd picked up on his way over, and stood next to Rachel. "They've improved heaps with controlling the ball."

"Good thing, too." Rachel laughed. "I was getting exhausted, running to get it."

It hadn't taken them long to work out each other's strengths. They now did half the warm-up and half the drills each, with Rachel constantly coming up with new ideas to improve skills.

The snacks had almost disappeared. "Make sure you have a good drink," Pete said to the players. "You know the other team is hard to beat."

"But, Mr Pete, we can beat them." Josh punched the air.

"Yes, you can—if you concentrate."

"We'll concentrate, won't we, team?" Josh led them running back onto the field. "Come on."

Pete took a last piece of apple and followed.

---

*P*ete and Rachel stood on opposite sidelines. The other team's coaches were refereeing this game, so their main task was to judge when the ball went over the boundary lines.

Once the competition started, they'd add Saturday afternoon games on top of the twice-weekly coaching. He and Rachel would probably have to alternate weeks, because the nursery didn't close until four o'clock. Maybe his father could supervise the nursery from one to four on Saturdays.

Rachel was running down the sideline, blonde hair tousled, keeping pace with whoever had the ball. He hadn't decided if he preferred Rachel's regular look or the chic look he'd only seen twice. He turned his head away. *Focus, Pete, focus.*

He'd never expected to enjoy coaching this much, but the players and their family members were highly motivated. It would take a grouch not to be impacted. Sure, some of the players were easily distracted—but a blast on the whistle would usually get them back on track. They made a joke of it by jumping to attention whenever he blew a long blast.

Every training day, Pete woke up with a song in his heart. Even Josh had commented that he was whistling and laughing more at work. It was hard not to be infected by the enthusiasm of the team.

Someone fouled Priscilla, the player who struggled more than the others.

"Time!" Rachel escorted a crying Priscilla off the field. She sent on another player and put her arm around Priscilla's shoulder. Their heads were bent together. Rachel was assuring Priscilla it was fine, she was loved and important, and it was a team effort.

In the time they'd been involved with Special Olympics, Rachel wore a new contentment. More laughter, more gentleness.

She was obviously growing spiritually too. She hadn't seemed embarrassed to tell him she was reading her Bible most days and praying out loud in the car on the way to work.

The whistle rang for half time, and the score was one-all. Rachel gathered the team for a pep talk, and he ran over to join them.

"Josh, remember that you're defending now. Don't rush too far forward and leave a gap the other team can get the ball through."

Josh saluted her with a mischievous glint in his eye.

"Jason, don't be scared of their forward. I know he's tall, but you're faster. Just zip in and take the ball from under his feet." Rachel looked up at Pete. "Anything to add?"

"Just keep doing the good work you're doing, and remember to have fun."

"Anything else?" Rachel added.

Pete pretended he'd forgotten, scratching his head and then turning to go, when Josh punched him on his shoulder.

"Come on, you know."

"Let's clap," Pete boomed out.

Josh led them. Clap, clap, clap.

"Let's stamp."

Stamp, stamp, stamp. The whole team loved these chants.

"Let's roar."

They roared like lions.

"Let's play."

And they rushed into their positions, yelling like maniacs.

They won two-one and still had enough energy to sprint over to their parents, chattering like hyperactive parrots.

Pete collected the stack of cones and checked for any forgotten water bottles and clothing. Only two items this week. He stored them in a box in the back of his car and turned to look for Rachel.

She was talking to two parents next to their car. A flash of blue and red caught his eye behind her. Someone in the playground? He moved his glance. Two primary-school children swung on the swings. He stopped abruptly, chest tight, a surging tide of panic spreading to his limbs. He turned as though he'd forgotten something and stumbled back towards the field. Once around the corner and out of sight, he bent over, gasping. Why did things have to be so hard? He was fine at work … most of the time. If something triggered him, he could usually walk away and take a few deep breaths and pray. He'd perfected the panicked 'help me' prayer.

He forced himself to take one deep breath, then another. He reached out a hand and hauled himself upright. The counsellor Binh had introduced him to had said these symptoms would lessen, but when?

He peeked around the corner. This was ridiculous. He was a grown man, hiding from two children. Had Rachel noticed anything wrong? He wasn't nearly ready to explain.

The parents were checking the children were buckled into their seats. He waited until their car doors slammed and then sauntered out towards Rachel as though he hadn't a care in the world. *Fraud!*

Rachel turned to walk towards her own car. He joined her.

"Did Josh tell you I took him kayaking on the weekend?" he asked.

"You think he'd forget to tell me something like that? He was so excited, he practically knocked me over on Monday morning."

"Apparently he had always wanted to go kayaking, but no one dared to take him. He saw my kayak at the back of the shed and asked if I would."

She winked. "It must have been okay. You didn't drown him."

"Yes, but it did take some thinking to get him in and out safely. I was terrified he'd get overexcited and flip us and then panic and forget how to get out."

"So, not an activity he can do on his own?" Rachel opened her car door and threw her bag across to the passenger seat.

He took a deep breath. Did he dare to ask her? Come on. He'd been thinking about it for three days. Even rung a company and made some enquiries.

The problem was that Rachel might think he was asking her out. The last thing he wanted was for things to be awkward between them, to ruin the ease of their friendship.

"Look …" He turned slightly away from her. "Would you be willing to come on a camping and kayaking trip with Josh and myself? I'd like to take him, but I'd want another person there just in case."

Rachel gripped the car door. "This is just as friends, isn't it?"

His throat went dry and sweat prickled his lower back. He nodded. "Just friends."

"That's all right, then. I'd be happy to come. I've never been camping."

Never been camping. Why not? Someone had mentioned hiking and camping at Esther's funeral.

"I've got a few minutes. What were you planning?" She closed the car door and swatted around her ears. "Mozzies, ugh."

They strolled up and down the car park with her stamping her feet and swinging her arms. He tightened his lips to prevent himself laughing. If she knew how ridiculous she looked, she might prefer to be bitten.

"Kangaroo Valley is safe, and easy to kayak. There's a campsite to stay at, and we can use my kayak and hire an extra one."

Two lines appeared between her eyes. "Are there any rapids?"

"Not where we'd be going. Mostly a leisurely river and some long stretches of flat water. Plenty of places to camp and swim."

"That sounds okay. I've never kayaked, and I wouldn't want to let you down."

"After seeing your soccer skills and hearing about your long swims, I doubt you'll have any problems. I can pair up with Josh to start with, and you can have my kayak."

She paused under the street light. "You sure?"

He nodded. "And I'll arrange the tents. I've got a two-man tent and a few singles. I had them sent over from Western Australia. Suddenly felt the desire to start using them again."

CHAPTER 17

*P*ete and Josh pulled out of the nursery at one o'clock on Friday afternoon, leaving Dirk and Colin in charge.

Pete towed a trailer with the kayak, tents, and other camping gear. They'd swing by Rachel's place on the way. The weather forecast predicted mild, sunny days with clear nights. Couldn't be better.

"You comfortable back there, buddy?"

"Yup. Do you know Rachel's friend?" Josh asked.

Perhaps Rachel hadn't been as comfortable as she'd seemed with the invitation. She'd rung him a week ago and asked if there was room for one more on their trip.

"Gina? Yes. You've met her before too. She was at Rachel's baptism. She's apparently an excellent cook."

A good cook was always welcome from Josh's point of view. Not that Pete objected either. If having a friend along made Rachel more comfortable, then so be it.

Rachel and Gina were waiting at Naomi's gate. Ten minutes, and their gear was loaded. Josh took one look at Gina's plump prettiness and started chattering away. He insisted Gina share the back seat with him, leaving Rachel to slide into the front.

At this rate, they might even get most of the way out of Sydney before rush hour traffic forced them to a crawl.

"Have you kayaked before, Gina?" Pete asked.

"Yes, a lot. We're a camping family, and my brothers were mad keen on anything to do with the water."

That was a relief. Having three beginners along might have been too much of a challenge. He'd give her a trial run with Josh in the morning and make the decision then about who would be best partnered with Josh.

Pete concentrated on the road and left the others to chat.

They managed to avoid nearly all the weekend traffic and when, several hours later, it came time to take the steep road down into Kangaroo Valley, Pete suggested Josh count the turns.

Pete geared down as they glided around the first curve.

"One," Josh said.

Driving this road was much more fun than the highway.

"Two … three." Josh continued counting from the back.

As they rounded the eighth corner, Josh asked, "What's that ping, ping noise?"

"They're bellbirds," Gina said.

"Mighty small bells," Josh muttered.

The road straightened out. Towering orange sandstone cliffs encircled the bowl of the valley. It was ideal weather. Plenty of sunshine and only the faintest breeze.

"We're going to make a brief stop for me to check the details with the kayak hire company."

They pulled into the car park. "Rachel, do you want to come in with me? Gina and Josh, you might want to stretch your legs." Pete pointed with his chin. "Bathroom's over there."

He open the screen door for Rachel and the shop's bell jangled. The shopkeeper hurried in from somewhere in the back, checked his book, showed them their kayak, and gave them plenty of water-proof bags to pack their gear in ready for the morning.

Arriving back at the car, Gina said. "Have we got time to buy some fresh milk? And the fudge here is famous too."

Pete glanced at the dashboard clock. "No problem."

He drove carefully over the narrow Hampden suspension bridge, with its mock turrets, parked in front of a bookshop, and followed them into the fudge shop.

The range of choices mesmerised them for a while but they finally emerged with a selection of vanilla-pecan, chocolate, and coconut fudge.

Once they arrived at the campsite, Pete said, "Gina, if you're looking after the food, I'll get Josh and Rachel to help me put the tents up."

Rachel proved a fast learner and soon they were sitting on four camp chairs near the water.

Rachel looked around the campsite, which was nearly empty. "You picked a good weekend."

"Lucky, I guess. There might be more people later." Pete took a long drink of orange juice. "We still have some daylight left, so why don't we all have a snack before I give Rachel a quick kayaking lesson."

"While you're doing the lesson, Josh and I will get the fire pit going and pop in the potatoes," Gina said.

"Good move, inviting Gina," Pete said with a chuckle.

Gina laughed. "I love outdoor cooking." She looked towards the trees on the landward side of the campsite. "The kangaroos should appear soon to keep us company."

Pete and Rachel hauled the kayak to the water, and he handed her a paddle. Within minutes, they were off.

"Alternate your paddle on the right and then the left." Rachel caught on as quickly as he'd expected.

"You don't need to dig the paddle in so deeply," Pete said and

Rachel immediately changed her technique. "That's right. If you're in front, then that's all there is to it."

"But the person at the back does more?" she said.

"The person at the back steers and turns the kayak." She'd learn faster by actually doing it. "Do you want to try?"

Rachel looked over her shoulder. "Let's switch, then take a few minutes to go around that corner and back. I don't want to abandon Gina for long."

Gina's light laugh and Josh's deep boom floated over to them. "I'm not worried about those two," Pete said.

Rachel paddled towards the edge. "Gina misses Esther, and her family don't live close by. I find her the easiest person to talk to at church."

Pete lined the kayak up parallel to the shore. "Put a hand on each side and lever your body out, keeping it low. I sometimes straddle the whole boat and stand up like that. If you prefer to get out on one side, I'll lean the opposite way."

She was up and out like a pro, and he followed suit. They switched positions, and he said, "Are you set back there?"

"Think so." Rachel pushed off.

It took her less than two minutes to work out the basics and only a few more to teach her to do turns.

Once they were heading upstream, he said, "Tell me a little about your church."

'It's really my grandmother's church, but Esther joined her soon after she left Victory."

"Is Victory where your parents work?"

"Not anymore." Her voice had gone flat and hard.

Something big must have happened to make them leave. Rachel was silent. She often talked about her mother, but he'd never heard her say anything about her father. Why was that?

They settled into a rhythm, his muscles warming to the task, and headed for the corner upriver. Rachel had the hang of things. He could feel the tiny movements when she adjusted their angle.

"I go to church with Gran now and Gina's there too. There's about a hundred people." Rachel paused. "Mostly older folk, with a sprinkling of families."

"And do you like it?" he asked.

"That's a question I've been struggling with recently. The pastor preaches from God's word, and the people love Jesus, but there aren't many people my age."

"Have you thought about going elsewhere?"

"I have, but I need to stay at the moment. For Gran's sake."

They reached the corner and Pete looked upriver to the next section. "Okay, turn us around."

The boat swung round, and he looked back along the kayak's water line to Rachel's paddle. Good, she'd worked out how to do a reverse stroke.

"Let's see how fast this thing goes," Rachel said, her voice tinged with enthusiasm.

"You bet." Pete was ready for a competition, even if only against themselves.

They dug in, muscles stretching and pulling against the water's resistance, smooth and fast.

CHAPTER 18

"That was some meal." Pete leaned back, rubbing his stomach. "Thank you so much, Gina."

"You cooked the meat," Gina said.

"But it was your magic marinade that took things to another level."

Gina flushed. "It will have to be much simpler tomorrow night."

Rachel stood up. "I'll do the dishes. The rest of you sit and relax."

As she headed off towards the public sinks, Pete unlocked the back of the car and pulled out his guitar. His hands trembled. This guitar had accompanied him and Mai on every camping trip. It hadn't been out of its case in three years, until a tune and a practice run last night. His fingertips were no longer callused, but they'd toughen up once he put in the practise.

He took a deep breath. Time to move on. Campfires and singing were inseparable.

Josh clapped his hands. "I like camping. Fires and food and now music."

"Wait until you hear me before you get excited," Pete said with a laugh, knowing Josh would applaud anything he played.

He strummed a few chords before moving into a song they sang at his old church. Josh joined in, singing joyfully but tonelessly. His volume covered the times when Pete stumbled over the chord changes. Then Gina joined in. Finally, Rachel came back from doing the dishes and listened. After a few minutes, she started singing, softly at first but growing in confidence. She had a great voice.

One song led to another until Pete took a breather and rested the guitar on top of its case.

Rachel indicated the closest campers. "I wonder what they think of our song choices. I can't believe I just sat and sang Christian songs for an hour." She looked at Gina. "It might not be so weird for you, but it is for me." She sat up straight. "And it's amazing how many of the words I knew."

Pete looked across the fire towards Rachel. Her skin and eyes glowed in the flickering light. He cleared his throat. "Rachel, I think the others know how you became a Christian, but I'd love to hear your story."

"I helped." Josh stabbed the fire with a poker and sent up a shower of sparks.

Rachel stared at the ground. Maybe he'd overstepped the mark. "If you don't want to, that's fine too."

"No. I'm willing, but I'm not sure how much detail you want. Do you want the one-minute summary or the ten-minute version?"

Pete looked over towards Gina and Josh. "I'd prefer the longer version if the others are happy to hear it."

"Me too," Gina said. "I only know snippets—just enough to know there were miracles involved."

Rachel took a deep breath and let it out slowly.

Pete wondered if the story was hard for her to share. He had things he struggled to talk about. Maybe she was the same. "You grew up in a church family—I know that much."

"Correct, but I didn't get along with my father." She folded her arms and stared into the fire. "He cared more about his reputation than his daughters, and demanded impossibly high standards."

He had to strain to hear her voice, which was now a quiet monotone.

"By the time I reached my teens, we were fighting all the time. It eventually got so bad that I ran away." She picked up a small branch next to her chair and stripped a leaf off it, then another, and another.

"I stayed with Gran for a while, but she talked about Jesus too much and I didn't want to hear about him, so I ran away from her too." She ripped off some more leaves. "That was a childishly stupid decision. I did lots of things I wasn't proud of." She avoided looking at him.

He shouldn't have asked her to do this.

"Because I didn't finish school, I ended up getting a job in a fast-food shop." Her head came up. "I hated it so much I decided I had to get a better job. I went to a second-hand clothing shop in Double Bay and found some designer clothes. Those, combined with my private school background, got me a job in the cosmetics section at David Jones."

She shrugged. "I did well at the job, but inside I was hollow and angry. A huge mess."

He could tell she was giving the edited version. Because of Josh, or because there were things she was too ashamed to mention? Many girls in her situation would have ended up on the streets. He shivered.

"I did have one Christian colleague, but I wouldn't let her talk about Jesus." Rachel shook her head. "Stupid me."

"How much better we'd all be, if we didn't run from Jesus," Pete said.

"Yes, but I ought to have known better. Gran's Jesus was different from the Jesus I'd had stuffed down my throat at home, but I was too hurt to notice."

She pulled the last leaf off the branch and leaned forward to drop it in the fire. The aromatic scent of burning eucalyptus filled the air.

"I got emptier and emptier inside, until one day I decided I'd had enough."

Rachel was choosing her words carefully for Josh's sake. It made Pete admire her all the more.

She sat up straight. "My car got a puncture right on the edge of a cliff." She smiled at Josh. "I couldn't drive the car anywhere. Who do you think was the first person God sent to find me?"

"I don't know." Josh scratched his head. "Who?"

Rachel turned towards Pete for the first time since she'd started her story. "Can you guess?"

"You're not going to say that this is how you met my parents?"

She nodded. "It sure is. They were in the car behind mine and pulled over when they saw me on the side of the road."

Josh's mouth dropped open.

"I was crying so hard, I didn't see Dirk clearly. He helped me change my tyre, followed me down the hill to a service station, and paid for a hotel room so I could get some sleep. I didn't even ask his name."

"Well then, how did you end up at the nursery?" Pete asked.

"Well, that was miracle number three. But there was another miracle before that one. Do you want to hear about it?"

He nodded, and gripped his knees. He had to hold something. Otherwise, he'd give Rachel a huge hug, and that would ruin everything.

"When I got back to work, I told my friend what had happened. Alice got all excited about God saving me and doing a miracle. Well, I was pretty upset with her, because I didn't believe in God. Or if I did, I didn't think he cared about me."

"He loves everyone, Miss Rachel," Josh said.

"You're right, but I didn't know that then. I was so annoyed about what my friend said that I told her I was going to set a test for God. If he didn't pass the test, then I had proven he didn't exist, and Alice wasn't to ever mention Jesus again."

God had obviously passed the test, but what would Rachel have come up with? Pete didn't yet know her well enough to guess.

"What was the test you set?" Gina asked.

Rachel laughed. "I was so confident there wasn't a God that I set something silly." She pulled her ear lobe. "I asked God to make a fifty-year-old man do a handstand right in the middle of David Jones, and I set a time limit of sixty minutes."

She had been as cynical as she was confident. Obviously, a God moment was coming up. Pete leaned forward.

"What happened?" Josh said in a hushed voice.

"Nothing—for fifty-nine minutes. I was delighted that I had an excuse to reject God, but poor Alice was upset. Really upset. And I didn't enjoy that part."

Pete reached over and poked the fire to distract himself. What had God done?

"At the last minute—literally—there was a collective gasp from all the sales assistants nearby." Rachel laughed, a relaxed spurt of joy. "I'd been so confident, I hadn't even bothered to look, but Alice was jumping up and down asking if that was my test. I had to ask her what had happened."

"And what did she say?" Gina asked, eyes wide.

"That a man had just done a handstand right in the middle of the floor. I still thought I'd won, because I'd set the condition that the man had to be fifty, and he looked much too young."

Rachel paused with a quirk of her lips.

She couldn't stop now. If Rachel wanted them to beg, he'd beg, "Well, don't leave us in suspense."

"I didn't think I'd be able to talk to the man and ask his age, because the security guards arrived to escort him off the premises. At the last minute, he veered towards our counter. His words shattered all my cynical confidence. He told me to go home. When I asked him which home he meant, he described my grandmother's front door in perfect detail."

The fire gave an explosive pop, and everyone jumped.

"I barely had enough wits left to ask him how old he was."

"What did he say?" Josh asked, awe in his voice.

"He said he'd turned fifty the day before," Rachel murmured, her eyes filling with tears.

Wow. Pete took a deep breath. He'd never heard a story like this. It reminded him of the miracles that the early Christians experienced in the Book of Acts.

Gina dug in her bag and handed Rachel a tissue. Rachel wiped her eyes and blew her nose. "I just fell apart."

Who wouldn't?

She shuddered. "Late one night, I went to my grandmother's. I never meant anyone to know I was there, but somehow Esther was awake. She heard me crying outside the door. And of course, Gran welcomed me in." Rachel grimaced. "I basically stayed in my room for weeks."

"Sounds like you had some sort of breakdown," Gina said.

Pete's heart clenched in pity.

Rachel nodded. "I didn't do anything for over a month. Esther nearly went crazy. Prior to my arrival Esther hadn't known I existed. Once she did, she wanted a grand reunion. The problem was, I wanted nothing of the sort."

"But how did you get to the nursery?" Josh said.

"After weeks of sleeping and eating, Gran convinced me to help her with some gardening. To my surprise, I loved it. Loved it enough to decide I'd try a career change, but all the jobs I applied for turned me down. Klopper's was last on the list."

"Not because it was your last choice, I hope," Pete said with a joke in voice.

"No, because it was the closest to home. I started with the jobs I least wanted and practised my spiel there first. When I reached Klopper's, Dirk wasn't there. I nearly missed him but I stopped for a cup of coffee. I was just about finished when Dirk came looking for me."

"Why, Miss Rachel?" Josh asked.

"That's the third miracle. Although I didn't remember Dirk, he remembered me. He'd spotted my car in the car park and rushed to find me." Rachel twirled the stud earring in her earlobe. "He offered me the job so fast I thought he must be crazy, but he didn't let me know why until weeks later."

"He knew you needed support and encouragement." When Pete was little, he'd sometimes resented the strangers his father brought home. Now he was older, he could see what such kindness meant to those his parents had helped. People like Rachel and Josh.

"But at this stage you still sound a long way from becoming a Christian," Gina said, stretching out her legs.

"Shh." Rachel put a finger to her lips and pointed to the river-bank with her other hand. The ponderous bulk of a wombat trun-dled along, rooting among the tender grasses.

"This campsite usually has lots of night-time visitors," Pete whispered. Once the wombat had gone, he looked back at Rachel.

"The rest of the story is more ordinary. I kept running, and God kept pursuing. He used Josh and your father to clear away the rubble of my warped views of God. My grandmother and others were praying in the background. Piece by piece, everything came together, until I overheard a Bible story and was intrigued enough to start reading the Bible for myself. The final step was reading Romans and understanding that Jesus loved me and didn't condemn me for my past." She shrugged. "I gave in. Shortly after-wards, I was baptised."

Rachel had glossed over a lot of the story. Understandable, really. Pete didn't share more than the barest minimum of his story with outsiders either. Maybe, just maybe, she'd one day feel comfortable enough with him to share the rest.

His stomach tensed. It would have to be a two-way street. He couldn't expect her to bare her heart if he wasn't prepared to do the same. He blew out a gusty breath.

Vulnerability was scary.

CHAPTER 19

*R*achel dipped her paddle into the smooth water. Not a breath of wind stirred. Josh had insisted on partnering with Gina and the two of them were paddling twenty metres in front of her and Pete. Gina sat in the back, neatly matching Josh's erratic rhythms.

The sun bounced off the water in tiny silver-gold splashes. She adjusted her sunglasses.

"Couldn't get a better day for it," Pete said behind her.

"I was thinking the same thing. Just right for beginners." Rachel jumped as a fish leapt out of the water in front of them.

She'd slept deeply overnight and woken refreshed soon after sunrise. She kept finding herself smiling to herself. Maybe the lightness in her heart was because of the scenery, but maybe it had something to do with telling her story. Each time she told it, parts of her past—including her suicide attempt and breakdown—lost their hold on her. Interesting. She pictured her past as the thick canopy of a forest opening up so shafts of light could reach the dark forest floor.

She dug her paddle into the water to the right and then the left, aiming for each stroke to be at the same angle and speed to keep the kayak as balanced as possible.

Pete and Gina must know she hadn't told them her whole story. Josh's presence had been part of the reason, but not all of it. Pete seemed to be a great bloke, but he'd grown up in a Christian family and stayed on track.

Her life hadn't been nearly so tidy. There may have been some excuses for her behaviour. As a runaway, she hadn't had the protective cushion of parental care and finance behind her, but she'd done plenty that now made her blush. Things she wished she could hit rewind and redo differently. Maybe that was normal for anyone who became a Christian later in life, but it didn't make her feel any more comfortable.

In her head, she knew Jesus had forgiven her, but it was hard to believe this deep in her heart.

The problem at church wasn't that there were no people to befriend, but that she wasn't willing to spoil their good impressions of her. They saw her accompanying Naomi and thought she was a model of selflessness. No one had ever thought that about her before.

Pete was probably the same. He knew her from work and soccer, activities that only revealed glimpses of her character. He didn't know the deeper stuff, the stuff people didn't show often or to just anyone. Once shared, it couldn't be withdrawn.

"Lizard," Josh yelled, gesticulating wildly.

There was a splash as the water dragon fled. They'd have to spot their own water dragons. She'd already seen several, sunning themselves on logs and exposed rocks.

"We'll have to teach him to be quiet if we're to have a hope of seeing any wildlife," Pete said, his voice bubbling with laughter. "I'm hoping for a platypus just before dark, but they're hard to see even without a noise-maker like Josh along."

"I've never seen one," Rachel said. "Have you?"

"Once, near the Snowy Mountains. The kayak hire guy gave me detailed instructions about where to camp and where platypuses have been spotted around here."

Their pick-up that morning from the campsite had been smooth. The kayak company had known they were also collecting Pete's kayak, and all four of them had already packed all their cooking, clothing, and tents in waterproof bags so everything would still be dry for their night of camping way upstream. A twenty-minute drive to Tallowa Dam, then a quick loading of their gear, putting on life jackets, and they were on the water.

There'd been significant rain in the last months, and the dam was full. The bleached white trunks of long-drowned trees lined one edge of the lake, a silent testimony of days before a dam existed.

"Let's weave in between them," Rachel said. "There might be birds nesting in the hollow tops."

"Gina," Pete hollered across to the other kayak. "We're just going to go among these trees."

Gina altered direction, and they all slowed down to creep forward.

"There's a possible nesting hollow," Pete whispered from behind her.

Rachel leaned back and looked. "I'm not sure anyone is home."

"Never mind. We'll keep looking." Pete kept the kayak drifting forward.

Rachel stopped paddling and dangled her hand in the water. She closed her eyes at its smooth coolness. So pleasant to be able to simply paddle along without having to plan where they were going.

Once clear of the trees, the waterway began to narrow. They'd only seen one other group of kayakers at the dam, but that other group had been far less organised and were now well behind Pete and Gina's kayaks. If they were lucky they wouldn't see any other kayakers the whole day.

It felt as though they were the first explorers of this valley. The only sounds were tiny slaps of water on the side of the kayak and the occasional shriek of parrots flying overhead, white sulphur-crested cockatoos or galahs.

They hung back until Gina and Josh were in front again and were soon back in a rhythm that kept them travelling about the same speed as the others.

"Thank you for sharing your story last night, Rachel."

A shiver of fear ran down her spine. Would Pete dig in the crevices she'd deliberately covered over?

"Thank you for being interested." She clipped her words together. That should shut off any further questions.

"And I want to thank you for not asking me my story yet," Pete continued.

Rachel dipped her paddle into the water. "Your father often reminds me that people will tell their story when they're ready."

"If I'm half the man my father is when I'm his age, I'll be happy." Pete lapsed back into silence and they continued to paddle. A half metre-long water dragon on the bank held its head erect and watched them with unblinking eyes, the sunlight showing off its green-brown skin. It slowly turned away from them as though expressing contempt for unwelcome aliens in its territory.

"Special Olympics offered me a children's team to coach," Pete said. "I said I couldn't."

An icy tendril of disappointment slithered in her gut, but she kept quiet.

"I find it hard to be around young children. You might have noticed at Josh's game." His voice shook.

Him too? Her stomach ached. She had noticed, because it had seemed so out of character. If anyone would be good with children, it would be someone like Pete. The kayak wobbled and she dug her paddle deeper to compensate.

"My children … my children would be seven and five—" He sucked in air. "And nearly three."

A coldness invaded her heart. She gripped her paddle so hard it cramped her hand. She'd thought only his wife had died. This was worse than she'd imagined. Much worse.

"I am so, so sorry," she mumbled. Such an inadequate thing to say. She was hopeless dealing with other people's grief. Too many years of bottling up her own.

"My father-in-law has been encouraging me to talk about what happened." His voice was monotone. "Said it wasn't healthy to have it all dammed up inside of me."

It certainly hadn't been healthy for her. It sounded as though his dam was ready to burst.

"The problem is that my story isn't the sort of story people want to hear."

She had to say something, but what? What were the right words to say to someone who had lost his wife and three children?

"I can see why you find it difficult." She stared ahead. Couldn't she do better than that?

"I don't want to burden anyone with it."

"Who else knows?" Rachel continued to paddle. At least in a kayak she didn't have to look at him. That was probably why he'd chosen to speak out now. He didn't know Gina, and she could see why he didn't want to tell Josh. Although, based on her past experience, Josh could probably handle this conversation better than she was. He knew how to help the hurting.

"Obviously my parents and father-in-law know. My friends in Perth know too, but most of them didn't stick with me afterwards." He paused. "It wasn't entirely their fault. I cut myself off. Couldn't handle seeing children at all for a while. That meant no church, no going near schools or playgrounds, and no socialising anywhere there might be children."

"That didn't leave you many options." The words burst out of her. She couldn't imagine Pete as a hermit, but he must have been.

"Dad's heart attack was actually good for me because it made me come here. Everything over there reminded me of Mai and the kids. I couldn't even handle seeing married couples together. That's when I started lunchtime swims and gym routines. Those were the easiest times for me to exercise and avoid triggering my grief." He paused for a few long strokes of his paddle. "It's good to be out in a kayak, and I started cycling again recently. I used to cycle fifty kilometres a day to and from work."

She had certainly noticed his lean, fit look.

"Tell me about your wife." Her voice was almost lost in a sudden burst of laughter from the other boat.

He was silent for a long time. Trust her to say the wrong thing. She kept paddling. The first of the cliffs were visible in the distance as the lake or river or whatever they were on continued to narrow.

"We met at church—as Binh and Mai were the only Vietnamese people in the congregation, they were hard to miss."

The water dripped off Pete's paddle.

"They were some of the first boat people to arrive in Australia, and Binh chose to come to Perth because he wanted to escape other Vietnamese and the reminder of everything they'd gone through."

"An unusual decision—not to go to Sydney or Melbourne."

"Binh is an unusual man."

Gina and Josh's voices were some distance behind them.

"I think Binh threw himself into church because he thought that was something Australians did." Pete chuckled. "But you'll have to check that detail if you meet him one day. Lots of migrants assume Australia is a Christian country and some become Christians before they discover their mistake."

A rock wallaby balanced on a small ledge. Rachel silently lifted her paddle and Pete stopped paddling too. The wallaby blended into its surroundings. She'd only been alerted to its presence because it had moved. They watched until it hopped out of sight.

"By the time I visited the church, Mai sounded more Aussie than the locals. Mai majored in piano at the Conservatorium, and taught at a school after she graduated. Once our eldest, Mark—" he stumbled over the name "—was born, she switched to teaching piano at home."

She kept silent. Telling her story had been part of her process of grieving. The least she could do was give him the same opportunity.

"Then came Amy, our little princess."

He gulped behind her.

"And on the day of the accident, Mai was six months pregnant." Again Pete stopped.

An ache radiated from the pit of Rachel's stomach. His nightmares must be terrifying. At least, she assumed he had nightmares. She'd had years of them herself. Trauma and grief seemed to invade her dreams.

"Pete, you don't have to tell me your story just because I told you mine."

"No, I need to learn to speak about Mai and the kids. They're part of my life. A big part. It's not right to deny they existed."

He took a big breath and released it with a whoosh.

"That Saturday morning was no different from most other days. Amy was in the middle of teething, so we'd had a sleepless night. Maybe that's why Mark was so cross." He dug his paddle into the water and sent the kayak surging forward. "It was one of those days you hear about. A grit-your-teeth-and-get-through-the-day-as-best-you-can kind of day." Pete's voice was low and slow.

Rachel's stomach pain intensified. She had no problem picturing the scene. She'd had days like that as a kid, being mad at the world and taking it out on everyone else. If she was honest, she'd had days like that as an adult, when she should have known better.

"If only we'd cancelled the visit to Binh." Pete sighed. "But the kids always loved spending the day at the beach with their grandfather. Mark had a new bucket ..." Pete's voice trailed off.

Rachel gripped her paddle, knuckles white. Trauma focused and magnified the tiny details. She would remember forever the details like the colour of a carpet or the smell of blood.

"Mark battled us from the moment he got out of bed." Another sigh. "That's what I hate—that I remember the battles of that last day more than all the good days before."

Rachel's shoulders ached with tension. She wanted to tell Pete there was no need to continue, but he had to get this out in his own way.

"Sorry to be all over the place." He sighed again, the sound of a man with too heavy a burden. "Mark started kicking the back of Mai's seat. When I told him to stop, he pinched his sister."

He paddled a few more strokes. "Of course, Amy started wailing. Mai tried to sort things out, but the size of her belly didn't allow her to twist easily. We were on the open road. There wasn't any traffic. The road was clear."

Rachel held her breath and closed her eyes, as if that could stop time. As if that action could take her back in time and stop whatever was about to happen.

"So I reached around to sort things out."

He paused, his breaths harsh in the silence.

"And the kangaroos—the kangaroos came out of nowhere—"

She froze.

"A split second." He shifted his body so the whole kayak tilted. "That was all it took."

He didn't have to say anymore. She could imagine the screaming, twisting melee of chaos. She'd hit a kangaroo once. It had looked fragile, but hitting the animal had been like running into a wall. It dented the whole front of the car.

"I'll never forget Mai's scream." There was a long drawn-out pause. "Or the dragging sensation and nausea as the car spun round and round."

Pete quit paddling. In the quiet she could hear him take one deep, ragged breath and then another.

She kept paddling. What else could she do? She was stuck in a kayak, unable to do much of anything. Unable to put a hand on his shoulder like a friend should. Unable to think of a single thing to say. The enormity of his pain washed over her. She'd attempted to drive over a cliff for far less reason than his. How had he gotten through the days and weeks and months after losing his entire family?

"You can see why I don't talk about this much," Pete said at last.

She nodded.

"Too much grief. Too hard for listeners to know how to respond. It's easier not to say anything."

He dug his paddle in again. "Thought you might understand."

"Uh-huh," she muttered, hoping she sounded empathetic. Her head spun with all the questions queueing up on her tongue. But whether she should ask them was another matter. Some people preferred to talk out their pain, while others didn't. Which was Pete?

"If you want to ask something, feel free," Pete said. "It's been three years. I ought to be able to talk about my family without breaking down."

She'd only had a single loss when she'd headed for the cliff. One single loss compounded by guilt. Guilt wasn't always justified, but she'd be willing to bet guilt was a daily struggle for Pete. She couldn't ask him why he hadn't committed suicide. There had to be a better way to ask her question.

Josh's laughter rang out. He and Gina were having heaps of fun.

For a second, she wished she'd been in any other boat than this one. She leaned forward and found the water bottle she'd tucked into a corner and gulped a few mouthfuls. "What kept you going?"

"Lots of things. All through my teenage years my parents had pounded into me that God's word is true whether you feel that it is or not. I clung to that."

A crow flapped overhead, its lonely *caw-caw* bouncing off the cliffs and surface of the water.

"I never doubted that my family were safe in God's protection. The thing I doubted was whether I could live without them."

Before Rachel had become a Christian, she had thought the whole idea of heaven was preposterous, a crutch for old women and children. Now she, too, clung to this hope. She'd had little time to get to know Esther in this life, but they'd have plenty of time in the future.

"I also had the best father-in-law a man could want. He turned up on one of my lowest days and stuck with me during the months I felt most alone."

There was a story there, but she wasn't going to ask any more questions. Pete had trusted her with this much of his story, and that was more than enough. For now.

CHAPTER 20

*R*achel laughed as Josh dunked Pete in the river.

"Where's that Joshua?" Pete roared as he popped up. "How dare he dunk me?"

Josh was laughing so hard he'd never make it back to shore. Pete sent a spray of water in Josh's direction. In five strokes, Pete had overhauled his prey. He morphed from a roaring lion into a kitten with claws sheathed, as he dialled back his power and dunked Josh.

Rachel closed her eyes and let herself sink into the cool dark river water, enjoying its silky caress, the muffled shouts of Josh and Pete echoing in her ears. Human beings were amazing creatures. They could pour out their grief in the morning and in the afternoon play as though nothing hindered their utter enjoyment of life.

She surfaced, shaking the water from her eyes and ears. "Are you coming back in, Gina?"

Gina dabbled her toes in the water. "Once more. Then I need to get moving on dinner. Those two ruffians can set up the tents."

Gina slid off her sun-warmed rock into the water and shrieked as she went under.

Spluttering, the two of them swam rapidly for half a minute to warm up. There. That was better. They struck out for the deeper water, away from the men.

Further out from shore, Rachel floated on her back, eyes towards the blue sky. The clouds drifted too slowly to change shape.

"What an amazing place," Gina said. "We need to do this again."

"It's hard work preparing everything," Rachel said. "But once you're here, it's magic."

Entering the Shoalhaven Gorge earlier that afternoon had reduced even Josh to silence. Orange sandstone block cliffs, twisted trunks of eucalyptus, and total peace. The sort of place where people talked in awed whispers.

They hadn't seen any other people since early morning. By choosing the campsite furthest away, they might have avoided other people completely.

"It must have been like this for Adam and Eve," Gina said. "Coming to new places for the first time."

"And exploring and simply enjoying them."

There was another shout from Josh, followed by more splashing.

Rachel lifted her head and sculled with her hands. "Come on. Let's get out and get changed while they're still playing."

---

*R*achel collected water to boil the pasta, while Gina sorted the food they'd stored in a waterproof bag.

Josh and Pete stood at the edge of the river, dripping water. Rachel's face warmed and she averted her eyes. Good thing Pete kept his shirt on at work. Although they might have more customers if he didn't ...

"I'll just put a shirt on," Josh said.

"There might be mosquitoes later," Pete said. "Long trousers might be a good idea too."

"Okay." Josh marched on the spot. "Don't like mosquitoes."

Pete laughed. "I don't think anyone does."

"Why did God make them?" Josh said, towelling his back.

"I don't know, buddy. Perhaps they were useful creatures before Adam and Eve rebelled against God."

"What did they do before they started biting us?"

Pete shrugged. "I have no idea."

Rachel's eyes widened. A man willing to admit he didn't know something? The men in her past always had to have an answer, even if they were making it up. But Pete? He was secure enough to admit he didn't.

"I'm going to change." Pete gestured towards the rock that Rachel and Gina had also used. "Then, when you're ready, we're going to get the tents up."

"Before it gets dark," Josh said.

"Right. Otherwise we'll end up losing half the tent pegs."

"The tent would fall down." Josh slapped his hands together. "Splat."

Pete laughed. "Exactly. I don't want my tent falling on me, and I'm sure Rachel and Gina don't either."

A few minutes later, Pete came out from behind the rock and gestured to them, finger on lips.

Josh started forward with a rush, but Pete held up his palm and put his finger to his lips again.

Josh looked over his shoulder at Rachel and she walked over, and took his arm. "He's probably found an animal for us to look at."

They crept around the rock and Pete pointed towards a fallen log. There was a faint scuffling, then Rachel spotted a brown, spiky back in a crevice.

Josh looked at her, eyes shining. "What is it?"

"An echidna. Wait and see if it comes out so we can see it better."

Gina went back to her cooking, but Rachel stayed with Josh and Pete, frozen in place. She kept her hand on Josh's forearm so he wouldn't shout in excitement if the echidna moved.

The rounded spiky bottom wriggled and backed out. She held her breath and squeezed Josh's arm. The echidna moved along the log, probing its thin snout into holes and picking up ants with its long tongue.

Josh's eyes widened and he opened his mouth. Rachel gestured for him to be silent. The creature gathered confidence and scuttled along the length of the log like a clockwork toy. Then it moved around the end and out of sight.

"I've never seen one of those," Josh whispered.

"I see them quite often, but you've got to be quiet to see most animals and birds," Pete said.

Josh giggled. "I'm not quiet, am I?"

Rachel let go of his arm. "You were this time, so you got to see an echidna eating its dinner."

"I hope our dinner tastes better than ants."

"If you hurry and get the tents up, then you'll be eating before you know it," Rachel said.

---

*R*achel watched Pete stroll over to the cooking area and sit down on a convenient rock.

"Need help?" he asked Gina.

"The pasta will be ready in about a minute. When it's done, it would be great if you could drain off the water." Gina handed him the specialised tool to carry the pot.

The delicious smell of frying food made Rachel's mouth water.

Gina deftly turned corn fritters on the pan. She already had a pile of crispy, golden goodness on the plate next to her.

When Pete came over with the drained pasta, Rachel stirred in the grated cheese. Once the cheese had melted, Gina added tuna and parsley. Simple, but it made Rachel salivate.

Their four bowls were clustered on a plastic bag on the ground, and Rachel divided up the pasta. Gina popped a few fritters on the top of each bowl, then handed the bowls around.

"Yum, yum," Josh said, licking his lips.

"Our family always sang grace before the meal when we were camping," Pete said. "Want to give it a go?"

Rachel's parents had hotel-hopped for holidays ... when they'd had them at all. Now she was here, she couldn't help wishing her childhood had included trips like this, although the thought of her parents camping was mind boggling.

It took them a few suggestions before they found a song they all knew. Rachel closed her eyes to dig up the words from her memory. She hadn't sung this one since she'd been dragged along to Naomi's church as a teenager.

"Great is your faithfulness, great is your faithfulness."

Pete's mellow voice rang out and anchored the rest of them. The evening star hung low down, bright against the slowly darkening sky.

"Morning by morning new mercies I see."

For the first time in many years, Rachel let the song fill her heart and overflow.

"All I have needed your hand has provided. Great is your faith-fulness, Lord, unto me. Amen."

Somewhere behind them were the muttered arguments of birds settling down for the night.

"You have a beautiful voice, Rachel," Pete said as he picked up his first corn fritter.

Rachel's face warmed. "I used to sing a lot in high school." Back when singing had been her escape from the endless conflict with William.

"Church would love to have more song leaders," Gina said.

Not likely, even in her dreams. It had been too long.

Rachel turned to look at Josh, who was almost halfway through his pasta. "Were you hungry, Josh?"

He nodded. "That kayaking was hard work."

"And you didn't fall in once." Pete winked at Josh.

"Nope." Josh puffed out his chest. "Didn't want Gina to get wet."

Rachel laughed and stabbed another piece of pasta. If only this weekend could go on forever.

After dinner and dessert, Pete washed up. Josh wiped each dish and handed it to Rachel to keep them off the sand.

Josh chatted away, which gave her an excuse to be quiet. If she spoke, she'd be sure to reveal something of the whirling emotions in her heart. Fear and excitement all melted together.

There was no guitar tonight, as Pete had left it locked in his car. Good thing. A musical Pete was yet another attraction, and she didn't want any more reasons to like him.

Josh yawned.

Pete followed suit and laughed. "It's only eight-thirty. Too much sun, fresh air, and exercise."

They finished the dishes and made sure no food or rubbish was around to attract the wildlife. She couldn't help noticing wherever Pete went, as though there was an invisible rubber band between them. She shook her head. She shouldn't have come. Should have recognised the danger.

"Goodnight, Rachel. Sleep well." Pete said quietly with a flash of his lopsided grin. Her stomach did a leisurely somersault. *Help!* This was worse than she'd thought.

She said goodnight quickly and turned towards her tent. Pete said goodnight to Gina then clapped Josh on the shoulder. "Come on, Josh. You're going to sleep like a log tonight."

Josh chortled. "How does a log sleep?"

She didn't hear Pete's reply, but she could still hear the muted rumble of their voices as she scrambled into her own tent.

Once in her sleeping bag, she squirmed this way and that. The nylon rustled as it moved over the mat beneath her. There was no way she could sleep. Not with Pete nearby, and not with it being way too early.

Outside the tent, the dead leaves covering the ground stirred in the light breeze. Two branches rubbed together. Occasionally, an owl of some sort hooted.

She rolled over again and tried not to think about Pete. Hopeless. His goodnight had unsettled her. It was all the fault of that dimple in the middle of his chin. Very distracting.

She'd better arrange to go in Gina's kayak tomorrow. Hanging around with Pete was dangerous. Much too dangerous.

If she spent too much time with him, she was going to get her heart broken. Big time. How could she compete with a dead wife who sounded perfect? Beautiful, musical, and mother to his children.

It was clear he wasn't anywhere near ready to give his heart away again, and even if he was ready, it was just a pipe dream.

Besides which, he was clueless about the nastiest parts of her story. The parts that still gave her occasional nightmares.

---

*R*achel awoke, stiff and cramped. The pale light of dawn glowed through the tent and revealed the heavy dew on the outside surface of the tent. Rachel looked at her watch. Not yet six.

She crawled out of her sleeping bag and contorted herself in various postures to dress in the small space and pull on her shoes. She crab-walked out of the tent and staggered upright.

The she-oaks along the edge of the water were silhouetted against a blush pink and gold sky, each needle-like leaf highlighted. The metallic grey water stretched out to the cliffs on the opposite side. Rachel walked towards the sandy shore, rubbing her hands up and down her arms. She'd left her jacket in the tent.

It was all so beautiful. She couldn't help thinking about God as creator here. The problem was that God so easily got pushed to the periphery of normal life. This scenery made her want to pour out her heart in prayer, a desire that would normally disappear under a mound of small yet persistent demands. What bills needed paying? What would she and Gran eat for dinner? What did her grandmother need help with?

Ever since her talk with Dirk about friends, she'd been thinking about finding someone she could meet up with to read the Bible and pray. She'd phoned Alice, from her old job, and had been touched to hear Alice had never stopped praying for her. Alice had been delighted that Rachel had become a Christian. It would have been great to meet with Alice, but she had young children and lived too far away.

Rachel walked along beside the river. Some animal had been digging in the embankments and left droppings scattered around. She skirted them.

Lord, this desire to meet up with someone must come from you. Would Gina be suitable?

She'd invited Gina to come on this trip at the last minute. She'd hesitated to ask her because Gina was so much younger, and because she was really Esther's friend. But maybe it wouldn't matter. Gina was one of those women who seemed to have been born full of common sense. Would Gina have time to meet? And would she be willing to come to Rachel's place? Gran needed Rachel around. She'd only been able to agree to this weekend away because one of the church ladies was keeping an eye on her grandmother.

Rachel reached the end of the tiny beach and turned around. If she managed to be in the same kayak as Gina, she'd ask her if she was willing to meet up. Even once a fortnight would be better than nothing.

CHAPTER 21

The following Friday, Pete turned the computer on and settled himself down for a day of accounts.

"Mr Pete, Mr Pete." Josh sounded excited.

Pete looked up to see Josh running in the main door and across the foyer to the office. Lyn followed in his wake, mouthing, "Sorry."

Josh skidded to a halt in front of him, beaming his ten-thousand-volt smile. "Mr Pete, guess what?"

It was more fun to play along. Pete scratched his head and scrunched up his face like he was acting in a silent movie. "Ah— your sister is having a baby and you're going to be an uncle." Josh had told him his sister had been married last year.

Josh shook his head. "Nope. Guess again."

Pete scrolled through the possibilities. Girlfriend? Unlikely, and he refused to tease Josh about it. Something at church, maybe? "You're going to perform in an orchestra at church?"

Again, the exaggerated head shake. "Na-uh. One more guess."

Pete leaned back in his chair and took his time. Any impatience would hurt Josh, and the longer this game went on the more Josh would enjoy it. Presumably, whatever it was had something to do with Lyn. She normally just dropped Josh off in the car park.

He stroked his chin and looked at the ceiling.

"Come on, Mr Pete. One more guess."

"Did you win something?"

Josh turned to his mother. "I didn't win anything, did I, Mum?"

"Not really. Well, not yet. Tell Mr Pete what's happened." Lyn laid her hand on Josh's shoulder.

"We got a letter, Mr Pete, a fancy-looking letter."

Pete leaned forward. "And what did the letter say?"

Josh looked at his mother. "You explain, Mum. You're better at it."

Lyn kissed him on his forehead. "No, you take your time and explain."

If Pete ever learned half of Lyn's patience, he'd be doing well. She was a fierce mother bird, gently but firmly tipping Josh out of the nest. Josh couldn't drive, but everything he could do himself, she made him do. Clothing, showering, shoes. Even lunches were obviously Josh's own work.

"You know I play soccer?"

"Yes." Of course he did, since he was Josh's coach, but saying that would only fluster Josh and delay things even further. Josh would get there eventually, although Lyn might have to explain the details.

"Every year there is a big competition ..." Josh looked at his mother.

"Keep going, Josh. You're doing a good job," Lyn said.

Pete nodded, a lump in his throat. At soccer practice, he'd often finish sentences for some of the players. It made sense in terms of efficiency, but every time he did it, he wished he'd bitten his tongue. It must make the players feel stupid.

"And they've asked me to do extra training." Josh glanced at his mother and she gave a tiny nod. "If I play well, then I can join the state team."

Pete jumped up, slapped Josh's shoulder, and pumped Josh's arm up and down. "Well done, buddy. Well done."

Josh stood up straight for a moment, then slumped.

"What's wrong, Josh?"

"The training is four days, when I should be working."

"That's no problem, Josh. We manage when you're on holidays, and this will be just the same."

Josh looked up at him, but the spark was still missing.

"What's wrong, buddy?"

Josh's lip wobbled. "If they choose me, I won't be able to play on our team."

Pete put his arm round Josh's shoulders. "We don't know if you'll be chosen for the state team, but if you do, it will only be for a short while. Representing our state is a huge privilege."

Josh nodded. "I know, and I want to do it, but I also want to play on our team. I like being with you and Rachel."

"Well, I like spending time with you, too." Pete gave a warm smile.

Josh's face lit up. "You do? Really?"

"I really do, Josh." Josh had a way of wriggling deep into people's hearts.

Before he could gather himself together, Josh enveloped him in a rib-cracking bear hug. "That's how much I love you, Mr Pete."

Mark and Amy used to hug him like this. Without Josh's strength, of course, but with the same enthusiastic, full-on commitment. No one else had bear-hugged Pete in recent years. Josh didn't see any of the walls Pete had erected around his heart. Even if he had, Josh would probably storm them anyway.

Pete hugged him back. "Thank you, Josh. You're the best kind of friend a bloke could have." He patted Josh's back. "Now, let's discuss the dates of the training."

Lyn smiled up at him, tears in her eyes.

He crossed over to the oversized calendar on the wall, marked in the four training days, and pencilled in the possible competition week. He turned to Lyn. "Where is the competition?"

Lyn grimaced. "Perth."

"Why the face? Perth is a great place."

She nodded. "It is, but it's an expensive trip. At least one of us would have to go too, and everything is either self-funded or you need to find sponsorship."

Maybe Pete could go. He'd been looking for a good reason to visit Binh and reconnect with some of his former friends.

"Why don't we pray about it?"

"Now?" Lyn asked, raising her eyebrows.

"Why not?" His dad never hesitated to pray for people. It was high time Pete followed that example.

The phone rang. Pete left it for Colin to pick up, and they bowed their heads.

Before he opened his mouth, firm footsteps came across the floor to his door. "Sorry to disturb you, but the potting mix delivery will be here in fifteen minutes," Colin said.

Pete looked up. "Perfect timing. We'll finish praying, then I'll send Sam and Dave up with the trolleys."

Colin backed out the door as though he'd been stung. Pete grinned. Judging by Colin's reaction, he'd better concentrate some prayer in that direction.

They bowed their heads again. "Dear heavenly Father, thank you so much for this opportunity Josh has been given. You know he is both excited and a bit nervous. Help him to do his best. Help him not to be upset if he misses out. Besides, that will mean he'll keep playing on our team."

Josh shuffled his feet.

"If he does well, remind him that you love him and will help him. You are more than able to provide the money he needs and the extra money for someone to accompany him. Help him have fun. In the name of Jesus, Amen."

"Amen, boss. Amen." Josh bounded towards the door and Lyn turned back towards Pete.

"Thank you, Pete. Ian and I do appreciate all the extra encouragement you give Josh."

"I benefit too. Your son has been reminding me of all that is good about life. That's a debt I can never repay."

CHAPTER 22

*P*ete strolled towards the back corner of the nursery. The morning was muggy and still, foreshadowing a hot day to come. He'd better get the big water container, as he and Josh were going to be digging up the compost heap.

Josh was in the shed, choosing his shovel.

"You ready for some sweaty work, Josh?"

Josh nodded hard enough for his head to fall off. "Ready, Mr Pete."

"Time for sunscreen." Pete moved over to the industrial-size pack.

A few minutes later, they were ready. Pete dug the shovel into the middle of the old compost pile and began loading the wheelbarrow to transfer it to where it was needed.

"Are you looking forward to the soccer camp next week?"

Josh grimaced and shrugged.

"It's normal to be nervous."

"I'm worried I won't be able to do it." Josh shuffled his feet. "I don't know the others."

"Your mum will take you each day, won't she?"

Josh nodded and kept shovelling.

"You'll have fun and learn some new things."

"But learning new things is hard."

Pete shovelled more compost into the wheelbarrow. "But you're good at learning new things, and the coaches will be patient. They want you to do well."

Josh wiped his forehead with his sleeve. "What if they don't like me?"

Was Josh worrying about whether they'd like him as a person or whether he'd do well enough to be chosen for the state team?

"Would you like me to pray for you, buddy?"

Josh looked up and beamed. "Yes, please, Mr Pete. Praying always makes me feel better."

The corners of Pete's eyes prickled. Such childlike faith. The faith his little Mark had displayed when he wasn't having one of his occasional bad days.

Pete walked over and laid a hand on Josh's shoulder. "Dear Jesus, you know the soccer camp is a wonderful opportunity for Josh. Give him courage to go and make new friends and do his best. Thank you that even if he doesn't get on the team, he can learn new things and have fun. Help him to trust that you'll help him. In Jesus' name, Amen."

Josh looked up at him. "Thanks, Mr Pete. You're a good boss."

"And you're a good worker." Pete gestured at the pile of compost. "Now let's get this done before it gets any hotter."

It was hot enough that they needed a drink every quarter of an hour. Pete ripped up some cardboard boxes piled nearby and layered them between the new compost they were making.

"Josh, if you'll shake that bag of leaves over the top, I'll rip up the last of the boxes."

Pete took two steps towards the boxes and grasped the top one. There was a blur of brown and a stinging pain on his left forearm where his long-sleeved shirt had ridden up and left a gap.

He jumped back with a cry, tripped over, and fell to the ground. A snake he recognised from his first-aid lessons slithered in the opposite direction.

Josh's eyes were wide, his face drained of colour.

Pete looked down at his arm. Two bite marks, a centimetre apart. He pulled off his glove and rolled up his shirt sleeve. Then took a deep breath, struggling for calm against the adrenaline surging through his system. He must keep calm or Josh would be of no use to him.

"Josh, I need your help." *Lord, help me speak simply.*

"Run to Rachel and tell her I've been bitten by an eastern brown snake." Surely Rachel would know to bring the first aid kit with its pressure bandages. "Then tell Colin to phone the ambulance."

He asked Josh to repeat the two instructions before he let him scramble up the path, heading for the main entrance.

Lord, let Rachel and Colin be there, and help Josh to be coherent.

Everything in his heart screamed at him to run and do this himself, but he'd done St. John Ambulance training earlier in the year, and knew he had to keep his arm immobilised after a snake bite.

Was the clamminess of his skin the venom working, or was it just fear? Brown snakes were supposed to be among the most poisonous snakes in the world.

He took another breath. *Help me, Lord, and get Rachel and the ambulance here soon.*

Pounding steps came down the path. He turned his head. Rachel, with the first aid kit swinging in her hand. Good. And Josh right behind her.

She was gasping as she dropped to her knees beside him and unsnapped the locks on the box.

"It's okay, Rachel. Take a deep breath."

"You're bitten by a snake and you say it's okay?" Her voice cracked.

"Please, take a breath. I need you as calm as possible."

She gulped.

"Is the ambulance on the way?"

"Colin was phoning while I grabbed the first aid kit."

Colin could be trusted to do what was needed.

"He told them it was an eastern brown and was giving the address as I shot out the door."

Pete used his right hand and pulled out the pressure bandage.

"You'll have to do it. Wrap it like I've sprained something."

She fumbled and nearly dropped the bandage. *Lord, help her remain calm.*

"Keep the roll on top, and put two loops round the bite site."

His voice seemed to steady her, because she only took a minute to do it.

"Now, can you and Josh push me on the trolley to the main entrance? It will save time for the ambulance officers."

They helped him sit in the centre of the trolley, gripping the edge with his right hand and keeping his left arm as still as possible.

Was that a headache starting? He was ignorant about what to expect in terms of timing or order of symptoms. Was he going to go numb or dizzy any time soon? Or would he stop breathing? His heart sped up. He had to remain calm and not pump the venom around his system any faster.

"Rachel, I'm going to leave Colin in charge. I need you to drive to Mum and Dad's and tell them what's happened. I'm hoping Dad will take over here, but then I'd like you to drive Mum to the hospital."

"And if both your parents insist on going to the hospital?"

"Then can you come back here and help the others. Someone needs to make sure that no one goes looking for that snake. We don't want anyone else bitten." Sam and Dave could easily treat this as a game and not think of the consequences. The snake was more likely to attack if it was cornered or afraid.

They were on a flat path, and Josh could now manage on his own.

"Rachel, can you please go ahead and check with Colin that the ambulance is on its way, then stand at the front gate to wave it in."

She touched him briefly on the shoulder, and gave a tight smile, then quick-marched away from them, through the back door of the foyer area.

"This is fine, Josh. We'll wait here."

Josh clicked on the brakes with his foot. "Are you going to be okay, Mr Pete?" He choked, and sat down abruptly on the ground, putting his head in his hands.

"Josh, do you remember what we did when you were feeling scared?"

Josh looked up, his dirty-covered face streaked with tears. Pete gave a shaky laugh. "Buddy, would you pray for me?"

Josh sniffed and rubbed his hand across his face, further smearing the dirt.

"You want me to pray for you?"

"I sure do, buddy. I need your prayers right now."

Josh squared his shoulders and said, "Dear God, Mr Pete has been bitten by a nasty snake. We don't want him to die. Please get the ambulance here right now."

In the distance, the drawn-out wails of an ambulance changed into the more rapid alternations of its siren.

"Jesus answered." Josh jumped to his feet.

"And you mustn't worry about me, Josh. The ambulance officers will keep an eye on me. I saw the snake, so we know what sort of medicine is needed."

The sound of the siren grew in volume and then cut off. They must have seen Rachel.

Now for the part he dreaded—the dose of excitement for everyone coming in from the car park and gawking from the café. He hoped Colin would remember to check the standard procedures manual for information about dealing with snakes on the premises. Rachel or his father would be sure to remind him.

Through the big windows he saw the ambulance pull into the space closest to the foyer. One of the ambulance officers opened the back of the ambulance while the other came over, took a quick medical history, and expertly reapplied the pressure bandage.

Now the ambulance was here, the tension in Pete's shoulders relaxed. These were people who knew what to do if the poison affected him.

"Pete, we'll need you to get up on the gurney," the taller medic said, as the second one wheeled the gurney over.

Pete grimaced. "I was afraid of that." He tried to make it sound like a joke.

The female paramedic raised the head of the bed. "Standard procedure, but yes, you do look fitter than many of our clients."

As he feared, every customer in the vicinity stopped talking and craned their necks to follow their progress through the foyer and out into the car park. What a disappointment he must be. No blood, no gore.

The gurney went into the ambulance with barely a bump. His last view of the nursery was Rachel standing next to Josh with her hand on his shoulder. Josh would be fine, and Rachel would do a good job of breaking the news to his parents.

CHAPTER 23

*R*achel watched as the ambulance pulled out of the car park and put its siren on. She swallowed. Pete might look fine, but how much venom was coursing through his body? She'd never known anyone who'd been bitten by a snake. Snakes didn't visit department stores like David Jones, and they wouldn't dare visit William's palatial home.

Rachel wrapped her arms round her waist. *Dear Jesus, don't let him die.*

She turned to Josh. "You okay?"

He nodded. "Me and Mr Pete prayed. He told me not to look for that snake."

She shuddered and looked directly at him. "Be sure to listen, okay?"

He gave her a thumbs up. "I'll go help Sam and Dave."

"I've got to go over and tell Dirk and Norma what's happened."

"You'll come back, won't you?"

She turned and hugged him, as much for her comfort as for his.

"He won't die, will he?" Josh whispered in her ear. He had a way of voicing her deepest fears.

She gave him another squeeze and broke out of the hug. "The ambulance officers said he'd be okay. They said the hospital had antivenom."

"What's that?"

"Medicine to make sure the snake's poison doesn't make him sick."

"Phew." He grinned. "You go and do everything Mr Pete told you, or you'll get in trouble."

Rachel saluted Josh. "Yes, sir. If I don't get back here before the end of work, I'll ring Colin and leave a message about how Pete is doing."

*I*t took an hour for Rachel to get to the house and break the news to Dirk and Norma, for them to adjust to the shock, and to get ready to go their separate ways. Dirk went to the nursery to make sure Josh, Sam, and Dave didn't let their curiosity lead them to search for the snake. Rachel drove Norma to the hospital.

The fastest way to the hospital was through the gorge. The hairpin curves distracted her from the tension in her muscles and the fear coiled in her stomach.

Ever since the kayaking trip, she'd been trying to convince herself Pete was just a friend. She no longer believed it. She cared.

She turned the steering wheel for the next hairpin turn, dropping to fifteen kilometres an hour. Pete had trusted her to safely deliver his mother to the hospital. She concentrated on the road in front.

A couple more turns and they'd be out of the gorge. Then back to the hospital she preferred to avoid, the hospital where Esther had worked.

"Sorry to be so quiet," Norma said. "I'm praying."

Rachel gripped the steering wheel. "Not much else we can do."

"I appreciate your driving me. I wouldn't have trusted myself to drive."

Rachel gripped the steering wheel. "Pete was quite clear in his instructions."

Norma laughed. "I bet he was. Thank you for being such a good friend to him."

Pete had been a good friend to her. It was the first time she could remember merely being friends with a man. It was unreasonable to suddenly want more. She had nothing to offer him but a truckload of regrets.

There is now no condemnation in Christ ... The words she'd been memorising leapt into her mind. It was all very well saying that God forgave her and there was no condemnation in Christ Jesus, but what about the condemnation she heaped on herself?

*J*t took Rachel and Norma awhile to find Pete. At last they were pointed towards an observation room next to emergency. They heard Pete's laugh as they approached the door. Norma clutched Rachel's arm. That did not sound like a dying man.

The nurse was just leaving as they crossed the floor, their shoes squeaking on the linoleum.

"Mum. Rachel." Pete's face lit up, the smile crinkling the corners of his eyes.

Rachel's breath hitched. Her face warmed and she stooped to tie a shoe that didn't need it.

Norma hugged Pete. "You're okay," she murmured. "Okay."

"Sorry to give you a fright. So far I've shown no symptoms, but they've taken a blood test and will do another." He grimaced. "The doctors think it was a dry strike."

"A what?" Norma said.

Rachel stood up and inched closer to the bed.

"Apparently snakes don't like to waste venom. Brown snakes are shy and usually slither away. Maybe that one was too warm and lazy to make the effort to strike properly."

Norma sat down with a thump on the only available seat.

"It's okay, Mum. It doesn't look likely that I'm going to leave you."

Norma leaned forward and took his sun-browned hand in both of hers.

Rachel swallowed and looked away. Pete was almost certainly fine. They'd be sending him home soon. There was nothing to fear. Inwardly she skipped, but she made the effort to walk sedately to find a spare chair.

As she carried the chair towards the bed, Pete looked up at her. "Thanks so much for bringing Mum and getting here so promptly."

"Of course," Rachel said, conscious that she was still in her work clothes. Not that Pete looked much cleaner. His work shirt was streaked with dirt and sweat and clashed with the pristine white of the hospital sheets.

She grinned.

"Don't laugh at me. There was no way I was going to wear one of those hospital gowns."

He'd guessed her thoughts. That was scary.

"Sorry I didn't think to bring clean clothes for you." Her neck heated. Not that it would have felt right doing so.

"Things were a little chaotic. The doctors insist I stay overnight, but I think it's just a precaution."

Rachel glanced at her watch. Three hours until the end of work. "I promised to phone your father to let him know what's happening, and to allay Josh's fears."

"Josh was a real trooper. I wasn't sure he'd remember all my instructions, but he did." He grimaced. "Bit embarrassed I wasted taxpayer's money, but the first aid classes insisted you shouldn't muck about if someone is bitten by a snake."

"Not with Australian snakes, anyway." A smile tugged the corner of Rachel's mouth. "At least you'll have a story to tell."

CHAPTER 24

A few days later, Rachel found another letter from her mother waiting when she arrived home from work. She went out to the back verandah to read it. Naomi had already opened it, saying she couldn't wait.

DEAR NAOMI AND RACHEL,

HOW ARE YOU BOTH GETTING ALONG? WE'LL DEFINITELY COME HOME AT CHRISTMAS FOR A FEW WEEKS TO AVOID THE BUSIEST TIME OF YEAR HERE. MOST LOCALS DO A HOUSE SWAP AT CHRISTMAS AND VISIT RELATIVES ON THE MAINLAND. REG IS HAPPY TO TAKE THE SERVICE FOR THE TOURISTS.

The corner of Rachel's mouth twitched. Already her mother sounded like an island local.

WE'RE HAVING A GREAT TIME ON LORD HOWE. THE CHURCH HAS TAKEN US INTO THEIR HEARTS. THESE FOLK HAVE SHOWN ME WHAT A CHURCH SHOULD BE. ALL THOSE YEARS AT VICTORY, I NEVER KNEW WHAT I WAS MISSING. MAYBE VICTORY GOT TOO BIG, BUT IT NEVER REMINDED ME OF A FAMILY, NOT EVEN IN THE EARLY DAYS. I ALWAYS FELT LIKE AN OUTSIDER.

And if the senior pastor's wife felt like an outsider, was it any wonder that so many others did too? William had always treated the church members as an audience or a personal fan club. Rachel clenched her jaw. The bigger the better, from his point of view.

Naomi shuffled out to join Rachel on the verandah, carrying a cup of tea. Rachel wanted to jump up and take the tea from her, but Gran insisted on her independence for anything she could still manage. Gran answered every one of Mum's letters immediately, and loved to discuss each letter after they'd read it. Pity her mother wasn't closer or telephone calls less expensive. Going to Lord Howe Island had made sense for her parents, but the separation was hard on her grandmother.

WE'RE SETTLING INTO A ROUTINE. WILLIAM AND REG READ THE BIBLE AND PRAY TOGETHER MOST MORNINGS. I'M IN A WOMEN'S BIBLE STUDY, AND I'VE BEEN ASKED TO LEAD THE GROUP FOR THE NEXT MONTH. I'M GOING TO EXPERIMENT WITH THE STORY METHOD JOY AND ESTHER TAUGHT US. THE SET OF DISCUSSION CARDS ARE READY, AND I'M LEARNING THE FIRST OF FOUR STORIES FROM EXODUS.

Her mother would be terribly nervous. All the years at Victory she'd supported William behind the scenes. She'd done heaps of hospitality and some craft—which she loved—but was never asked to lead a small group or teach the Bible. William didn't encourage anyone close to him to develop teaching gifts.

WE LOOK AFTER DAVY ON TUESDAY EVENINGS SO THAT REG AND IVY CAN HAVE AN EVENING TO THEMSELVES. WILLIAM—

Rachel shuddered. If she could wipe out all her memories of William and replace him with someone like Dirk, Rachel would do it in an instant.

She looked over at her grandmother, who was sipping her tea and waiting patiently for Rachel to finish the letter.

—AND I GO SNORKELLING WITH DAVY EVERY SATURDAY MORNING.

Someone less suited than William to hang around with children Rachel couldn't imagine. He'd seldom had any contact even with his own children. He shouldn't have had children in the first place. Maybe he'd wanted to prove his manhood. Bah. It served him right to have daughters. He was the kind of chauvinist to care about such things. The Victorian era with its children-should-be-seen-and-not-heard attitude would have suited him better. All the emotion, mess, and clumsiness of childhood was her mother's department, and he had insisted it be kept out of sight. Bile burned in Rachel's throat, and she tightened her lips.

"You okay, Rachel?" her grandmother asked, peering at her.

"Sure," she muttered, turning back to the letter.

THE HIGHLIGHT OF LAST WEEK WAS THAT THE HUSBAND OF ONE
OF THE OLDER CHURCH MEMBERS BECAME A CHRISTIAN.

This was more like it. Something that she and Gran could rejoice over.

HE HAS BEEN THOROUGHLY OPPOSED TO HIS WIFE ATTENDING
CHURCH ACTIVITIES EVER SINCE SHE BECAME A CHRISTIAN, THIRTY
YEARS AGO.

Presumably the wife had become a Christian after they'd married. That would be hard. Probably hard on both sides.

Rachel looked out over the garden. It was unlikely she'd ever marry. But if she did, there was no way she'd date a non-Christian. Not that dating a Christian was any guarantee of a good marriage, but it must increase the probability of success if both people put God first, like Dirk and Norma.

She blew out a tired breath. Why waste time thinking about marriage? She didn't even know any single men between the ages of twenty-five and ninety at church, and only Josh and Pete at work.

Pete. He kept wandering into her mind, and she kept pushing him out. Caring for Pete would likely lead to heartbreak, and she'd had enough of being hurt. And presumably, so had he.

Pete was kind, considerate, and a good friend, but she didn't have the guts to tell him her whole story. If she ever had a reason to tell him, she didn't look forward to seeing his back as he fled.

Gran shifted her feet as though to remind Rachel to finish the letter so they could discuss it. Rachel focused on the page again.

THE WIFE WAS ALLOWED TO ATTEND EITHER THE SERVICE OR
BIBLE STUDY, BUT NOT BOTH. SHE MOSTLY ATTENDED BIBLE
STUDY, FOR WHICH MANY PEOPLE CRITICISED HER.

Rachel would have made the same decision as this woman. A church service could too easily be something you attended passively, without any real involvement. At a Bible study, you could ask questions, interact with others, form friendships, and be held accountable.

EDNA HAS PRAYED FAITHFULLY FOR HER HUSBAND, DESPITE HIM
BECOMING MORE AND MORE CANTANKEROUS AS HE AGED.

This woman's husband was a controller. Like William. One of the reasons Rachel liked Pete so much was that he was nothing like William. He'd never given any indication of controlling others.

WILLIAM VISITED HIM LAST TIME HE WAS ON THE ISLAND BECAUSE
REG SAID HE MUST. WILLIAM SAID IT WAS A HORRIBLE VISIT, SO
IMAGINE EVERYONE'S SURPRISE WHEN THE MAN ASKED WILLIAM
TO VISIT HIM IN HOSPITAL!

Rachel's mouth twisted in contempt. William loathed hospital visits. Having refused to visit his own daughter, it was unlikely he'd answer the summons of someone he disliked.

YOUR FATHER AND I WENT OVER TO REG AND IVY'S AND SPENT A GOOD TIME IN PRAYER. THEN WILLIAM WENT OFF TO THE HOSPITAL, WHILE REG, IVY AND I STAYED BEHIND TO PRAY.

Rachel's eyebrows rose towards her hairline. She'd been wrong.

IMAGINE OUR SURPRISE AND DELIGHT WHEN WILLIAM BOUNCED BACK (HE REALLY DID BOUNCE) AND SAID THE MAN HAD BECOME A CHRISTIAN. OF COURSE, WE WERE FULL OF QUESTIONS.

Naomi put down her empty teacup on the table in front of her.

WILLIAM SAID HE WAS TERRIFIED TO FACE THE MAN AFTER THEIR LAST ENCOUNTER, BUT HE PRAYED FOR PEACE. HE FIGURED HE'D ASK WHY THE MAN HAD SENT FOR HIM AND SEE WHAT HAPPENED.

The man Rachel had known as a teenager wasn't a prayerful man. He'd been Mr Independence and conqueror of all he surveyed. He certainly never asked God or anyone for help. Anything he disliked doing, he avoided. He especially avoided visiting sick people and anyone who might criticise him.

WELL, THE STORY WAS THIS. WHEN HIS WIFE BECAME A CHRISTIAN, HE'D ASSUMED THE 'RELIGIOUS' PHASE WOULD SOON PASS. HE MADE LIFE DIFFICULT FOR HER, BUT EDNA CONTINUED

TO SHOW PATIENCE AND RESPECT, NO MATTER WHAT HER
HUSBAND SAID OR DID. HE WATCHED HER FOR THIRTY YEARS AND
FINALLY BEGAN TO HAVE A GRUDGING RESPECT FOR HER STALWART
ATTITUDE. OF COURSE, HE WAS TOO STUBBORN TO LET HER SEE
HIS CHANGE IN VIEWPOINT. THEN HE HAD A SECOND HEART
ATTACK.

Whoa. God had needed to strike this man as hard as he'd struck Rachel.

HE HEARD THAT WILLIAM HAD CHANGED AND THOUGHT IT WAS A
HOOT THAT THE PREACHER HAD BEEN CONVERTED.

SO WILLIAM TURNED UP, KNEES SHAKING, AND WAS
IMMEDIATELY ASKED TO TELL HIS STORY. GOD USED WILLIAM'S
STORY TO KNOCK DOWN THE MAN'S LAST OBJECTIONS.

"Have you reached the part where the man becomes a Christian?" Gran asked.

Rachel looked up. "Just finished that section."

Her grandmother's cheeks were flushed. "I've been praying that William's transformation would impact others."

Of course her grandmother was praying. She'd also be praying that Rachel and William would be reconciled and live happily ever after.

Rachel loved her grandmother, but knowing she was being prayed for sometimes felt like manipulation. Why was that? Was it something to do with humans appealing to the divine to change someone, rather than allowing the person to work through things themselves?

She read the last page and a half of the letter.

"Isn't it encouraging?" Gran said.

"Mmm," Rachel said. What else could she say? If the subject of the letter was anyone other than William, she'd be thrilled. But the subject was William. It riled her that a man who used to hate hospital visits not only did them now, but was used by God to lead people to new life.

People had told her how much she was changing, and she couldn't deny it. She'd even caught herself humming a song of praise to God this morning. The Bible said that when a person was converted, they became a new creation. Why was she so reluctant to accept that William could change? Her shoulders tensed. There must be something wrong with her, because she wanted to find excuses not to forgive him. Reasons to keep hating him forever.

CHAPTER 25

*P*ete's parents had given him a slow cooker for Christmas last year, and the tantalising smell of chicken cacciatore wafted towards him as he pushed open his front door.

By the time he'd washed the day's grime off, the meal would be ready. He had a Dick Francis thriller calling his name, and he could read during dinner. There was no one here to care.

When he was clean and changed, he took a spoonful of chicken and vegetables, blew on it, and sampled it. Delicious, and enough for tonight and the two nights of coaching.

He'd never expected to enjoy coaching so much. The question he hadn't yet settled was whether he most enjoyed the sport, Josh and his teammates, or Rachel.

Probably all three, if he was honest. Rachel was undemanding and never flirted with him. In fact, she behaved like a sister towards him. Sisters were wonderful, but he didn't want Rachel to treat him the way she treated Josh. Not any more. For the first twenty minutes after the snake bite he'd thought he might be done for. His main regret was that he would never get to know Rachel better.

What did Rachel think of him? It was obvious she didn't detest him, but not detesting someone was a long way from liking them enough to pursue things further.

He switched off the slow cooker, dished out a helping, and left the lid off to allow the leftovers cool. Then he sat down at the kitchen table, finished his meal, and had read six chapters of his book when the phone rang. Binh.

He closed the book, put his plate in the sink on the way to the kitchen phone, and pulled out a bar stool.

"Hello, son. How have you been this week?"

"It's been rather exciting. I got bitten by a snake."

"What? Are you okay?" Binh's concern reverberated down the line.

Pete leaned back and told the story.

Binh listened with several small exclamations before saying, "And how have you seen God at work in all this?"

Another of Binh's favourite questions.

"The most obvious way is protection. I'm glad to be a dry strike statistic and not a death one."

Pete had never heard of dry strikes last week, and now he sounded like an expert.

"The best part was several opportunities to talk about Jesus."

"Great, son, great. Tell me more."

"First I was able to joke with the ambulance officers and slip in that it was a good thing I'm a Christian, since we don't need to fear death."

Binh laughed. "You Aussies. Always joking about serious things. I couldn't understand it when I first arrived."

Pete shifted on the stool. "I guess it is strange, using humour to keep serious topics at an emotional distance."

"At least Aussies sometimes talk about death. Vietnamese mostly avoid it. I certainly didn't know how to deal with it when I needed to."

But God had taught Binh how.

Pete switched the phone to his other hand to give his right ear a break. "I felt a total fraud in hospital. The other man in my room was really ill, and I had two tiny puncture marks in my arm and was perfectly well."

Pete paused. If he'd been a betting man, he'd lay a bet on what Binh would say next.

"I hope you didn't waste your opportunity."

Bingo. Pete laughed. "I knew you'd say that. So I'm lying there, feeling grumpy, and suddenly I thought of you. I imagined you saying, 'Son, it is no mistake you're in hospital at this time, so look for why God might have put you here.'"

"Am I so predictable?"

"Afraid so, but it's something I appreciate about you. You are always thinking about other people and whether they know Jesus."

Somewhere on the Perth end of the phone, a lawnmower roared into life. It had been far too long since Pete had been back to Perth, and unexpected homesickness swirled through him.

"If I don't look to Jesus, I become overwhelmed by my own problems," Binh said.

Rachel had told him something similar about her sister. Esther had concluded that part of the reason she had cancer was to put her in the path of people who needed Jesus. There'd been a man at Esther's funeral—Pete couldn't remember his name. Esther had led his wife to the Lord while she was in palliative care. A little later, the husband had come to Christ too.

"So did you use your time wisely?" Binh asked again.

"I knew you'd ask, so I prayed that I'd get at least one opportunity." Pete grinned at himself in the kitchen window. "You know about the ambulance officers, but God, being God, gave me three more."

"He does love to give us more than we ask."

Pete blinked. The pain of the last few years had blinded him to the truth of God's generosity.

Pete quickly told Binh about two more of the opportunities God had given him with the nurse and a doctor. Then he stood and stretched. He'd been for a run during his lunch break, and he was a little stiff.

"Are you planning on coming to Perth any time soon?"

Could Binh be lonely? Pete was the closest person Binh had to family. They talked on the phone every week, but that was no substitute for actually spending time together.

"I wonder …"

"What are you wondering, Pete?"

"Josh was selected to represent New South Wales for soccer, and the competition is in Perth."

"Were you thinking of coming to support him?"

"The thought had crossed my mind."

What were the chances of convincing Rachel to come too? He so wanted Rachel to hear Binh's story, but it would be better for her to hear it from the man himself. It would be interesting to see the two of them together. Surely if Pete took Rachel to visit, Binh would realise Pete thought Rachel was special. He'd have to be stupid not to, and no one would call Binh stupid.

"I'd love to meet Josh," Binh said.

Whenever Binh had visited Pete and Mai in Fremantle, the children would run or crawl as fast as they could towards the front door, even before the doorbell stopped its chime. Once inside, Binh would squat down and hug them both at once in one big, writhing armful. If Binh met Josh, Binh would sense the heart of Josh in a second.

Pete swallowed. His own pit of grief had been so deep and dark, he often forgot he wasn't the only one grieving major losses. Binh had lost the last members of his family too.

"Binh, I'm sorry I was so caught up in my own grief that I didn't pay attention to how you were coping that first year."

"Son …"

Pete's heart clenched as it did every time Binh called him 'son'. His parents and others had taught Pete about grace from his childhood, but the way Binh treated him after the accident had driven the lesson deep into his heart.

"Son, I remember what losing a family was like. I didn't cope well either."

"But you weren't a Christian then."

"That's true, but it's not wrong to grieve deeply. We grieve much because we loved much."

Pete's grief was twisted with guilt. Whenever his grief receded, his guilt surged up and entangled him again. As Binh had pointed out several times, Satan wanted him prostrate and focused on self-survival.

"I sense you've finally begun to live again," Binh said. "Am I right?"

Pete stared out of the kitchen window. The first stars were visible, tangled in among branches of the taller trees.

"Thanks to your prayers, and Mum's and Dad's." He thought back over the past weeks. "I think I've begun to turn the corner."

"I've prayed that you would be freed from your past." Binh sighed. "My past bound me for too long. Kept me punishing myself for my losses." He paused. "Almost as though I didn't deserve to be happy because my family never had that chance."

Pete had been so self-centred. As though the thoughts that nearly crushed him were his alone. As though he was the only one in all history to experience them. How arrogant!

"It's Satan who destroys joy," Binh said. "I couldn't seem to understand that my family would never want me to feel unhappy on their behalf. My feelings of guilt didn't help them at all."

As always, Binh had given Pete plenty to think about. He hadn't told Binh about the fourth, and best, opportunity to talk about Jesus.

He wanted to tell Rachel first.

CHAPTER 26

$\mathcal{T}$he doorbell rang as Rachel finished setting the table. Gran had suggested inviting Gina for dinner on the nights they did Bible study. That made it easier for Gina to come straight from work and avoided a late night for everyone.

When Rachel opened the door, Gina was holding a bunch of roses. "Please don't think you need to bring flowers."

Gina kissed Rachel's cheek. "Actually they're for Naomi. I know how much she loves flowers."

"Come in," Rachel said, leading Gina down the hallway. "Dinner is just about ready. Nothing fancy."

Gina laughed. "I never say no to a night off from cooking."

Gran was already in the dining room. Gina handed her the flowers and Gran buried her nose in them. "Beautiful. Thank you so much."

"If Rachel will give me a vase, I'll arrange them for you."

Rachel and Gina went through to the kitchen and Rachel found a vase. "I'm nearly finished here. The sink area is all yours."

After dinner Gran volunteered to do the dishes while Rachel and Gina headed to the lounge and found a chair each.

Gina gave a tight grin. "I'm not used to meeting one-on-one with people who are older than me."

Rachel smiled. "Think of me as spiritually younger, if that helps."

Gina took her Bible out of the bag on the floor and put it on her lap. She looked across at Rachel. "I suggested Ephesians because I've studied that recently. Did you get time to read the whole book through?"

Rachel nodded. "I read it twice."

"Let's start by praying and then talk quickly about the background. The clues to Paul's letters are usually in the book of Acts."

"I must admit, I looked at Acts last night."

Gina grinned. "Were you the teacher's pet at school?"

She had been until she'd run away. Now Rachel would be a misfit at a school reunion among the doctors, lawyers, and high-powered businesswomen.

Gina prayed that their time together would be helpful to them both. Then she reached into her bag again to bring out another book. She laid it on the coffee table. "I use a Bible atlas all the time. This one is for you to keep."

"You didn't need to do that," Rachel said, a wobble in her voice.

Gina flipped to the page she'd already bookmarked and Rachel leaned forward.

"Paul's second missionary journey." Gina traced the towns in Asia Minor. "He revisited many of the towns he'd been to on his first journey, encouraging and teaching as he went. Then he headed further west." She tapped her finger on the map. "Ephesus was on the coast and had a harbour. It doesn't nowadays, as the harbour silted up and the city died. You can visit the ruins."

"That would be fun to do someday, if we had the money."

Gina nodded. "It's on my wish list. Now, there's something else about Ephesus that's a bit unusual." She smiled and waited.

"Paul stayed much longer than usual."

Gina nodded.

"And so many people became Christians that the silversmiths got angry at the loss of their business and staged a riot," Rachel said.

"Wouldn't that be wonderful?" Gina leaned back in her seat. "I don't mean the riot bit, but seeing so many people becoming Christians."

Since Rachel had become a Christian, she'd been content to cruise along enjoying the benefits. Most of the time she forgot about Jesus altogether, and didn't remember that others needed him. Paul had such a burning hunger to share the good news.

They talked a few more minutes, then Gina curled her bare feet up under her. "Why don't we read the whole chapter once more? Then I've got a few simple questions. We don't have to stick to them if we decide to discuss other things."

Studying the Bible with only one other person made Rachel relax. She'd felt unable to ask all her questions in the group with Esther and the others, because the others were way ahead in their spiritual journeys.

Rachel read the first half of the chapter and Gina the second.

"Since the chapter is in two halves, I thought we'd consider up to verse fourteen first," Gina said.

"The blessings part, you mean?"

Gina nodded. "Which blessings mean the most to you?"

Rachel looked down at the verses. "The first one moves me. It's an incredible thought that God chose us before the foundation of the world." She shook her head. "I was so angry at him, yet he never gave up on me."

A thought struck her, and she drew in a sharp breath. She'd given up on William. Even her mother had lost hope for a while, but Mum had still gone back to her marriage before everything was resolved. Now every letter bubbled over with the changes her mother was seeing in William. It made Rachel boil with fury. The evidence was stacking up that William had come to new life. Her continued anger grated on Rachel's conscience.

"And we were chosen for a purpose," Gina said. "Not only are we now children of God, but we're to be holy and blameless."

"But that's just it. I don't feel holy or blameless."

"Mmm," Gina said. "Someone once used 2 Corinthians 5 to explain it to me." She flipped through her Bible and waited for Rachel to do the same. "Here, in verse 21 it says, 'God made him who had no sin to become sin for us, so that in him we might become the righteousness of God.'"

Rachel raised an eyebrow. The verse was a mishmash of abstract concepts in her mind.

"Imagine … imagine if our clothing got another spot of dirt every time we went our own way instead of God's way." Gina touched her own clothing. "But Jesus never rebelled, so his clothing was spotless white."

"Okay, got that bit."

"Then we come to the cross," Gina said. "It's like all our dirty clothing was piled on top of Jesus. God looked down on Jesus and saw our sin."

The picture was clear in Rachel's mind. "Got it now. Jesus who had no sin became sin for us."

Gina nodded. "Now everyone has a choice. We can keep our dirty clothing, or we can let Jesus take it, and accept the new clothing Jesus gives us. Once we're in Christ, then God chooses to see Jesus' perfection and not our sinfulness."

"Whoa." Rachel shook her head. "That concept is going to take me awhile to get my head around. It doesn't seem quite fair."

"We all struggle to grasp the magnitude of what Jesus did on the cross. Our viewpoint is so limited." Gina took a drink of water. "Being forgiven means a lot to me."

Rachel's eyes widened. "I wouldn't have thought you had much sin to worry about."

Gina looked up at Rachel. "That's another thing we do—we compare sins and judge some as worse than others."

"But aren't they? Isn't murder worse than lying?"

"To us it is." Gina rubbed her ear. "But I'm not sure God sees things the way we do."

"I don't understand that," Rachel said.

"You remember how Jesus said that to hate someone is equivalent to murder, and lust is equivalent to adultery?"

Rachel nodded.

"Jesus seems to care most about our heart attitudes. The prophets often talked of how God hated the Israelites' religiosity when their hearts were actually far from him. God said he would prefer them to obey him rather than to make sacrifices that didn't mean anything."

Hope pushed up a tiny, green shoot in Rachel's heart. Could it be true that in God's eyes, her past was no worse than all those people's who sat in church? If that was so, the feeling that she was still dirty was false.

She shook her head. Mind-blowing. Before she lost the thought, she jotted it down in her notebook.

"Paul lists a lot of blessings here," Gina said. "Can you think of any other advantages he doesn't list?"

"Lots more." Rachel sat up straight. "Being a Christian gives me a sense of purpose. It gets me out of bed in the morning. I used to be isolated in my own selfishness and self-pity."

"And now you're coaching at Special Olympics." Gina glanced at her watch. "Let's look at the prayer next week. I learn a lot from analysing what Paul prays for. But for now, why don't we thank God for the presents he has heaped on us."

Rachel blinked. Yes, 'presents' was the right word. 'Blessings' sounded too spiritual and otherworldly. In her mind, she saw a great mound of brightly wrapped gifts under the Christmas tree.

Red, green, blue, and silver. Ready to be opened and rejoiced over.
Until now, she'd mostly been stuffing them under her bed.

Unopened and unused.

CHAPTER 27

*T*he following Tuesday, Pete's phone rang before he finished his rushed dinner. It was unlikely to be Binh, as it wasn't his usual night to call.

He picked up the phone, "Good evening, Pete speaking."

"Pete, it's Rachel."

His heart sank. Was she cancelling?

"My car was slow to start after work, and now it won't start at all. I think the battery's dead. I can't see how I can make it."

She wasn't cancelling if he could help it. Soccer wouldn't be the same without her.

"I'll come and get you." He glanced at the clock on the wall. Six fifteen. "There's still time." If the traffic cooperated.

"I hate to be a hassle."

"And I'd prefer the extra driving than having to do the training on my own. I'll be on my way in five minutes."

"Thanks, Pete. I appreciate it."

"My pleasure." And it was. The bonus was that he'd get an hour of uninterrupted time to talk and he'd offer to pick her up tomorrow morning too. He grinned and rushed to get his keys and wallet.

*T*he traffic wasn't heavy, and they were going to make it to soccer right on time.

"Did Josh tell you that he made the state team?" Pete changed down a gear as they went up the first of two big hills.

"Uh-huh. He's equal parts over the moon and terrified."

"He'll be fine. After I talked to my father-in-law this week, I made the decision that I'm going to go and visit him at the same time as Josh's state competition."

"Josh will love that, but what about the nursery? Will Dirk look after things for however long you're away?"

"I've been thinking about that. You know how the public bathrooms have needed an upgrade for a while? Well, I checked with the bathroom company and they're available that week. I'm thinking of asking Dad to supervise."

"Close down the nursery, you mean?"

He nodded. "Yes. Everyone could take time off or do some of the other tasks that we seldom get time to do." His fingers drummed on the steering wheel. "I'm borrowing a house from friends going overseas so that both Ian and Lyn can afford to go with Josh."

"They'll love that."

He took a deep breath. "And I wondered if you'd like to join us. You said you'd never been to Perth."

"But I can't. Not with my grandmother as she is." The words burst out of her.

Was it disappointment in her voice? He hoped it wasn't just because she'd miss seeing Josh's games and going off on an adventure.

"Could anyone stay with your grandmother? What about Gina?"

Rachel sighed. "I don't know if I'd dare ask her to do something major like that."

He watched the tail lights of the cars in front. How he wanted her to come. To show her the beautiful city of which he was so proud. To introduce her to Binh.

"I will think about it," Rachel said.

At least the door wasn't completely closed. He'd be praying.

The traffic was flowing well because they'd missed the worst of the rush hour.

"I wanted to tell you about something exciting that happened while I was in hospital."

Rachel turned her head to look at him. "Exciting? I expected you to be bored."

"Excitement comes in many forms." He flicked her a glance and concentrated on the road. "Do you remember telling me Esther's diaries were full of stories of people she talked to about Jesus?"

"Yes?" Rachel said, confusion in her voice.

"How she used to pray for opportunities and expect God to give them to her?"

"Uh-huh."

"Well, after you all left the hospital, I took a long hard look at my attitude. I was annoyed at having to waste a night in hospital when it was obvious I was fine. But I remembered how both Binh and Esther would have responded and asked God to open my eyes to spiritual opportunities."

"And?"

"Suddenly I saw, really saw, the other man in the room. He lay with his back to us the whole time you were visiting."

Brake lights on the car in front glowed red and it turned abruptly into the petrol station. He braked to avoid running into it.

"I prayed for him, then dithered about getting up and going to visit him. In the end I did, because I figured I'd never see him again."

He paused.

"To my shock when I got closer, I discovered he'd been crying. Not something I expected from a man in his fifties."

"What did you do?"

"I coughed to let him know I was nearby and gave him time to collect himself. Then I said, 'It doesn't seem fair that I have all the visitors when I'm only here one night.'"

Pete stopped for a red light. "Bert said he'd been in another hospital more than a month and admitted he hadn't had a single visitor."

"Poor guy."

"After I'd told him why I was there, he told me he had end stage liver cancer and was waiting to be transferred to a palliative care unit. I wasn't sure I was ready to handle that, but something urged me to stay."

"Did he tell you his story?" Rachel asked.

Pete nodded as the traffic light turned green. "He'd been an alcoholic. He had no visitors, because he'd wrecked his marriage and his sons would have nothing to do with him."

"I wouldn't have had a clue what to say."

"I didn't either and felt way out of my comfort zone. There was a war in my head. One side urged me to walk away because I didn't need anyone else's burdens to add to mine." Pete shook his head. "But another thought urged me to stay and tell this man he didn't ever need to be lonely again."

"Esther talked about that mental battle in her diaries. I've found her experiences convicting," Rachel said. "I've tried to convince myself that she was a 'super' Christian, but I don't really believe that." Rachel sniffed. "Esther was no saint. She could be pretty annoying." She chuckled. "At least, she annoyed me. The Esther in her diaries shows an ordinary person who didn't hide her doubts and fears."

Pete heard her swallow. It was great to hear Rachel talking

about her sister. His grief had gone rancid because of his isolation. Talking things out was much healthier.

"I didn't know how to start either," Pete said. "So I prayed. Hard."

"And how did God answer your prayer?"

"I sensed that I was to tell my story and explain the difference being a Christian makes. The poor man got more than he bargained for, because I was soon crying as well."

Telling another bloke that he cried was one thing, but it didn't bother him to tell Rachel. Not much, anyway.

Rachel shifted in her seat. "How did he cope?"

"I think he was relieved to discover other people could cry too."

Pete turned the car right, heading for the soccer fields.

"Did he respond to what you said?"

"He listened but at the end he said, 'It's nice that being a Christian helps you, but Jesus would never want me.'"

Rachel harrumphed. "I thought exactly the same thing. What did you say?"

"I was still praying, and the story the Chinese lady told at Esther's funeral drifted into my mind."

"The thief on the cross?"

"Yes, the way she told it was so vivid."

He swung the car into a parking space and turned off the engine.

"Joy is a good storyteller."

"Yes, but the story itself is gripping. I hadn't practised telling it, but Bert seemed to grasp it. He asked some good questions and I ended up telling him the story of the Pharisee and the tax collector, and a couple of others."

Someone rapped on the window and they jumped. Sam and Dave stuck their mischievous faces near the driver's side window.

Pete wound down his window. "We might regret inviting you to play, if you scare us like that."

Dave chortled. "No, you won't. You like us too much."

"You're right," Pete laughed. "Now let me put the window up and get out of the car, and we'll take you over and introduce you."

---

*A*fter soccer practice, Pete and Rachel got back in the car. Once Rachel had buckled her seatbelt, Pete drove out of the car park.

"I don't think you finished telling me what happened with Bert," Rachel said.

He turned onto the main road. "I don't remember exactly what Bert asked, but I dredged up a Gospel outline I learned in high school and shared that as best I could."

"A Gospel outline?" Rachel wound down her window to let in the cool night air.

He'd used Christianese. Sometimes he forgot she was a new Christian who didn't know some of the things he took for granted.

"There are lots of outlines out there, but the one I used has a series of drawings."

"You'll have to show me one lunchtime."

"Of course, and I could teach it to you. It's handy to have, as I discovered with Bert." He clicked on his indicator and overtook a car crawling along well below the speed limit. "Not that I did a good job of it, but I did my best."

There'd been a refrain in his head telling him he sounded foolish, but at the same time he'd felt the quiet joy of knowing God was with him and helping him.

"And how did Bert respond? I presume the presentation gives you a chance to decide if you want to follow Jesus."

"Yep, and Bert grabbed my arm and said, 'Yes, I want Jesus to save me.'"

Remembering the hunger in Bert's eyes made him want to stop the car and leap into the air a few times.

"See? You must have done a better job than you thought."

"No." He shook his head. "That's the point. It's not whether we do a good job or not, but whether God opens their spiritual eyes and gives them new life."

"Esther said something similar in her diary. That nothing seemed to happen on the days she thought she'd done a terrific job of communicating, and just when she thought she'd messed up, people wanted to know more."

"It's one of those mysteries that make being a Christian such an adventure. God seldom works the way we expect him to."

"Mmm," Rachel said. "It was Josh's total sincerity that had the biggest impact on me."

"Yes, like the woman in John chapter 4. She just said, 'Come and see the man who knows everything about me.' And Jonah. He was wildly successful, and he didn't want his listeners to repent at all."

Rachel giggled. Not a sound he would have associated with her, but a delightful light-hearted sound.

His heart rate accelerated. If God could use the reluctant Jonah, surely he could use Rachel and himself.

He swallowed and said as casually as he could manage, "I promised Bert I'd go back to the hospital on Saturday to visit. Would you be willing to come too?"

There was a long silence.

Stupid! You'd think he was an awkward teenager. He restrained himself from pounding the steering wheel. He'd bungled things and scared her off. She reminded him of a deer stepping out into a clearing, ready to leap away at the slightest noise. As the silence stretched between them, he wondered if maybe he was the deer. Frozen in the headlights. Scared and exposed.

What was he thinking? He should have made a more conventional invitation instead of asking her to come as a sort of sidekick.

Or a prayer partner. But he hadn't wanted to ask her to dinner. Hadn't dared to jump ahead that fast.

"Of course, it's fine if you can't come. I understand," he said.

Popular convention said never to date anyone from work. He should have taken that wisdom to heart. If she fled, they might lose her at work too. He tightened his hands on the steering wheel. *Please, Lord. Don't let her run away.*

"No—" Rachel said.

He clenched his jaw. The whole idea was going down in flames because he'd sprung things on her.

"—Sorry, I can't leave Gran more than I already do. The doctor has put her on medication for her heart. I need to be there for her."

She looked across at him. "But I'll certainly pray. Actually, I'm sure Bert will be happier to talk to you on his own."

Phew. He breathed out a long breath. All wasn't lost. If she needed to be at home, he'd have to come up with reasons to visit her there.

CHAPTER 28

*R*achel and Gina helped Naomi out of the car and safely onto the footpath.

"Gina, if you'll stay with Gran, I'll go and park the car." Rachel went back around to the driver's seat and drove off.

After parking the car, she walked over to where Gina and Gran were waiting.

Her grandmother narrowed her eyes. "What are you up to?"

Rachel winked. "You'll have to wait and see."

By parking at the back, they'd not only avoided the stairs but also avoided the banners advertising the event. Rachel took her grandmother by the arm and Gina walked on the other side.

"Girls, do give me some clues."

"Well, you told me how much you miss visiting the art gallery. This will be a much smaller version."

And one with far less walking.

"Is this that painting and photography exhibition I saw advertised in the paper?"

"Maybe," Rachel said.

"You precious girl." Gran stopped walking and reached up to kiss Rachel's cheek. "Just the sort of art I like."

"I'm glad our choice meets with your approval." Rachel breathed a sigh of relief. She hadn't known anything much about her grandmother's tastes in art, other than the few paintings hanging on the walls at home.

Gina stood with Gran while Rachel bought three tickets. Rachel had wavered between asking Pete or Gina, but hadn't wanted to give Pete any wrong ideas. Besides which, he was visiting Bert at the hospital. Asking Gina was less stressful, and if today went well, Rachel was going to raise the idea of the Perth trip and see how Gina responded. After several weeks of Bible study together, Rachel was fairly confident that Gina would feel comfortable enough to say no if staying with Gran was not feasible for her.

"Come on," Rachel said, taking Gran's arm again.

Early Saturday afternoon had been a good choice. There were only about ten people in the first room.

"Do you want to roam on your own or all look together?" Gina asked.

Gran smiled at her. "Feel free to do whatever you like, but I enjoy looking at each picture together, because then we can talk."

"Okay, together it is," Gina said. "Lead on."

After viewing the first room, Gran said, "Can we sit down for a few minutes?"

"You're in charge." Rachel lowered her grandmother to the bench in the centre of the room.

"Anyone have a favourite?" Gran asked.

Gina pursed her lips. "There are plenty I'd be happy to hang on my walls." She pointed to a photograph and a matching painting. "Maybe that pair, with all the sailboats skimming across the harbour on a breezy day. Reminds me of happy days watching the small boat races on weekends."

Rachel pointed to the right. "I'm going for that photo with the glimpses of cliffs through the mist and the single twisted tree peeping out."

Gran put her head to one side. "I haven't decided if I prefer the black and white photos or the paintings best. I love the shadows and starkness of the photography."

Rachel checked her watch. Pete would be visiting Bert about now. *Lord, help Pete to explain more of your truth to Bert. And help Pete to be encouraged as you use him to reach someone who so desperately needs you.*

"Okay," Gran said, struggling to her feet. "Let's keep going."

There was an attendant standing near the doorway into the next room. As the woman moved to let them past, she revealed a painting behind her. Gran put her hand to her throat and stopped. "No, that one's my favourite."

The waterfall in the painting flowed down the sandstone cliffs and gathered in a pool before plunging down to the next level.

"Wentworth Falls," Gran said. "My uncle had a house there, and we used to go for two weeks every year. All the cousins together in a rambling old house. The older boys put up tents in the garden."

It was easy to forget her grandmother had been a little girl once upon a time. It reminded Rachel she must ask to see some of the old photos. Gran wouldn't live forever. Now was the time to hear the stories of her childhood. Stories that made her the woman she was. Prayerful, courageous, and always with a twinkle in her eye.

The second room contained flora and fauna pictures, and the remaining two rooms concentrated on single objects. A bold, red waratah flower; a praying mantis; or a tightly curled fern frond.

They sat down on the bench in the middle of the last room. "I can't make up my mind whether I prefer the wide angle or the close-up view of the world," Gran said.

"Both are beautiful," Rachel said. "It makes me ponder the amazing creativity of God. Every detail perfect, and every plant or flower unique."

"Yes," Gina said. "God could have created one kind of tree and called it 'tree', or made every person look identical, but he didn't."

"We serve a great God, don't we, ladies?" Gran said, rubbing her right knee.

"Are you ready to go and get a cup of tea, Gran?"

"Now you're talking. I hope it isn't far to walk."

"Is your knee giving you pain?"

Gran nodded. "But there's nothing that can be done, this side of glory. Soon it will be as good as new. Then I'll be dancing. I used to be quite the foxtrotter."

Rachel had left nothing to chance and had booked a table for four o'clock. The café was only next door. Soon they were seated and drinking tea from a proper teapot with cups and saucers.

"Ah, that's good," Gran said, putting down her cup and leaning back in her chair. "Thank you so much for bringing me on this expedition."

"Our pleasure," Gina said. "But you do have to give us something in exchange."

Gran's eyebrows rose towards her hairline.

"Nothing scary, but would you be willing to tell us some of the big lessons God has taught you?"

"I've lived more than eight decades. How much time have you got?" Gran leaned forward again and took another sip of tea. "I'll need a serving of scones with jam and cream to give me the strength."

"Good thing I already ordered them. Here they are," Rachel said, as the waiter approached the table. "And some of the passionfruit cheesecake."

"You sure know how to motivate an old lady."

As her grandmother tucked into her afternoon tea, Rachel smiled across at Gina. It was reassuring to see how easily Gina related to Gran. Rachel had been a little embarrassed to ask for Gina's help for this short trip. Now she was considering asking her to live at their home for a week. That was much more of an imposition.

Gran finished the last crumb of her cheesecake and dabbed her mouth with a paper serviette.

"One lesson I learned early on was not to be too independent." Gran paused, as if to look back over the years. "After my son and husband died, I had no one to rely on. If my husband's secretary hadn't marched right into my home and forced me to come walking with her, I might not have recovered from my melancholy."

"She's the lady who brought you to Christ, isn't she?" Gina asked. Gran had shared her story with the quilting group.

Gran nodded. "Louisa was the first one to show me the church is a family and we need to help each other out. Over the years, I've cooked meals for families with new babies and I've driven old people to medical appointments." She laughed. "And now I'm the old lady who needs others to drive me."

She smiled across at Rachel and Gina. "Invest in helping others, and not only will you reap the rewards of satisfaction and joy, but one day you might end up being the recipient."

Rachel nodded. This was a lesson she needed to learn.

"And it's a good witness to others outside the church," Gina said.

"One of my dreams has always been that the church cares so well for each other that non-Christians will be envious and want to know why we do it," Gran said.

"That's a dream I can get excited about," Gina said, enthusiasm tingeing her voice.

"Is it Louisa's picture on your dressing table?" Rachel asked.

Her grandmother nodded. "She was like a sister to me. I'm excited that I'll see her soon."

"Please don't die yet, Gran."

"I can't go on forever. Every day is one day closer." She patted Rachel's hand. "I used to be scared of death, but I'm not now. Too many of my friends are already in heaven. I imagine them lining the entrance ready to cheer me home."

Rachel's eyes moistened. And Esther would be one of the welcoming committee. It was easy to picture Esther bouncing on her toes and waving to get her attention. Rachel hugged her arms around her body. She and her sister would finally have an eternity to get to know each other properly.

Gina brushed some scone crumbs off her skirt. "What other pearls of wisdom can you share?"

"You make me nervous, dear, calling them pearls of wisdom."

"I like to learn from other people's experiences," Gina said. "Sometimes it saves me from making similar mistakes."

"Another thing I learned was not to judge people too quickly." Gran tilted her head to one side. "I came from quite a privileged background, and I tended to look down on people without much education. I had a hard time seeing beyond externals to the treasures underneath. God had to give me his heart for people."

It was all too easy to assume Gran had sprung out of the womb as she was now, but of course she hadn't. No one was ever born mature. God had changed Gran and was changing her, so why did the thought of God changing William annoy Rachel so much?

The key factor on the human side was humility. As much as Rachel didn't want to admit it, William seemed to be growing in that virtue. That was already the miracle of the century.

"You know, most spiritual journeys have similarities," Gran said. "Any follower of Jesus has to learn to trust him. The actual trust lessons might be different for each person, but the overall lesson is the same."

"Can you explain that a little? I mean, only if you want to." Gina poured herself another cup of tea. "Anyone else?"

Rachel held out her cup.

"Well, I had to learn to trust God with lots of practicalities after Norman died. In my era, women didn't deal with the taxes or bills or household repairs." Gran sneezed. "Excuse me. Now, where was I? Oh, yes, trust. The hardest thing for me to learn was to continue to trust God with William and the rest of my family."

Gina reached across and touched Naomi's arm. "The way you've prayed for more than thirty years inspires me to not give up on my family. Even the ones I don't know yet but who are out there somewhere."

Last week, Gina had told Rachel she was adopted and was considering whether to search for her biological family or not. More trust lessons.

"And all of us have lots to learn about forgiveness."

Rachel's stomach cramped.

"Forgiveness is yet another application of the same lesson. Can we trust God to judge fairly? Can we trust him to protect us or help us deal with further hurt?"

Rachel's shoulders tensed and a headache pounded at the base of her skull. Was this her problem? That she wanted to be the judge, jury, and executioner as well. That in order to avoid further hurt, she didn't trust God to walk with her through whatever happened. Yet every time she wanted to run from the issue, God brought it back to her attention.

Yes, being forced to face issues was for her own good, but sometimes she wanted nothing more than to stuff the issue into a cupboard and leave it for a better time. Whenever that might be.

CHAPTER 29

*P*ete cheered as Josh used a straw to blow a ping pong ball along his parents' lounge carpet. It was Josh's birthday, and Pete had organised a small party. Asking Rachel to organise the games ensured she'd want to come. Inviting Naomi had clinched it.

Now the room was full of adults playing children's games. Josh and Pete were one team, competing against Rachel and Josh's dad.

On the other side of the room, Ian blew tiny puffs to manoeuvre the ping pong ball around the half-way post, a glass jar.

"Well done, Ian," Rachel said.

He lifted his head. "I'm not sure that I'm going to forgive you for this loss of dignity."

Rachel laughed. "I was only trying to find games Josh would enjoy. After all, it's his birthday."

Her laughter was so different from when Pete had first met her. The gut-knotting cynical edge had almost entirely disappeared.

Josh wasn't far behind his father. Pete and Rachel were going to have to fight it out in the second leg of the relay. Josh coughed, and his ping pong ball shot off at an angle from his line of travel.

Naomi laughed, then patted her chest as though she was trying to catch her breath. "Don't give up, Josh."

"Naughty ball." Josh scurried along the carpet like an overgrown mouse to chase his ball.

"Nearly there, Ian." Rachel dropped into position, ready to start her part of the relay. Their ball crossed the line, but Josh was only a few seconds behind.

Rachel, competitive woman that she was, had probably practised at home, because her ball was halfway to the turning point with only two blows.

Josh sent their ball over the line. Pete took over and blew it forward. He was going to gamble on bigger breaths, so he didn't have to bend too often. Rachel reached the halfway point and turned. She was intent on winning and blew a hard breath. The ball shot forward towards him. He shifted his head and blew it sideways and backwards.

"Cheat, cheat." Rachel gave him a what-do-you-think-you're-doing? look.

"I thought we were playing croquet rules." Pete used to play croquet with school friends on their back lawn. Nothing like being able to send the opposition miles out of their intended path. He blew, and his ball inched past the halfway point.

He scrambled forward and got the ball round the glass with minimum fuss.

"Go, Mr Pete, you can catch her." Josh's excited jump set all the fancy dishes in Norma's sideboard dancing.

"Not so much jumping," Lyn said.

"Oops." Josh fell back into the seat behind him.

Pete blew another long breath and the ball rolled forward, straight towards the finish line.

Rachel's ball veered across his line of travel. With a mischievous glance over her shoulder, she planted herself right where he wanted to be and blew her ball over the finish line.

"Humph," Pete said. "Not sure that was in the rules."

"Son," Dirk said, his face red from laughing. "I'm not sure you can object after your behaviour. She beat you at your own game."

Pete put his hand on Josh's shoulder. "We'll just have to beat them in the next game. Come on, Rachel, what's next?"

Rachel reached behind the sofa and pulled out two bags. "This one needs all of us. Dirk and Gran, you're on our team. Lyn and Norma, you're with Pete and Ian."

"I didn't think I had to play anything," Norma said.

"Well, it's really your shoes we need." Rachel walked over to one end of the room and put down one of the bulky bags. "The goal is to build the tallest freestanding tower you can with shoes. I'll get Dirk to judge. He won't cheat."

"How do you know?" Dirk smirked. "I'm related to Pete."

Rachel wagged her finger at him. "I'm relying on you as a mature adult and pillar of the community."

Pete sniggered as his father saluted Rachel. She was getting her fair share of flak from the Klopper family tonight. She'd handle it. Would he ever be able to convince her to join the family?

"I'm not sure I'm going to be any help at this," Naomi said to Rachel.

Rachel squeezed her grandmother's hand. "With you as consultant, Ian, Josh, and I should manage."

It was hard not to stare at this new Rachel. Somewhere in the last few months, her hard edges had been smoothed away.

"Okay, Dirk, give us seven minutes," Rachel said.

Josh managed to knock the tower down halfway but eventually they had something standing tall.

"Dad, you'd better come and measure this before it collapses." The other tower looked about the same height—they'd used shoelaces to link the shoes together and give more stability. Clever, but not enough. Their team had used fewer shoes, but each shoe was a bigger size. One-all.

Josh shone at the next game, transferring peanuts from a bowl at one end of the room to the other while walking on his knees. He still managed to drop each peanut off his teaspoon at least once, but that didn't diminish his absolute enjoyment of the process. Their team won again.

Once they'd finished calming Josh down, Rachel said, "Josh, if you'll sit down, we'll bring in your birthday cake." She disappeared into the kitchen with Lyn.

Josh smacked his lips and rubbed his stomach.

The cake should meet with Josh's approval. Rachel had said she could bake an acceptable cake, but decorating wasn't her thing. Pete had suggested something related to soccer, and she'd asked him to make her two little goals and find some soccer figurines. She'd do the rest.

Pete reached to turn off the lights, and Rachel brought the cake into the lounge, lit only by the glow of the candles. They all sang 'Happy Birthday' as she set the cake down in front of Josh.

"Look, Mum and Dad," he said, eyes round. "It's a soccer field, and there's me." He pointed. Sure enough, Rachel had put one figure in Josh's usual position and labelled it with a big 'J' hanging around its neck.

"Well done," Pete said, for her ears only.

She blushed and his stomach did a slow cartwheel.

"Bye," Pete called as he and Rachel stood waving off Josh and his family. He turned to her with a smile.

"That was a grand success," she said.

"You chose some of those games to maximise laughs."

Rachel put her head to one side. "You think?"

A breeze rustled the dried leaves on the road edge and wafted the sweetness of mock-orange flowers from the nearby hedge.

"Look." Rachel pointed at the sky. "Shooting star."

A streak of green shot across a patch of sky. This part of Sydney had less light pollution than the centre of the city, and the sky was ablaze with stars. A sickle moon hung suspended above the nearby hill.

A tingle of nerves danced at Pete's fingertips.

Lord, is this the time to speak to Rachel? Please help me not to mess up our friendship.

He took a deep breath. "I noticed that your grandmother needs help with her shoes now. Are you having to give her quite a bit of assistance?"

Maybe he shouldn't ask. He wanted her to think he was caring, not interfering.

Rachel stepped back and sat on the low brick wall. He joined her.

"It's only been the last month or so. Her heart isn't pumping as efficiently as it did, and she's getting less and less flexible. Slip-on shoes would be great for independence, but they're not safe."

"Would it help if you took off an hour earlier in the afternoons?"

She turned her head. "Work fewer hours overall, you mean?"

"That's one possibility."

"I have been considering my options."

No! His chest tightened. He couldn't lose her from the nursery. From his life.

"Apparently even if I apply for a carer's pension, I can still work about twenty hours a week outside the home."

He let out his breath slowly. So she wasn't thinking of abandoning them entirely.

"I'm planning on talking things over with Gran. Much as I don't want to, I'll have to stop coaching soccer."

He'd been expecting her to say that for weeks. His heart rate sped up and he took a deep breath.

"You know I'll miss you, don't you?" He was out of the habit of saying anything like this. Not that he'd ever had to say much with Mai. Their relationship had drifted into love so gradually that he barely had to raise the topic. It had just been natural. In some ways, his friendship with Rachel was similar. But now? Now he wanted more.

Rachel leaned forward, gripping the edge of the wall with both hands.

He had no idea if she could sense the tension he felt. Whether she was waiting for him to say more, or, hoping he wouldn't.

He took another steadying breath. His blood pumped in his ears.

"This might not be the best timing, but I don't want to talk about personal things at work, and you need to be home with your grandmother in the evenings and on weekends." He still hadn't said what was really on his heart. At his age, this should be easier. He knew she liked him as a person and a Christian brother, but did she like him more than that?

Rachel stared at the ground. He was making a mess of this, but she hadn't stopped him talking. Maybe that was a good sign.

"What I'm trying to say is that I'd be interested in getting to know you beyond just friends." He swallowed loudly. He sounded as dorkish as a pimply teenager asking out his first date.

Rachel didn't move. Was she offended? Angry? Trying to work out how to turn him down without offending him? He didn't have a clue.

A tear slid down Rachel's cheek, and then another, each gleaming like crystal in the moonlight. Her shoulders shook and she took a shuddering breath. What was going on?

"You wouldn't want anything to do with me if you knew the whole story," she said through her tears.

All he wanted to do was gather her in his arms. He'd known she hadn't told him everything, but reject her? Never.

"We've all got things in our background we're ashamed of." He took a shaky breath. "I killed my family."

She rounded on him, face contorted. "You need to get something straight." Her breath snagged in her throat. "You did not kill your family. They died. Maybe your actions contributed, but their deaths were not your fault." She thumped her thigh. "You didn't intend for them to die."

She took three panting breaths. "But I intended my baby to die." Her knuckles gleamed white as she clutched at the wall. "I killed her because allowing her to live would have got in the way of my plans." She stabbed her forefinger on the wall. "My plans for my life."

Abortion. His heart ached for her. He'd grown up among people who believed certain sins were worse than others. Abortion was always near the top of such lists.

"I sit in church every week and feel dirty." Her voice harshened into scorn. "I know you'll say I'm forgiven." She held up her hand. "I do believe God has forgiven me, but I don't feel it when I'm around you or Gina. You're amazing people. Someone like Gina is the right kind of woman for you."

He wasn't interested in Gina. He opened his mouth to say so, but only a croak came out. Rotten timing.

"I probably should have told you my whole story before, but it's hard to know when it's appropriate." She laughed, the harsh cynical laugh he hated. "Maybe I should wear a sign with 'committed adultery and abortion' around my neck to keep men like you away."

"Rachel, I—"

She turned her face away from him. "Could you please go and bring Gran out to the car? I don't think I can handle seeing your parents."

He unpeeled himself from the wall and touched her shoulder.

Rachel withdrew as though he'd burned her. "Don't touch me.

Please." She stood with her back to him. "I'll get my things from the hall, if you'll get my grandmother."

He turned to go.

"Please, thank your parents for their hospitality. You can explain later what happened."

"Surely you don't want me saying anything to them?" Finally, his voice worked.

"Your dad knows the whole story. I assume he's told your mother." Rachel rubbed her sleeve across her eyes. "The abortion and the nightmares and why I tried to end it all."

Lord, help. He struggled to take a full breath. *Show me how to stop Rachel believing she is unworthy of love.*

CHAPTER 30

*R*achel barely waited until Pete re-entered his parent's house before she scurried after him to grab her things. Oh, if only she could get home and not have to talk to anyone else for a few days.

Pete. It hurt even to think of his name. *Pete.* She groaned. Inside the house was light and laughter, but out here the darkness no longer felt romantic. Only damp. Oh, everything was a total mess.

She sneaked through the front door and unhooked her handbag from the stand in the hall. Out of the corner of her eye, she caught a glimpse of something different from last time she'd been here. Admittedly, it had been a while. She looked more closely. Yes, there was no longer a gap in the family photos on the wall. Instead, there were two photos she hadn't seen before. A photo of Pete and two adorable children. She peered closer. She'd have gotten along with his son—he had scallywag written all over him. Her gaze shifted to the photo of Pete and Mai on their wedding day, gazing at each other with adoration.

Her breath caught in her throat. She'd have given anything to have Pete look at her like that. She shook her head. Stupid fantasy.

She'd turned him down. Had to turn him down. He wasn't the type to date without having honourable intentions, and she didn't want him to date her out of pity. He was made to be a father. It was obvious in the way he coached soccer. In the way he'd played along with Josh tonight. She sucked in a breath.

"Dirk and Norma, thank you so much for your hospitality. Rachel and I had a terrific time." Her grandmother's voice floated down the hall.

Good on Gran, for trying to cover for her not being there. Rachel ghosted out the front door she'd left open and pulled it behind herself. No need to present her tear-ravaged face to everyone. Pete would explain everything to his parents.

Once Naomi came outside, Rachel helped her into the car, buckled her seatbelt, then climbed in the driver's side and started for home. There was silence for a few seconds.

"Are you okay, Rachel?" her grandmother asked.

Rachel muttered something noncommittal and put her foot on the brake as she approached the turn out of the Klopper's street.

"I take it that means you're not doing well, and I'm guessing it has to do with Pete. I can't imagine you not thanking Dirk and Norma, and Pete looked white around the gills when he came in to collect me."

She should have known Gran would spot something was wrong.

"I've been praying for you and Pete. It's been obvious how much you like and respect him."

"Mmm." There was no use denying it. She'd been in danger of heartbreak ever since they'd started coaching soccer together. The kayaking trip had only made things worse.

"Based on the way you two were horsing around tonight, I'd say he feels the same about you." Naomi shifted in her seat. "If you want to talk about it, I'm willing to listen."

Rachel gripped the steering wheel. "You can probably guess."

It would be easier to tell Gran now, in the relative darkness of the car.

"He doesn't know your story?" Naomi asked.

"He does now." And he'd been silent. How could he not have been horrified? All those years ago, she'd ignored her conscience and focused on dealing with her problem. Problem! Her child had not been a genderless problem, or a random bunch of cells. Dehumanising a baby made things easier, but it didn't make it right.

Rachel sighed. "I'd already told him how I became a Christian, but I left out the abortion." Weariness wrapped itself around her. "Even at the time, I knew there might come a day when I needed to tell him the whole story, but it's always hard to know when to dump information like that on someone."

Share it too early and people feel uncomfortable. Share it too late and it can be devastating. Hurting Pete was the last thing she'd ever wanted to do.

Naomi reached across and touched Rachel's hand. Oh, how she'd wanted to let Pete's hand linger on her shoulder, but she hadn't dared. She had to make a clean break before things got even more entangled.

"Dearie, how did he respond?"

"I was too upset to notice." By rejecting him, she'd probably lost the friendship as well and blown the trip to Perth, which she'd been looking forward to. She blew out a gusty breath.

"You've both got the rest of the weekend to process things. I daresay he'll be praying as hard as I will."

Rachel reached sideways and patted her grandmother's knee. "Thanks, Gran. But Pete would be crazy to keep pursuing me."

"Why? It seems to me that you'd be quite a catch."

"Gran, you're an absolute darling, but your love blinds you to the facts."

"What facts?"

Did she really have to spell them out? Rachel sighed. "For a start,

I'm older than Pete. Most guys care about that, especially at my age. Pete is father material through and through. Who knows if I can even have a child."

Because her abortion had been the street kind - an unmarked bottle from a stranger - she hadn't been told having an abortion might lower her chances of having another child. She'd found that out years later.

"Having children is God's business," Gran said. "He has a history of giving children to older women."

Yes, well, that was back in biblical times. Rachel hadn't heard any stories of post-menopausal women having babies nowadays. Not that she was that yet, but it could be just around the corner.

Rachel cleared her throat. "Pete should be looking for some lovely Christian woman. Someone younger. Someone like Gina."

"It might be too late for that," Gran said with a hint of a joke in her voice.

Rachel pushed her grandmother's words aside and put on her indicator to change lanes. "It was only a matter of time before he recovered from the loss of his family. Here he is, feeling better, and I happen to be the woman on the spot. If I get out of the way, he'll be able to see many more suitable options."

Gran laughed softly. "You forget that God sometimes has other plans."

"I doubt Pete is in God's plans for me."

"Dearie, I think you still misunderstand God's love and forgiveness. When he says you are not condemned, he means it."

"But it wouldn't be fair if I could be forgiven without any consequences."

"You've had plenty of consequences."

Rachel clenched her jaw. The nightmares had been horrendous. And they'd been set off by the smallest of things. By children laughing or running to hug their parents. By children reaching up to hold their mother's hands or by joyously skipping down the footpath. Maybe that's why she'd done well in cosmetics. Most parents kept their children far away from all that expensive glass and those breakable objects.

"Any consequences were still a small price to pay for my choices." Rachel wiped the sweat off her forehead. Exercising her choice prevented her child from ever having a choice.

"After my son and Norm's deaths, I lingered much longer in my melancholy than was healthy." Her grandmother paused. "As though somehow my misery would even up the balance on some divine scales. As though I was a monk doing penance with a hair shirt rubbing my skin raw. In a horrible sort of way, it made me feel better."

Maybe that was what Rachel had been doing.

"We might say Jesus' death was on our behalf and we're forgiven, but we deny it in our hearts. In some perverse way, we want to pay for our sin by beating ourselves up."

Gran's words made some sort of sense. Their conversation had wandered a long way from Pete, but these were issues Rachel had been avoiding.

Rachel pulled a tissue from the box jammed between the seats and blew her nose. "I stifled my conscience. When I think of all the people who would have loved to raise my child, I hate myself." Bile rose in her throat. "Maybe I thought if I couldn't have my child, then no one could."

Her grandmother wriggled in her seat.

"Uncomfortable?" Rachel asked.

"A little. I'm not used to sitting in cars any more."

Rachel stopped for the red light. "Only five minutes until we're home."

"If we continue beating ourselves up," Gran said, "it's as if we deny Jesus' crucifixion and tell him his death wasn't enough."

Rachel blinked.

"If Jesus' death was one death for all our sin, then you are forgiven. Full stop."

Full stop.

"No need for penance. No need for any contribution on your part. No need to think you don't deserve happiness." Gran laughed, a sound like a shaft of moonlight bursting through the gloom. "We didn't deserve anything in the first place. None of us did. That's the whole point of the gospel. That's why Jesus is such good news. He gives us everything we don't deserve." Gran paused. "Like forgiveness, a clean start, and a new life. Then he heaps on joy and peace and contentment for good measure."

Rachel would love to believe it. In her head she knew Jesus could forgive her, but she wallowed in the thought that she'd never be happy, that it was right and proper that she'd never be happy. Could Jesus really want to give her far more than he'd already given her?

"But was I right to tell Pete the whole story?"

"Absolutely. These things have a way of coming out. Hiding it wasn't going to do your relationship any good." Her grandmother clasped her hands on her lap. "But I think your motivation might have been wrong. Did you tell him as a way to say, 'see, you should have nothing to do with me. I don't deserve any happiness'?"

Rachel clenched the steering wheel and took a deep breath. "Maybe. I'll think about it when I can think straight."

They sat in silence for a few moments.

"Have you considered going to a counsellor to talk about some of these things?" Gran asked.

Rachel shook her head. No, definitely not.

"We didn't have counselling available in my younger days, but a friend went a few years ago and found it helpful. It might be worth looking into."

"Gran, I don't promise to go, but I will think about it. Right now, it's your prayers I want."

"Dearie, you'll certainly get those. And if Pete is half the man I think he is, he'll be praying too. He'll do what God tells him to do."

Her grandmother had great faith, but Rachel wasn't so sure. If she'd been in Pete's position, she'd consider the whole situation too difficult and would withdraw gracefully to pursue less complicated women.

And who could blame him?

CHAPTER 31

*T*he jacaranda trees were in full bloom all along the street. Pete and Dirk's shoes crushed the purple bell-shaped flowers underfoot. The day's heat was defused by a playful zephyr of a breeze. Somewhere, there was the faint buzz of a lawn mower.

Pete and Rachel were supposed to be accompanying Josh and his parents to Perth next month. The last thing Pete wanted was for Rachel to pull out of the trip, so he didn't have much time to convince her he could handle just being friends.

"Dad, are you still happy to supervise the builders at the nursery while we're in Perth?"

As well as the public bathrooms upgrade, builders were also going to add a new, covered outdoor dining space for the café. All the workers had chosen to take the week off, and it was much easier to do both projects at once.

"Don't you worry about anything. You'll only be gone a week." Dirk kept silent for a long moment. "But you haven't come toddling along with me for your health. You prefer to be out cycling or kayaking on a Sunday afternoon."

Pete swallowed noisily. He'd nearly skipped church this

morning to nurse his pain at Rachel's rejection, but he wasn't going to isolate himself again. The sermon, on the parable of the persistent widow, had been like an arrow to his heart.

He'd gone straight home, eaten lunch, then poured his heart out in prayer. Rachel had seemed to be warming towards him the last few weeks. Then, snap. All the barriers were up, and the door was slammed in his face.

When he'd finally prayed himself to a standstill, he had rung his father to ask if he could accompany him on his daily walk.

Dirk took a few more steps. "I presume you want to talk about Rachel. It was obvious something happened between you after Josh's party."

"I didn't expect you to miss that there was a problem."

"And are you sure she'd be happy for you to talk with me?"

"Yep, she told me you already knew her whole story and nothing would shock you."

"Ahh," Dirk said, pushing back the rim of his hat.

"Yes, she told me about the abortion."

His father kept walking. "And how did you respond?"

"I messed up. Couldn't think of anything to say."

Dirk took a few steps. "Once she simmers down, I don't think she'll hold that against you. What made her tell you about it?"

Pete cleared his throat. "Ever since our kayaking trip, I've been more and more convinced that I'd like to get to know her better."

"And you told her that last night?"

Pete nodded. It was a conversation he'd like to rewind and start again.

"Being Rachel, she probably threw the abortion at your head as a reason you should run a mile."

Pete rubbed his eyebrow. "You do know her well."

"She's talked a lot to me over the last year. Maybe she feels we have things in common since both of us became Christians as adults."

They continued walking.

Dirk glanced towards Pete. "What was your initial reaction to what Rachel told you?"

Pete sighed. "Shock, sadness … disappointment that she'd chosen that option …" He hesitated. "Confusion, really. Lots of emotions piling up one on top of each other." Even after his time of prayer, his stomach heaved at the thought of abortion. Losing his family in an accident had been bad enough. Rachel had made it clear that she considered her actions were in a different class.

"Dad, why would she just tell me like that?"

"Can't you come up with some possibilities?"

Not another question. Pete wanted answers, not questions. He thought for a few moments. "Maybe I'm similar … I don't tell everyone I meet about Mai and the children, but it's always lying below the surface." He sighed. "When a friendship reaches a certain level, I feel I have to mention it."

The tricky thing was working out when it was appropriate, who needed to know, and in how much detail. "When I do mention it, it feels as though I've burdened others with something they shouldn't have to carry."

They began walking up the hill.

"Why do you think she ran away from you?"

Pete rubbed the back of his hair, which was damp with sweat. "Dad, I don't know. I thought she liked me more than a little."

"I think you're right. Maybe that's why she ran. Both of you have trouble forgiving yourselves and don't think you deserve happiness."

Pete cracked his knuckles. "She was angry about how I continue to beat myself up about the crash. Said my situation was an accident but hers was a choice."

Dirk chuckled. "She's right. You have beaten yourself up too much." He took a swig of water from the bottle in his hand. "Survivor's guilt is common after accidents like yours. But in every situation, we have to practise using our sword of the Spirit."

"I've never really understood that analogy."

"If you'll let an old man get to the top of the hill, I'll be happy to explain it to you," his father said as he puffed.

Pete had been so deep in thought he hadn't noticed his father needed to stop talking for this steep bit of the path. They walked on without speaking. It was a clear day; there would be a beautiful view from the top.

They crossed the small car park at the top of the hill.

"I'm going to sit on that seat," Dirk said, pointing to the best viewpoint. He walked over, sat down, and took another drink from his bottle of water. "Ahh, that's better. I'm not used to talking while I walk. Mostly I pray. But when I get here, I love to look at that view."

The long line of the mountains was a smudgy blue across the horizon. Pete could see the corner of his parent's house far down below, and a tiny red dot in the back garden. That would be Mum.

"I wonder what she's up to?" his father muttered. "She's supposed to be putting her feet up and reading."

"I'm not sure that Mum is good at taking much time for herself."

Dirk laughed and patted the seat next to him. "Sit down. You're giving me a crick in my neck talking to you up there."

Pete didn't need the break, but he did want to hear more about sword fighting. "I've always found the armour of God imagery a bit abstract."

"I did too until I had a Bible study leader who used to be a fencing coach. He made it more concrete. Reminded us how long people have to practise to not only get fit, but also for the sword strokes to become second nature."

Dirk held an imaginary sword in front of himself. "A fencing sword is relatively light, compared with one they'd have used to fight with in the Middle Ages. Back then, young knights were constantly practising. You didn't fight well without years of training."

That made sense.

"Paul commands us to take every thought captive. Every time one of Satan's lies enters our head, we need to remind ourselves what Scripture says on the issue."

"So, if we think we can't be forgiven for something—" Pete drew out his words as he considered the idea. "We need to remind ourselves that Jesus died—and he removes our sins as far as the east is from the west."

Dirk nodded. "Exactly. You choose the Scriptures based on the issue you're struggling with. The fencing coach suggested we memorise a few key verses for each issue and repeat the appropriate verse every time the lie comes into our mind."

"Sounds like hard work." Pete stretched his back and neck. "After the accident, lies kept circling in my head like vultures. Most of the time, I let them feast on me."

"Satan never plays fair. He attacks when we're at our weakest and that's when we most need to remember God's truths." Dirk flicked an ant off his leg. "Sometimes we need other people to help us sword fight."

"That's what you and Binh tried to do, but I was too depressed to see it."

Dirk grunted. "Both Binh and you have gone through things most people can't even imagine. That's probably why he was better able to help you."

"I hope you didn't feel left out." Pete put his hand on his father's shoulder.

"I understood, but I think your mother found it pretty hard. I had to remind her that praying was our first responsibility. We especially prayed that Binh would be given God's wisdom to help you."

"Well, God heard that prayer."

In less than two weeks, he'd be able to see Binh in person, instead of only talking on the phone. Binh had been the hardest person to leave behind when Pete moved east.

Please help Rachel not to cancel the trip to Perth. I do want her to meet Binh. And it would be even better if they got along. Rachel already loved his parents. If she took to Binh too, maybe it would be enough to make her warm to Pete's request for more time together.

Dirk stood up. "Ready to go? I should be able to talk going downhill."

As they crossed the car park, Dirk said, "What do you think God wants for you?"

"I think the sermon we heard this morning was God's reminder to me to keep praying and not give up."

His father looked sideways at him. "I don't think it's going to be smooth sailing."

"That's okay." Pete cleared his throat.

His father kept quiet.

"Society talks about marriage as though it's all romance and attraction." Pete rubbed his ear. "With Mai, everything started with friendship, and love sort of caught us unawares." His neck heated. "Not that I'm against romance." He cleared his throat. "But now I'm older, I hope I'm also wiser."

His father put his hand on Pete's shoulder. "You know we'll be praying."

He was counting on it.

CHAPTER 32

*R*achel put her key in the back door and pushed it open. There was no Naomi sitting, waiting for her. Odd. She was usually there every day, ready to talk after a long day on her own.

Rachel hesitated, listening. No sound at all except the ticking of the carved wooden clock on the wall.

"Gran, are you home?" she called.

Nothing.

Her heart rate ratcheted up a gear. *Lord, help her to be okay.*

She checked the kitchen. Nothing.

Gran's bedroom. Nothing.

"Gran?" her voice cracked. "Gran?" A rising panic clogged her throat. Oh, why hadn't she arranged for the panic button thingy that elderly people hung around their neck? It had been on her to-do list. *Lord, let her be all right.*

The bathroom was empty. That was a relief. That was the worst room to fall in, with its cold tiles and hard edges.

What was that? She whipped her head around and strained her ears. A tiny thump from Esther's old room.

"Gran, I'm coming." She rushed down the hall.

Gran was behind the door, sprawled on the floor, her left leg twisted at a grotesque angle. Her skin colour blended in with the pale carpet.

"Oh, Gran." Rachel dropped to her knees beside her. "What happened?"

"I tripped." Her grandmother grimaced. "Think I've broken my other hip."

Rachel had to dip her head to even hear Naomi's reply.

"How long have you been here?" Rachel's hands shook as she smoothed the hair on her grandmother's clammy forehead.

Gran drew in a quavering breath. "Just after lunch."

Rachel bit her lip to keep from dissolving in a puddle of tears. *Think. First things first.* Shock. That was first. She stood up. Her knees threatened to give way."I'll get you a blanket, then ring the ambulance."

It was bad luck that no one had used the bed for a while. There were no blankets on it, and the bedspread had been out of her grandmother's reach. She pulled a blanket off Gran's bed and brought it back to tuck around her.

"Don't leave me," Gran said in a near-whisper.

"I have to ring the ambulance. I'll be right back."

If Gran had broken her hip, which looked almost certain, then she'd need another surgery. Her weakening heart must mean there'd be more risk this time.

"Good girl. Thank you."

Rachel didn't feel good at all. She felt a failure. Gran had been weakening every month. Rachel had been thinking about decreasing her work hours and arranging for someone to be here during the other times, but she hadn't gotten on to the practical details. These things should have been her first priority.

No time for beating yourself up now.

Rachel stood and headed for the telephone. With a trembling

hand, she dialled the emergency number and gave the details of Naomi's name, age, condition and their address as if on automatic pilot.

She put the phone down. What next? *Open the front door.* She hurried to prop the door open, then returned to sit on the floor next to her grandmother. Rachel took her hand and stroked her finger over the back of Gran's hand. So frail, with all her rings hanging loosely.

Gran's eyes were dull with pain. *Lord, let the ambulance get here quickly.*

"Rachel, you need to be ready—" Gran took several shallow breaths "—in case I don't make it."

That was not what she wanted to hear. "Gran, the ambulance will be here soon."

"Dearie, I'm old, and ready to go home."

Rachel's eyes filled with tears.

"Don't be sad for me. God has answered all my major prayers." The corner of her grandmother's mouth lifted in what might have been a smile. "You and William were the greatest miracles."

Rachel put her grandmother's hand down and shifted her position on the floor. Five minutes had passed since she'd called the ambulance. It might take another fifteen.

Gran's eyes closed. Should she quickly pack a few overnight things?

"Gran?" Her grandmother didn't move.

Rachel's heart rate accelerated. She wanted to shake her grandmother to check she was still breathing, but it would cause too much pain. Instead, she leaned forward and put her cheek next to her grandmother's mouth. A tiny puff of air tickled her cheek. Rachel counted under her breath while she waited for another. Three, four, five. After two more breaths, Rachel stood and tiptoed out of the room. She hated to leave Gran, but there wasn't anyone else around to help.

There was a small bag at the bottom of her grandmother's wardrobe. She packed two nightdresses, some underwear, her Bible, notebook, and glasses, and then went to the bathroom to collect her grandmother's toothbrush, toothpaste, and other sundries.

Rachel zipped up the bag. It would have to do. She'd go in the ambulance if they let her. She'd better get her handbag as well—she'd probably have to catch a train home. And she needed to find her mother's phone number. She'd memorised the work one, but didn't know the Lord Howe number.

There was a groan from Esther's room.

"I'm coming, Gran," Rachel called. She left the two bags sitting on the floor handy to grab on their way out.

She took Gran's hand and checked her pulse. It was weak and erratic. *No, Lord. I'm not ready for this.*

Gran took a deep, shaky breath. "The important papers—" Two more little breaths. "Are in the top drawer of the filing cabinet."

Rachel wanted to plug her ears with her fingers, as if doing so would stop her ever needing to know this information.

A siren wailed, the sound increasing in volume as it got closer. The siren cut off. Rachel squeezed her grandmother's hand. "I'll let them in and shut up the house."

Gran's eyes were dull with pain. "But you'll come with me?"

"If they'll let me. Otherwise, I'll follow in the car. Don't worry, I'm not leaving you."

Rachel scrambled to her feet. Outside there were footsteps and a rattle of a gurney. This was getting ridiculous. Two ambulances in a month.

"Come in," Rachel called as she walked down the hall. "My gran is through here."

She held the door open. The two paramedics left the gurney outside the door and came in. She led them towards where her grandmother lay.

"Have you moved her?" the female paramedic said.

"No. She's in too much pain. I don't know how long she's been there, but it could be several hours."

The paramedics looked at each other, faces serious. "We'll give her some good pain medication before we move her."

The woman went around and knelt on the floor. "Mrs Macdonald, I'm Jill and that's Mike. Can you tell me what happened and point to where you're hurting?"

Rachel crossed her arms over her stomach. It didn't stop her shaking.

They took a quick medical history and Gran mumbled her answers. The paramedics reached into their medical box, pulled out some sterile packages, and proceeded to insert a needle near Gran's wrist. Rachel left the room and leaned against the wall to compose herself. She'd leave them to it and start locking up the house.

By the time they got Gran on the gurney, her colour had improved a fraction and her breathing had strengthened.

"Are you coming with us?" Mike said to Rachel.

"Can I?"

He nodded and raised the gurney. Rachel followed them out.

---

*T*he siren wailed as they turned onto a main road. Rachel squeezed into a corner as Jill worked to set up an IV. "Mrs Macdonald, you'll be dehydrated after all that time on the floor."

"Rachel?" Gran called, her voice only a loud whisper.

If Rachel leaned forward, she could just manage to touch her grandmother's free hand. All she wanted to do was grip it and never let go, but she contented herself with gently stroking it.

Her grandmother had her eyes closed.

"The painkillers are strong," Jill said. "She'll be drifting in and out of sleep for the next while."

"I presume she'll have x-rays?"

"Yes. She'll need them before any surgery."

"I was afraid she'd need surgery."

"Almost certainly, but surgery might not be until tomorrow."

Rachel kept stroking her grandmother's hand. "I guess it was silly of me to imagine she'd be wheeled straight in."

"No, not silly, but there is likely to be a queue. Waiting until tomorrow means we can get some fluids into your grandmother, and bring up her blood pressure. Are you going to be able to stay with her?"

Rachel nodded. "I'll have to ring my parents, but they're working on Lord Howe Island. I don't know when they'll be able to get here. It could be a few days."

Lord, get them here as fast as possible.

Even if it meant seeing William again, she'd do it. Gran would definitely want to see him.

———

*O*nce her grandmother was settled, Rachel went down to the hospital lobby to use the public phones. She'd phone Pete first. She still hadn't figured out how she'd phone her parents. She had no phone card. Probably just as easy to phone from home.

She dialled the work number. If Pete wasn't still in the office, it would switch through to his home phone. It rang a few times.

"Klopper's Nursery. Pete speaking."

His steady voice calmed her nerves.

"Pete, it's Rachel. I'm at the hospital."

He gasped. "Are you okay?"

"I'm fine; it's Gran." She gnawed her lip. She mustn't cry now, not with random strangers passing by. She turned her back on them. "She fell, and it looks as though she broke her other hip."

"Will she have surgery?"

"Not tonight, but maybe tomorrow. She's really weak." A tightness encircled her chest. "She keeps talking about heaven and telling me what to do if she dies."

Pete went silent at the other end of the phone line. Absorbing the news, praying, or wishing he didn't have to be involved?

"I don't think I'll be able to come into work tomorrow."

"Of course not. I wouldn't expect you to. Do your parents know yet?"

"No. I couldn't leave Gran once I'd found her. She was on the floor all afternoon." A wave of guilt washed over her.

"Have you got your car?"

She gripped the phone harder. "No. I came in the ambulance."

"Would it help if I drove over there?"

Would it? It had only been two hours, and already she was exhausted from too much emotion and multiple small decisions.

"I'm presuming you won't be at the hospital all night," he said.

"I'll be kicked out at eight." She'd have stayed if she could, but the hospital was strict about visiting hours. Anyway, her grandmother would need her rest if she was going to cope with the surgery to come.

"Would you like me to pick you up and take you home?"

Not having to walk the kilometre and a half to the train station sounded more than appealing. "Yes, please. If it's not too much trouble."

"Where shall I meet you?"

They arranged to meet in the front lobby just after eight. Rachel hung up, then called Gina. She'd also want to know what was happening.

Gina immediately offered to come over and stay the night, but it would have to be a little later in the evening, as she had guests.

Rachel didn't say no. Having someone at home might keep her mind off the fear burrowing in her heart that this might be it. That her grandmother might not make it.

CHAPTER 33

*R*achel jerked awake at five. It didn't seem right to have slept so well.

She stretched and yawned. *Jesus, help Gran to know you're with her. Help her not to be scared or lonely.*

Esther's diaries had revealed how hard it had been the last time Naomi fell. How difficult it had been to watch someone suffer and not be able to do anything about it.

Last night, Gina had turned up soon after Pete had driven Rachel home. Gina, being Gina, had insisted on fixing up the guest room for herself, then made hot chocolate for them all while Rachel rang her mother.

William and her mother were going to phone the airport when it opened at nine to see if there were any seats still available on today's flight. Then they'd phone Rachel to let her know what was happening. Hospital visiting hours started at ten, and Rachel would be waiting on the doorstep. She didn't intend to miss a single minute with her grandmother.

A bird sang outside the window. Gran would say it was a reminder that God was still in control. He who cared for the sparrow and the flowers would care for them. Rachel's throat constricted and she blinked away the hot tears pooling in her eyes.

It had been Gran who'd given Rachel a love for gardening. Her first attempts at mowing the lawn and potting plants had been laughable, yet look at her now.

But it wasn't just gardening that Gran had introduced her to. Nowadays, she got more pleasure from simple things like playing board games and looking at old photos. So different from her old life, which had seemed full but was really only a hectic pursuit of pleasure, beauty, and fitness to make up for the emptiness in her heart.

Her grandmother was a special person, someone who delayed judgement and had proved to be full of practical wisdom. A woman who knew that prayer changed things. Even before Rachel had become a Christian, she had sensed Gran prayed because she loved people and wanted the best for them.

Thank you Lord, for giving me this time with Gran.

Rachel moved her pillow against the bedhead and clasped her knees to her chest.

Pete hadn't stayed long last night, but he had led them in prayer, a prayer that was as good as a hug. She'd had to turn her head away so he wouldn't see her cry. How she'd survived so many years without friends like Pete and Gina was impossible to imagine. Friends who put themselves out for her. Friends who cared when she was hurting.

Pete had assured her he'd recruit his parents to pray—something she should be doing right now.

*R*achel was at the nurses' desk in Gran's ward by ten on the dot. She waved to gain attention and a nurse came over.

"Good morning. I'm Rachel, Naomi Macdonald's granddaughter. I'm wondering if there is any news about surgery."

"I'll get her nurse to come and talk with you."

Rachel stood and waited. The noticeboard next to her gave instructions on post-operative care. Would Gran walk as soon as the board said? Especially given she'd recently had a hip replacement on the other side.

The nurse arrived. "Are you Naomi's only relative?"

"Her son, William, is on Lord Howe Island. He's hoping to arrive here by tomorrow evening."

The nurse wrote in her notes. "And William is your father?"

Rachel nodded. Strange, but sometime recently she'd begun to acknowledge William again as 'father'.

The nurse was asking another question. No time for Rachel to consider the implications of her softening on the issue of how she referred to William.

"Naomi has listed you as her next of kin."

A warmth spread through Rachel's chest. She hadn't expected that.

"Your grandmother has already had her x-rays, and the doctor will want to talk to you when he does ward rounds in the next hour or so. Will you be here?"

Rachel nodded before heading towards her grandmother's four-bed room. Two of the beds were obviously being used but their occupants must be elsewhere.

Her grandmother's skin was no longer papery-white. Rachel leaned in and kissed her cheek. It was smooth and soft, like the ultra soft tissues Gran always bought. "Did you get any sleep?"

"More than I expected. Having a catheter makes things easier, and the nurses packed pillows around me to prevent me moving accidentally."

Not moving prevented one problem, but lying still couldn't be good for someone her grandmother's age.

"Last time I had surgery, I had to do regular deep breaths to avoid chest infections. I've been trying." Gran demonstrated, but her deep breath wasn't what Rachel would call deep, and Gran winced a little, as though she was holding back because of the pain.

"Mum called this morning. If the weather holds, they'll be on tomorrow's flight from Lord Howe and will be here around dinner time."

"That's good news, dearie." Gran patted the bed gently. "Can you put the side of the bed down and sit close to me? I've had a long snooze and I'm drugged up."

Rachel fiddled with the knobs until the side of the bed folded down, then pulled her chair as close as she could.

"Glad you're here. Wanted to talk." Gran closed her eyes.

Rachel waited.

Her grandmother's eyes opened. "First, I wanted to thank you for this last year."

"Thank me?" Rachel's breath caught in her throat. "It's I who should be thanking you. Without you, I would have been a mess." Gran's place had been the home she'd never had.

"You've gone well beyond the call of duty," Gran said.

"I've been beating myself up for not doing enough." Rachel touched her grandmother's arm.

"You've done plenty. I know you come home as soon as you can in the evenings. There are plenty of other things you could be doing."

It had been a privilege.

Footsteps approached the doorway of the room. A lady wearing a pink apron approached, bearing a blooming purple-blue hydrangea.

"Delivery for you," the woman said with a warm smile.

"Absolutely beautiful," Gran said. "Rachel, would you open the card?"

Not that Rachel needed to. She'd been selling dozens of pots of these same flowers for the last month. She opened the envelope and read it.

DEAR NAOMI, THESE FLOWERS COME WITH MANY PRAYERS FOR YOUR RECOVERY. YOURS IN CHRIST, PETE, DIRK, AND NORMA KLOPPER.

Rachel blinked back tears. Wonderful, wonderful man. The kind any woman in her right mind would be honoured to know and be loved by. He deserved the best.

"How kind," Gran said. "I've often thanked God for leading you to the nursery."

Rachel moved the flowers so her grandmother could see them without much effort. She had a sneaking suspicion she knew what Gran wanted to talk about.

Rachel sat down again. The one advantage of Gran being forced to lie flat and stare at the ceiling was that Rachel could avoid eye contact.

"Rachel, I wanted to talk to you about—" Gran said.

There was a chatter of voices outside the door, and a small group of doctors walked into their room, nurses in tow.

"This is Naomi Macdonald and her granddaughter, Rachel," the nurse said.

The doctor nodded to Rachel and smiled at Naomi. "Sorry to have you back here—twice in as many years." He flipped back a page in the notes. "According to the notes from your previous visit, your last lot of rehabilitation went reasonably well."

"I'm not sure I'd give me a pass mark, young man. I went from being able to live alone to needing a walking stick and family living with me."

"Yes, the whole ageing thing isn't much fun." He ran his finger down the notes in front of him. "I'm a little concerned about your recent heart issues. They're not serious on their own, but combined with surgery, they might be." He glanced towards Naomi. "If this were an optional surgery, I'd recommend against it. But the x-ray showed a clear break, and we can't leave you with a broken hip."

Rachel drew in a sharp breath. She'd been concerned too, but worry was harder to avoid after hearing what the doctor had to say. She wasn't ready for anyone else in her family to die.

"You're saying I might not come through the surgery."

The nurse beside him looked at the floor, and he tightened his lips. "It wouldn't be right for me not to tell you the risks."

Gran gave him a crooked smile. "It's okay. I'm prepared. My life's in God's hands, and I won't be upset if I go home to him. It has to happen sometime soon."

He didn't even blink. He'd probably heard all manner of things from patients.

Rachel tightened her lips to prevent herself laughing out loud at her grandmother's words. Esther had written in her diary that Gran had said something similar to her doctors last time.

"You should be able to go into surgery at four."

"And I'll remember to do deep breaths to keep my lungs in tip-top shape," Naomi said.

"Exactly. I can tell you've done this before." He handed the notes to the nurse and led the group to the door.

Her grandmother patted the bed beside her. "They'll give me more pain relief soon, and then I'll be gaga. I need to talk to you about your father."

"I know, Gran, and I know what you want to say. You want me to forgive him."

"Yes, dearie. I'm tempted to ask you to do it for me, but that would be wrong. You need to do it for yourself." She reached for Rachel's hand. "The cost of not forgiving him is too high."

Rachel sighed.

"If we keep saying no to God, then it gets easier and easier to do so. But the more we say yes, the easier it gets. Like a muscle getting stronger."

Gran wasn't telling her anything new, but oh, she didn't want to hear this. Rachel's shoulders tensed, and it was hard to breathe. Forgiving her father seemed to imply that what he'd done was all right. Acceptable. But it wasn't. Fathers were supposed to love and encourage and protect their children, not make their life a constant comparison game.

"If we refuse to forgive, eventually we might not want to read the Bible or be around Christians, because it will make us too uncomfortable."

Rachel's cheeks burned. Twice this week, she'd deliberately skipped Bible passages referring to forgiveness. Her father had cut Gran out of his life for decades because she'd dared to tell him the truth. How ironic if Rachel kept her father out of her life and, in so doing, became like the person she most hated.

"Gran, I can see forgiveness is important, and I can't deny that God thinks so, but how do I do it? How can I make myself want to forgive?"

Gran squeezed her hand. "There are many things in life we don't feel like doing. I don't much feel like having surgery today, but I will go through with it because I hope for a good outcome. Sometimes we have to choose to obey. It can be a long process of making the same choice again and again. Eventually feelings follow."

Her grandmother's words made sense. There were many things in life like that. Rachel seldom wanted to exercise, but she did it because exercise was good for both her body and her emotional well-being.

"We often demand joy first, but joy is the result of obedience. First, choose to forgive. The more you choose forgiveness, the more you'll feel like forgiving."

"Gran." Rachel's throat constricted, and she had to take a few breaths before she could speak. "Sure, I want that lovely forgiveness feeling, but forgiving him seems so unfair. Why should he get off scot-free?"

"Do you really think he gets off scot-free? Hasn't he already paid a high price for his choices?"

"What price did he pay? It was me paying the price." The words spewed out of her mouth.

"Dearie. He has paid in the loss of his daughter. He didn't get to see you grow up. Your father has many regrets. He has to live knowing he dishonoured Jesus for years and led many people away from God." A tear trickled down a runnel in Gran's cheek. "Sometimes forgiving ourselves is the hardest thing. He's mentioned his guilt and regret several times in his letters."

"I didn't know he wrote to you."

"He's been writing every week. I assumed you wouldn't want to hear about it."

That was news. Her father had always been a man who lived in the moment and passed off humble tasks like writing non-essential letters to others. The evidence that Jesus had indeed changed his heart was continuing to pile up.

"Rachel, I'm going to have a snooze. Can you stay?"

"I'm planning on staying as long as they'll let me, and I brought your hymn book. I'll sing a few for you while you rest."

---

*G*ran had been asleep for ninety minutes. Rachel had sung her way quietly through the hymns she knew. The ones she didn't, she'd read out aloud as poems. She'd have to do this more often—there was such depth in the words. The hymn writers were like the psalmists, aware of the complexities and difficulties of life, yet still choosing to focus on Jesus.

Jesus, I need you now. I wish Mum was here. And she wished her father wouldn't have to come too. She was nowhere near ready to deal with him, not on top of everything else. But she could at least be polite. Politeness wouldn't kill her.

Her grandmother groaned and opened her eyes.

"Gran, I'm still here." She reached and took Gran's hand again.

"I was having a beautiful dream about Esther."

Rachel shivered. Gran would get annoyed at her if she attached any superstitious meaning to the dream. She stroked her grandmother's hand.

"Darling girl, I have to go sometime. When I was young, I dreaded the thought of death, but now I'm rather excited. I do so want to see Jesus." A pale pink flush stained her cheeks. "And so many of my friends are waiting for me."

"I can't even imagine what meeting Jesus will be like," Rachel said.

Gran smiled a smile of such sweetness that Rachel's breath caught in her throat. Maybe once she'd followed Jesus as long as Gran had, her hunger to finally see him would be greater than her desire to stay here. The last entries in Esther's final diary had said something similar. Maybe Jesus and his kingdom became more and more tangible as this earth faded.

Rachel leaned forward and put her forehead on the bed. Gran smoothed her hair. "They'll come to take me to the operating theatre soon. Will you pray for me?"

Rachel blinked. Pray for Gran? How could she pray for someone who was so far ahead spiritually?

Rachel sat up straight. "I'll do my best, Gran."

"Your best will be more than adequate, dearie."

Rachel took a deep breath. "Dear Jesus, thank you that you are here with us. Especially thank you that you're here with Gran, helping her cope with the pain." Her voice wobbled. "Thank you for the medical staff, and that we live in a country with a good health system. Thank you that Gina was able to come and stay with me."

The more Rachel thanked God, the more she was able to believe Jesus was in control.

"Thank you that you know what you're doing. We'd prefer that Gran bounces back from this operation, but even ..." A tear trickled down her cheek. "Even if she doesn't, and even if your plan is something different, help us to trust you." Another tear leaked out, and another. "Thank you for these last months. Gran has been such a gift to me. Thank you for all her wise advice, and thank you for what you're doing in our f-family ..." Rachel swallowed, unable to say any more.

"In Jesus' name, Amen." Naomi ended the prayer.

The nurse arrived to give the painkiller and Rachel leaned forward to whisper in her grandmother's ear. "You do know how much I love you, don't you Gran?"

Her grandmother smiled. "I sure do. My heart is chock-full of thankfulness. It's like that phrase in the Bible: the years the locust has eaten, you've restored to me."

Rachel couldn't recall the phrase, but she could picture a locust-ravaged field. No green thing left.

"God has restored to me nearly everything I prayed for, and I'm going to trust him for the rest."

The rest was Rachel's restoration with her father. From her vantage point, it seemed a miracle too far even for God. She'd have to see William tomorrow.

The dull headache was back, throbbing behind her left eye socket. William. God would have to give her the strength, because she was running on empty.

CHAPTER 34

*T*he next evening, Rachel hurried downstairs to the main foyer of the hospital and threw her arms around her mother. "I'm so glad you're here."

Her mother hugged her back. "We came as fast as we could. How is she?"

"Not good." Rachel choked up. She broke out of the hug and pulled a clean tissue out of her pocket. "She still hasn't regained consciousness."

The doctor had said that Gran had a stroke during surgery.

"I'm sorry you've had to handle this on your own."

Rachel clutched the tissue. "I haven't been on my own. Gina and Pete have been great."

Pete had dropped in at the hospital yesterday late afternoon and stayed with her while Gran was in surgery. He'd gone and found her something to eat and practically force-fed her. He'd been there when the doctor explained what had happened during the surgery and then he'd followed her car home to make sure she got there safely.

Gina was still staying over and had rung the church prayer

chain coordinator. The pastor had already been in this morning to pray for Naomi and Rachel.

"I'm guessing there's a limit to the number of visitors," her mother said.

Rachel held up two fingers. If she talked, she cried. Since last night, a headache had encircled her skull with a tight band.

"Why don't you and I go in first. When William comes in from paying the taxi driver, I'll go in again with him."

Gran lay on her back in the bed, her face almost unrecognisable with its flatness of expression. Tubes and lines were attached to many parts of her body. Alien things. Fearful things.

"The nurses said we should talk to her and assume she can hear," Rachel said.

Her mother moved to the head of the bed and took her mother-in-law's hand. "Naomi, it's me, Blanche." She checked over her shoulder.

Rachel understood—talking to someone who couldn't respond didn't feel quite right.

"William and I just arrived from Lord Howe. William will be in soon to talk to you. We've booked in to a motel right next to the hospital so we can be here at any time."

Rachel had been relieved they hadn't asked to stay with her. Her mother would have been welcome, but having her father around would have been more than difficult. Gina said she would keep staying with Rachel until she wasn't needed. Whenever that might be.

Rachel glimpsed her father peering through the glass section of the ICU door. She took a deep breath. She could do this.

She pointed towards the door and mouthed, 'William' at her mother. He may as well come in now. Rachel headed out the door to the waiting area.

William was pacing up and down, muttering to himself. He

turned and saw Rachel. He gave a lopsided smile and then caught himself. "Hi. How is she?"

He sounded as awkward as she felt.

"You can go in now," Rachel said. "Mum is talking to Gran."

His whole face lit up. "Oh, is she conscious?"

She hadn't intended to be cruel. "No, but the nurses encouraged us to talk to her. They hope it might wake her up."

The hope appeared to drain out of him like water out of a bath.

"Right then, I'll go in." He stumbled once before he reached the swinging doors and pushed them tentatively.

Poor man. Rachel's sense of pity surprised her.

Jesus, I'm going to need some help here. Heal Gran and help me to be kind to William, even though I don't feel like it.

She couldn't pray anything else. Gran would have asked her to pray she'd go peacefully if that was God's will, but Rachel couldn't pray that. Some things were too hard.

---

*O*n the third morning after her grandmother's surgery, the home phone rang at eight. Rachel's hand trembled as she picked up the handset.

"Rachel, it's Mum."

The breakfast she'd just eaten threatened to come up. Gina hovered in the doorway, gnawing her lip.

"The hospital just rang and said she's worse. They've asked us to come in as soon as we can."

A pulse beat in her neck. *Oh, Gran.* "I'll be there as quickly as I can."

She put the phone down and stared at the floor.

Gina walked over to her and put a hand on her shoulder. "Has she gone?"

Rachel shook her head, throat tight and tears prickling her lashes. "Not yet, but she's worse. The hospital asked us to go in."

"Can I drive you?"

A heaviness weighed Rachel down. She nodded and went to get her bag. She checked her wallet automatically and added a book— something she could use to avoid talking to her father if they were hanging around all day. Not that she'd have the concentration to read anything.

---

*H*er mother was waiting at the hospital entrance. Rachel stopped, took a steadying breath, and walked into her hug.

"Too late?" she asked in a whisper.

"She just took a few breaths, sighed, and slipped away."

Rachel buried her face near her mother's neck. "Oh, Mum."

Blanche stroked her hair. "It was so peaceful. A lovely way to go."

"Lovely for her," Rachel whispered. The scab over the gaping hole left by Esther's death had ripped open again. How many more times was she going to have to do this?

She took a shuddering, sobbing breath and looked back over her shoulder. Gina was still standing there. "Sorry, Gina. I forgot all about you."

"That's totally understandable. I'm so sorry. We're all going to miss her. Naomi was a wonderful woman of God."

Why were there so few variations on how people could express their empathy? If Esther's death was any indication, she'd hear almost identical words over and over in the next few days until she'd want to scream. Scream at the tediousness of it. Scream at the emptiness and loss. Scream at the pain left behind.

Gina might not be family, but she'd known Gran almost as long as she had. Rachel pulled Gina into a group hug. "Thanks, Gina, for bringing me here." Stupid words. Mere noise.

The three of them broke out of the hug and Gina reached into her ever-handy bag, pulled out a packet of tissues, and handed them round.

They grinned foolishly at each other and blew their noses.

"Are you going to be okay driving, Gina?" her mother asked.

"I'll probably have a little cry and pray for you all. Then I'll head to work."

"We'll appreciate the prayers, especially for William," her mother said.

A tiny stab of sympathy pierced Rachel's heart, but she pushed the emotion away.

Gina swung around and headed back in the direction of her car. How Rachel wished she could go with her instead of dealing with the monstrous to-do list that stretched in front of them. She took a deep breath and tucked her mother's arm under hers.

CHAPTER 35

*P*ete had only known Rachel a little over a year. It felt much longer. In the last year, she'd come to know Jesus, been baptised, seen her sister die, and now here they were again. At a funeral, at the same church where they'd farewelled Esther.

There were about a hundred people spread out around the room. Someone like Naomi deserved more, but most of her contemporaries were gone. Those here today were either members of this church or people like Pete and his dad, here to support the Macdonald family.

He craned his head to look towards the front row. He'd met Blanche before, but William was a total stranger. Knowing how Rachel felt about William, it must be awkward having to sit on the same pew with him. But what else could she do?

Lord, let Naomi's death be a means of restoring relationships within her family. That was her heart's desire, and it's what you desire too. Help Rachel to get through today, and help our being here today to be a support.

Pete looked down at the order of service. The cover showed a beautiful photo of Naomi as an older woman on her back verandah, surrounded by hanging baskets of flowers. He turned the folded A4 sheet over to look at the back. Photos of Naomi on her wedding day, one with two primary-school aged sons, and a final one as a middle-aged woman.

The eulogies would be given by William and Rachel. *Oh Lord, give her courage.*

The same pastor who'd conducted Esther's funeral led them through the songs and began his sermon. Pete and his father were six rows behind the Macdonalds. He was acutely aware every time Rachel cried.

Several times Rachel and Blanche clutched each other's arms. Blanche was caught in the middle, because at times she also held William's hand. He must be feeling rotten. So recently reconciled with his mother, now losing her again.

The pastor finished his sermon and gestured to William, who walked up to the small podium and laid down some notes. He was a suavely handsome man. Grey suit, crisp white shirt, and a discreet tie. His tan was presumably natural, given he'd spent several months on Lord Howe Island.

William took a deep breath and let his shoulders sink before he lifted his head. "Naomi June Macdonald. My mother." His Adam's apple jerked. "I really have no right to be standing up here talking about her. It should be one of you, her friends. Most of you have never even met me. It's a sad story and entirely my fault. I'll get to that, but first I want to tell you some of Mum's early story."

Pete had enjoyed listening to eulogies before Mai and the children died. They revealed many things about a person and what made them unique. Pete gripped his knees. Nowadays his heart ached for how much it cost anyone to stand up and speak about their loved one.

"My mother was born on the seventh of June, 1910, the eldest of four children, into a moderately well-off and progressive family. By progressive, I mean that she was encouraged to complete her schooling and attended secretarial college. It was considered radical at the time to train women who'd likely soon leave work to get married. Mum ended up as my father's private secretary. Sure enough, she did leave work shortly after they were married."

William waited until the laughter eased. "My parents attended church because that's what people of their class did, but Mum said she never heard the Bible taught clearly. Not like we've just heard from Steve." He nodded towards where the pastor was sitting off to the side.

"Mum ran the household, looked after my older brother and myself, and volunteered in different organisations." He reeled off an impressive list of charities.

"My parents lived in a big house in Hunters Hill and owned one of the first cars in the district. Dad played golf and went to work and his club. Ian and I were mostly raised by a nanny."

Pete was paying close attention to the family history. Maybe some of this was new to Rachel too.

"Losing Ian and my father so close together sent Mum into a severe breakdown. We didn't know much about mental health in those days, and I remember being mad because she didn't pay me any attention."

Pete shuddered. Depression in the years after the second world war? No thanks.

"Kids are selfish, and I wasn't any better or worse than most. I dealt with my grief by working hard and focusing on being a success. It didn't take long until my mother and I drifted apart. I was at boarding school most of the time and didn't know what my mother was going through."

William gripped the podium. "But God didn't abandon her. In his mercy, he sent the woman who'd replaced her as Dad's secretary, and that woman loved my mother into God's kingdom."

Pete could see the back of Rachel's head as she bent forward. *Oh,*

Lord, do a miracle. Rachel will never be free until she forgives him. Let her soar free.

"Some of you might know Naomi well enough to wonder how I even know some of this story. You're right. At the time, I didn't know. From the end of high school I avoided my mother and eventually cut her out of my life. It's only as we've been writing these last few months that I've discovered some of these details."

He pulled a handkerchief out of his pocket and wiped his eye.

"Please don't be a fool like I was. Family is too precious to ignore."

Was Rachel listening? *Lord, help her not to break down or walk out. Help her to hear any useful things William says.*

"My mother was a special woman. She loved me enough to warn me about the consequences of some of my choices. I refused to listen." He peered around at his listeners. "We need people in our lives who speak the truth. Honour them by listening. I didn't, and it led to years of pain and regret." He gripped the pulpit. "But no matter how I treated her, my mother never gave up. She is an example to all of us of faithful, persevering prayer. She didn't just pray for us to be reconciled. More importantly, she prayed that I would be reconciled to God."

Blanche blew her nose in the front row and Rachel put an arm around her shoulders. Rachel's estrangement from William had to have impacted her relationship with her mother.

"And my mother was the kind of woman who persevered until God answered. Then she was waiting to welcome me home. No grudges, no 'I told you so,' no emotional distance to punish me." He covered his eyes and his shoulders shook.

Lord, help him finish.

"My mother is a model to all of us. Of prayer, of forgiveness, of doing the tasks God put in front of her. She could so easily have complained, or withdrawn. Instead, she chose to use her life to bless others. How many are here today because Naomi taught you English and helped you adjust to Australia?"

At least a quarter of the people raised their hands. Like Pete, Rachel had swivelled to look around. When she saw him and his dad, she gave a tight smile and a little nod. Did that mean she was happy to see him? He hoped so.

"Naomi June Macdonald." William gulped. "Mum. Thank you for being an example of what it means to follow Jesus. Because of your prayers, I'll be seeing you again."

He folded up his notes and put them into his pocket before walking back to the front row. Blanche whispered to him and kissed his cheek.

Pete gazed at his feet, a lump in his throat. Like Blanche, Mai had been his greatest cheerleader. He looked up. Rachel was already at the podium. He couldn't stand next to her, but he could pray. *Lord, she looks so pale. Stricken. Help her to say something honouring to you.*

"Thanks for telling us something of Gran's background." Rachel nodded in William's direction.

Her lip trembled and Pete gripped the edge of his seat.

"I'm going to say a few words of what Gran meant to me as a granddaughter." She clenched her teeth and leaned against the podium, head down. "Gran only had two granddaughters. As you know, we … we lost Esther."

Help her, Jesus, Pete prayed.

"It's been a tough year. One really tough year." Her voice wobbled. "But Gran—" She began to cry. "Sorry—"

If only he could jump to his feet and go and wrap his arms around her, but it was impossible. *Lord, help.*

Footsteps creaked across the old floorboards. *Thank you, Lord.*

Gina headed for the front with a glass of water and tissues. She handed Rachel the glass and whispered something. Then she leaned into the microphone. "Rachel's written down what she wanted to say in case I have to read it, but she wants to have a go at saying it herself."

There was an affirming murmur and nods from everyone. Rachel took a good gulp of water and stood up straight. Gina sat down behind her.

"Twice in my life, Gran took me in, no questions asked. When I turned up nearly eighteen months ago, I tested all Gran's patience. She showed me what it means to love others and demonstrate grace. I was a horrible house guest, but she never said a cross word. She never complained that I didn't do anything to help her, and she never made me feel unwelcome. Maybe she remembered what it was like to have a breakdown."

Rachel hesitated.

Come on, Rachel, you can do it.

"Gran was a trooper." She gave a weak laugh. "One grand-daughter with cancer and one who didn't want to talk to anyone, but Gran just kept loving us and praying for us. What I especially appreciated was that she didn't talk about Jesus in those first few months. She just revealed Jesus through her actions."

The corner of her mouth quirked.

"Gran would never claim to have been an evangelist, but in the end her methods had a huge impact on me, and I became a Christian."

Rachel had kept her eyes down for most of the eulogy but suddenly she raised her chin. "I know it is odd for someone my age to be living with their grandmother, but it has been a real privilege. A privilege to see what it means to age gracefully. Gran showed me what it means to follow Jesus step by step. I'll always be thankful for that. I'm thankful too, that she used her last words to urge me to obey Jesus more. I've still got a long way to go, but if I can be anything like she was, then I'll be happy."

Rachel turned and hugged Gina.

She'd done it, and Pete was proud of her. Now that the service was over, he had a task to do for Rachel. She'd rung yesterday and asked him to make sure William didn't feel out of place, since he'd know almost no one at the funeral.

His heart clenched. Rachel's request for him to care for someone that she struggled to even look at proved she was Naomi Macdonald's granddaughter.

CHAPTER 36

*R*achel drove to work the following Tuesday morning. Before she'd got in the main door, Josh enveloped her in a big hug, nearly knocking her over.

"I'm so happy you're back," he said.

Her father had headed back to Lord Howe Island after the funeral, but her mother had stayed a few extra days. From tonight, Rachel would have to get used to living on her own again. Although, it might not be for long. She was praying about whether to ask Gina to share somewhere with her.

"Miss Rachel, Miss Rachel, it's you and me today." Josh gave a little skip.

Rachel chuckled. He did like working with her, but the mulching machine was probably the bigger attraction. The noise and the fact that he was trusted to do it never failed to give Josh a thrill. She was there to do the actual pruning and make sure he didn't get too excited and become careless. So far, he'd always justified Dirk's faith in him.

She high-fived his raised hand. "Let's get the barrow and shears, and make a start."

"And the mulcher." His eyes shone.

She grinned. "Don't worry. We won't forget your favourite machine."

"It makes such a nice roaring noise as it gobbles up the branches."

And it was so much easier to end up with a pile of mulch than with heaps of unwieldy branches.

Both were soon equipped with heavy leather gloves.

"Let me first get a good heap of branches before you run the machine," Rachel said. "You might love the noise, but I don't."

He capered on the spot. "Okay, Miss Rachel. Mr Pete asked me to take special care of you today."

A tingly warmth crept up her neck and she turned away so Josh wouldn't see it and comment. Pete had been so brother-like over the last ten days that she'd decided they had no chance. But he had done as she'd asked and stuck with her father at the tail end of the funeral. Maybe that had significance. Or then again, maybe not.

It only took two hours to mulch the entire heap of branches, and she kept a wary eye open for snakes.

"Okay, let's clean and clear away the machine. Then Sam and Dave can come with their wheelbarrows and put the mulch around the plants that need it."

The two guys already had their instructions. She and Josh could get back to weeding. Weeding was the right task for today. Brainless and undemanding.

They cleaned the machine and Josh took its handle. "Okay, Josh, let's go."

They went via the storage shed to drop off the mulcher and then towards the area where they'd be working. The pots that needed weeding were on a raised table. Hooray for no bending. Josh went down one side, and Rachel took the other.

"I liked your grandmother," Josh said when they were a quarter of the way down the row.

"So did I." Josh hadn't been at the funeral. Lyn had been afraid he might get upset and overexcited. It was only another week until Josh and his parents left for the Perth competition.

"She was fun." He snickered. "She laughed a lot at my party."

Rachel's throat narrowed. That was the last outing they'd had.

"Mum says she's in heaven now."

"That's right, Josh. One day, you and I will be there too."

"I can't wait. In heaven, I'll be able to do everything."

She looked across at him. "Does it bother you? Not being able to do everything?"

He stopped weeding with one hand in the air. "No, not really, but I don't like being laughed at."

"Nobody likes being laughed at."

"That's why I like Special Olympics. No one laughs at me there."

"They only laugh with you, and that's okay, isn't it?"

He nodded and pulled out some more weeds. "I like laughing."

"And you're good at it. Even better, you help other people laugh."

He put his head to one side. "I think there'll be lots of laughing in heaven."

She'd had one dreadful year being bullied at school. Josh had probably had it much worse.

"Josh, what did you do when people laughed at you?"

He rubbed his nose. "What Mum and Dad told me to do."

"And what was that?"

"To smile and walk away, even if I didn't want to smile." He grinned. "Sometimes I wanted to hit them, but Dad said that wouldn't make Jesus happy."

Josh was a strong guy. If he'd hit people, it could have ended badly. He'd probably have been smashed to a pulp himself.

"Jesus forgave people who hurt him," Josh said. "So that's what I did." He smeared dirt across his forehead and sighed. "Jesus gave me a lot of practice."

"Did you ever refuse to forgive people?"

Josh pursed his lips. "I didn't want to forgive Philip." His jaw clenched. "He was at my first job and he was mean. Really mean. I told Mum and Dad that I couldn't forgive him. They told me a story."

"Do you remember which story?"

He nodded. "Yep. One about the man who couldn't pay back the money." Josh spread his arms wide. "He owed more than years and years of money that I get for working here. The king forgave him. Then he went and got mad at someone who owed him a little bit of money. Threw him into prison."

This story had been going around Rachel's head for days, along with the phrase, 'Forgive us our sins as we forgive those who sin against us.' The more she held on to her anger and insisted it wasn't fair that her father be forgiven, the more God's words pursued her. Those who crucified Jesus didn't deserve any mercy, yet Jesus still pleaded that they be forgiven. William hadn't deserved forgiveness any more than they had, yet God chose to forgive.

Rachel took a drink. "Did the story help you forgive Philip?"

He nodded. "Yep, but Mum and Dad said I shouldn't work there anymore." He beamed. "And soon after, I got a job here." He pulled more weeds. "I hope I can stay here forever."

"I think Mr Pete and Mr Dirk want you to as well."

He stood up tall. "Yeah, they're good people. They wouldn't let anyone hurt me."

Gina would say Rachel was crazy to turn a man like Pete away. She hadn't done it because she wasn't interested in him. She'd done it for his sake. And, because she was afraid. Afraid he'd be disappointed once he really got to know her. Afraid she wouldn't be able to give him everything he deserved.

They worked steadily down the row. When they finished, they stood, stretched, and had a long drink of water. "Looks good, doesn't it, Josh?"

"I like weeding."

She did too. Such a simple task, but it gave a sense of satisfaction. The sort of satisfaction that comes after making a delicious meal or leaving a bathroom squeaky clean.

They started on the next row. "How are you enjoying soccer?"

He gave a thumbs up. "Are you still coming, Miss Rachel?"

Everyone would understand if Gran's death meant she pulled out of the trip, but she'd prayed with her mother about the trip and Mum had urged her to go.

"Wouldn't miss you playing, Josh."

She'd never been to Western Australia. If this trip had been before Josh's birthday party, she'd be more than excited. But spending so many days close to Pete. Could she do it? And she'd been looking forward to meeting Binh, if only because Pete raved about him.

But perhaps Binh wouldn't want to meet her. Not after how she'd treated Pete. But then again, he might be relieved she was now only Pete's friend. There was no longer any possibility she'd replace his daughter.

CHAPTER 37

*P*ete yawned as he came downstairs. It had been a late night after a busy workday and then a five-hour flight. Ian had collected them in a rental car at midnight.

Lyn already had breakfast on the table, and Ian was sitting ready to eat. Lyn smiled a welcome. "This is such a great place. There's no way we could have both come if your friends hadn't been so generous."

"It was lucky I heard that they were going overseas and they hadn't loaned it to anyone else." Pete pulled out a chair and sat down. "How is Josh coping with the excitement?"

"Since the first game was played, he's had a wow of a time," Ian said, sipping his coffee.

Josh and his parents had arrived four days ago, and Josh's team had already defeated Tasmania and Victoria. This afternoon they'd play against the much tougher Western Australian team.

Rachel strolled in, somehow looking fresh and alert, despite the lack of sleep.

Lyn went into the hallway. "Josh, breakfast is ready," she called up the stairs.

"Coming, Mum." He thumped his way down the stairs, slid on his socks across the wooden floor, and threw his arms around Rachel. "You're here. I didn't hear you arrive."

"I'm not surprised. I expect you slept heavily with all the exercise you're doing. Are you having fun?"

He nodded vigorously and came over to high-five Pete. "You coming this afternoon?"

"Wouldn't miss it. Must see our star player in action."

Josh's smile stretched so wide his skin should have cracked.

"Rachel and Pete are going cycling first," Ian said. "They'll meet us at the sports field in time to watch your game."

"Ooh," Josh said, "You going on a date?"

Rachel flushed but managed to answer, "Josh, you know how you and I are friends? When we go out it isn't a date, is it? Well, Pete and I are friends too."

Good deflect, Rachel.

"Sorry," Lyn mouthed at Pete.

Pete gave a casual wave. Josh's comments never had any spite behind them. He had no idea of the undercurrents beneath the comfortable surface of Pete and Rachel's friendship. Rachel bowed her head and closed her eyes for a few moments before looking up and serving herself some muesli and tinned peaches.

Lord, you know I hope Rachel reconsiders her answer, but thanks for the peace you've given me about the whole thing.

Was Pete torturing himself by coming to Western Australia with Rachel and spending a whole week together? Others would say so, but his friendship with Rachel had remained relatively bump-free despite her rejection of his pursuit of a deeper relationship.

Her response had certainly rejuvenated his prayer life. God must get so frustrated with people. Forgetting him for long periods of time when life was smooth. Or ignoring him, even sulking, when life was painful, and only talking to him when they wanted something. It wasn't how Pete would want to be treated.

*P*ete stood on the drive and pumped up the bike tires. His friend had told him to help himself to their bikes. The family were avid riders, so the bikes were all a decent quality.

"Would you be able to look in the garage for a helmet for yourself? I don't need one as I brought my own. There should also be some cycle bags so we can carry the picnic."

Rachel headed back into the garage and came out a few minutes later with the required items.

He screwed the tire valves on and stood up straight. "Almost ready?"

"Be with you in five," Rachel said. "You stow the lunch, and I'll fill the water bottles."

The bikes had easily adjustable seats, and it took only a moment to get them right.

"Ready to go?"

"Right or left out of the street?" Rachel said over her shoulder as she sailed past him.

"Right," he called, setting off after her.

The timing for this week had worked perfectly. In the end, they'd closed the nursery for the planned upgrades. When Pete had worked as an accountant, organising holidays had been a somewhat simple case of booking a week or two off after month end. He was going to have to work out how to schedule breaks now he ran the family business. Rachel would soon be capable of running the place while he was gone. Although, if he had his way, she'd be with him on all his future holidays.

Please, Lord, change her heart.

Perth was a city made for cyclists. The Swan River wound through the centre of the city and was accessible along both banks.

Rachel said she hadn't cycled for years, but she set a good pace. He'd asked Ian to attach the bike rack to the car in case she'd had enough by the end of the soccer game and didn't want to cycle the five kilometres home.

"Left," he called as Rachel approached the bike path. They were only a kilometre from the river. Once on the riverbank, she'd see why he'd wanted her to experience the city from a bike.

He sped up to close the distance between his bike and Rachel's. "We'll turn right when we intersect with the river, but do feel free to stop any time you want to enjoy the view."

He sniffed the air, a mixture of sun on hot earth and eucalyptus. A smell that used to mean home. Would Mai have liked Rachel? The children would have, but Mai? Yes, of course she would. She'd have seen the hurts hidden out of sight and delayed judgment.

When he'd first met Rachel, she'd been prickly with anyone apart from his father and Josh. He was his parents' son, so he'd been polite, but she'd been too obviously a woman on the run.

The blue-grey river was hundreds of metres across, and sparkles of light danced off its surface. Rachel stopped her bike, pushed it off the path, and leaned it against the back of a wooden park bench. Scullers in two-, four-, and eight-man boats leaned into their strokes, heading upriver in a smooth unity of purpose. A motorboat puttered along nearby, and the river was dotted with kayakers, sailboats, and a smattering of hired rowboats.

"It's amazing," Rachel said, her face glowing with enthusiasm. "It must have been hard to leave here." She swallowed. "Sorry. Of course it was hard. Shouldn't have said anything."

"Yeah," Pete said with a slow nod. "But I'm glad to be reaching a new season where I'm ready to talk about my family." The reminder of them was a dull ache, tinged with love. "Mai and I often rode here before the children came along." They'd been unforgettable days. "We'd just started teaching Mark to ride a bike."

Rachel pointed skywards as a wedge of black swans flew overhead, plummeted down, and skidded to a stop on the water before sinking back to swimming elegance.

"We should see lots of other birds before the day is over."

"Where are we headed?"

"I'll show you." He pointed at the map on a metal board ahead of them. Rachel followed as he pushed his bike towards it.

He ran his finger along the planned route. "I was thinking we'd do this loop over Garratt Road Bridge right back to Narrows Bridge. It's a little over twenty kilometres, but it's mostly flat."

Rachel made no objection.

"There are other bridges, so we can cut the ride short if we're feeling tired."

She swung her leg back over her bike. "I'll see how I go."

Since it wasn't the weekend, the park was quite empty, and they could ride side by side. That way, he could point things out along the way.

They cycled on.

"This is one long series of parks," Rachel said. "Perfect for children."

Did Rachel still hope to have children? Not that Pete could raise the topic with things the way they were at the moment.

The sun warmed his shoulders, and they carved their way through the kilometres. Rachel declined the option of cutting the ride short.

"The bike path runs out up ahead. We'll go on back streets and cross Garratt Road Bridge." He sneezed. "We'll probably have to walk the bikes across."

"That'll give us time to admire the view," Rachel said. "I keep wanting to stop but don't want to do it too often."

"We'll stop for our picnic when we're closer to the city. Then we should easily make it to Josh's three-thirty game."

$\mathcal{S}$ hortly after twelve, they crossed Narrows Bridge and arrived back at Pete's favourite riverside park. He picked the spot with the best views of Kings Park and the city.

"I brought a small cloth to put the lunch on." Pete pulled it out of the pannier.

"That might allow us to finish eating before the ants and other creepy crawlies find the food," Rachel said with a laugh.

She'd breezed through the ride. He'd enjoyed pointing out some of the area's spectacular flowers, including banksia and both yellow and red kangaroo paw.

He sat down on the grass, in the shade of a tree. "Ahh, this is the life."

"It certainly is beautiful. I can see why you loved living here."

"Sydney is bigger and doesn't have the cycling infrastructure. Here in Perth, you're never far from a cycle path, beach, or the bush."

"Do you ever dream of coming back?"

"I couldn't leave Mum and Dad or the nursery now." Yet his heart was anchored here as well. Binh was equally a father to him, and he was all Binh had left. But that was a question for another day. Today he was here with Rachel, and he was going to make the most of it. "Would you be happy for me to thank God for the food?"

Rachel nodded.

Keeping his eyes open, he said, "Father, thank you for all your gifts. For great weather, great company, time to be away from work, and this food. Amen."

Rachel handed over his container of sandwiches. Corned beef and lettuce on crusty farm bread.

After he finished his first half, Pete asked, "How have you managed since the funeral?"

"I've been sitting here, feeling guilty because I'm enjoying myself. It's only been such a short time." He swallowed another mouthful of sandwich.

Rachel dabbed her eye with her shirt sleeve. "It feels like it's wrong to laugh, appreciate beauty, or enjoy the taste of food."

"From what I knew of Naomi, she'd want you to squeeze all the joy out of life."

Rachel reached for a carrot stick. "You're right. She told me almost exactly that before she died. But it will take time. Everything happened so suddenly. I'd hoped for a few more years." She sniffed. "I knew she was struggling with her health and I was already thinking about how I'd handle that—whether we should hire someone to stay with her during the day."

A line of pelicans on the edge of the river shuffled into the water and floated sedately by.

"The house was always going to feel empty." She munched her carrot stick. "Gina stayed with me the first week, and Mum was there a few days."

He knew nothing about Rachel's financial state, but she'd been living with her grandmother ever since he'd known her. "Is the house going to be sold?"

Rachel turned her head away from him. Oh no, maybe he'd overstepped the mark or trodden on a tender spot.

She was silent and then took a big breath, her shoulders rising and falling."No." Her voice shook. "Gran has given me the house."

Yes. He did an imaginary fist pump. No need to imagine her having to struggle and start again.

"Her will and the accompanying letter said my father already had enough. She'd planned to split her estate between Esther and myself, but rewrote her will after Esther died ..." Rachel's voice trailed off and she turned away from him. Again. This time she pulled up her knees and wrapped her arms around them.

How he longed to pull her into his embrace, but it was impossible. Not now, not when she was this vulnerable. Not when his action could send her fleeing in the opposite direction.

He got up and rummaged in the bike pannier. Somewhere in there he had a clean handkerchief. *There.* He pulled it out, walked across, and offered it to Rachel.

"Thanks." She used the handkerchief to wipe her eyes. "I still can't believe that the house is mine to do what I like with. When the doctors told us Gran might not make it—" She sniffed.

"The handkerchief's yours. Feel free to use it any way you like."

"I'm so ashamed, because I was worrying about where I'd live if she died. I'd already thought about renting somewhere with Gina."

She began to cry in earnest.

Now he'd done it, although it would probably do her good. He'd only seen her crying at the funeral. She'd always been rigidly in control at work. He'd followed the same regime, and all it had done was tie him in knots and plunge him into darkness. Rachel was not going to be left alone.

Not if Pete had anything to do with it.

CHAPTER 38

*R*achel followed Pete into the soccer stadium. They'd had no problem finding it. Now if only she could get through the game without any more embarrassing bouts of tears. Not that Pete had made her feel uncomfortable—far from it. He'd treated her like a sister, but without the hugs.

That was a good thing, wasn't it? She'd told him to back off, and he was respecting her wishes. So why did disappointment sit heavy in her chest? She shook herself. Stupid. Finally, a man who treated her with respect, and she still wasn't content.

"Here they come," Lyn said, gripping her arm.

The teams came onto the field from opposite sides, the Western Australian team running under a bright yellow-and-black banner, and New South Wales under a blue banner.

"There's Josh," Pete said.

He wasn't hard to see, bouncing every few steps like an energetic kangaroo, resplendent in his new uniform. He scanned the scaffold seating. Rachel raised her arm and waved the small blue flag they'd brought. Josh saw them and jumped up and down, waving both arms.

Lyn pointed to her eyes and then to the coach, to remind Josh to keep his mind on the game. He turned around and the players went into a team huddle.

"I worried this competition was going to overwhelm him," Ian said. "But he takes things in his stride and keeps telling me, 'It's only a game, Dad.'"

The whistle blew. Within seconds, Josh's team had possession of the ball and were dribbling it down the field. An opponent took it off the blue player and kicked it back, but Josh was there. He coolly stopped the ball, looked for one of his teammates, and sent it forward again.

Ian jumped out of his seat. "Way to go, son." He looked around and chuckled before sitting down again.

The ball went back and forth for the first half with each side scoring two goals. While the teams took a break, they all took the opportunity to walk and eat a snack before coming back to their seats.

"The problem is that the teams are evenly matched," Pete said.

"Yes, it's by far the best game we've seen," Ian replied. "Some of the early games were a bit of a romp in the park."

The whistle blew, and a short while later Josh's team took possession of the ball. Their passing was smooth and the ball moved up the field towards Josh.

Lyn held her breath, fingers gripping the bag on her lap.

Josh received the ball and dribbled it rapidly down the field, all his hours of practise coming together in one smooth series of movements.

"Go, Josh, go," Rachel muttered.

He approached the goalie's box and glanced round to check where the other players were. He never took the shot for himself if someone else was better placed.

The opposing team's goalie was bouncing side to side, hands ready.

Josh looked him in the eye, moved forward, and with a deft flick, kicked the ball at an angle. Pete had practised the exact move with Josh until he could score ninety percent of the time. The goalie didn't have a chance. The ball skidded past him and into the corner of the net.

Pete jumped out of his seat. "Way to go, Josh. Way to go."

Josh took a bow in their direction and Pete looked around at Rachel and winked. "Oops, got a bit excited and forgot not to distract him."

Rachel's face heated and she turned away and pretended she needed something from the bag on her far side. *Concentrate on the game, girl. Concentrate.*

*A*fter the game, Rachel stood near the team locker rooms with a crowd of the New South Wales team's friends and supporters.

There was the rumble of voices from behind the closed door, followed by a few cheers and running footsteps. The door opened and the players poured out. Josh was in the middle of the throng.

He rushed over to them, hugged his parents, and knocked fists with her and Pete. "Did you see me help with the third goal?" He pantomimed a kick.

"We certainly did, son," Ian said. "You and the team played very well. Excellent teamwork."

It didn't seem to matter to Josh that they'd lost when the other team scored two late goals. Now they'd be playing for the bronze medal.

Josh gave them a thumbs up. "Let's go home, I'm—"

"—hungry," Pete and Rachel chorused together.

Josh frowned. "How did you know?"

Pete chuckled. "You're always hungry."

*A*fter dinner, Pete drove south along the Kwinana Freeway heading for Binh's place in Mandurah. It was less than an hour's drive, but they'd be staying overnight. Of course, they could have gone in the morning, but Pete wanted as much time as possible there before Josh's next game.

Rachel idly looked out the window. Traffic was light, and there wasn't much to see in the darkness.

"Glad you came?" Pete asked. He didn't glance her way.

"You know, I am glad." She hadn't expected to be. She'd come because she didn't want to let Josh down, and cancelling tickets and chasing refunds would have been a huge hassle. It was easier to simply come.

Coming here had given her the time to process some of what had been happening. Western Australia felt like a different country, separated from the eastern cities by thousands of kilometres of seemingly empty space and vast deserts.

Desert. The word was in her mind because Gran's final letter to her, which accompanied her will, had mentioned the desert. She'd read the entire letter so many times she almost had it memorised. Each word written by a hand shaky with age, yet full of truth nonetheless.

You have been in desert times for decades. Arid years. Years of being parched and alone, but now you've met Jesus, the Water of Life. May he pour his life-giving water into your heart and bring about the promises of Isaiah 35 for you: 'The desert and the parched land will be glad; the wilderness will rejoice and blossom. Like the crocus, it will burst into bloom; it will rejoice greatly, and shout for joy.'

The imagery resonated somewhere deep inside her. Gran had been right; Rachel's heart had been a desert. Still was, in parts. *Oh, Jesus, please let me bloom again.*

She stared out at the dark silhouettes of trees racing by outside the car window. *Yes, Jesus, I know what stands in the way. My relationship with Dad.*

Pete said that Binh had learned to forgive far more than most people. Maybe his story could help her.

She flicked a glance towards Pete, driving at her side. And Pete? He hadn't given her the cold shoulder or made her feel embarrassed. In fact, he was rapidly becoming the best friend she'd ever had. She flushed in the darkness. This morning she'd dared to pray that she hadn't missed her chance. To believe that even when she hesitated to ask any more favours from God, he was a father who delighted in giving good gifts to his children.

CHAPTER 39

*R*achel tied her shoelaces and stepped outside to join Binh. The sun had been up for almost an hour, but the air still held a crisp coolness that would burn off later in the day. Pete had suggested Rachel join Binh on his daily walk so she could hear his story.

Now they strode along the footpath, on what Binh said was his regular route. A few runners passed them, and she could smell the salty tang of the sea.

"Pete always refused to tell me your story. Said it would be better coming directly from you." Rachel laughed. "I guess he assumed we'd meet."

"And now Josh's soccer has given you the opportunity to come here," Binh said, swinging his arms.

He might be short and wiry and twenty years older than she, but the man could move at a fast pace without puffing.

"It was a great excuse to visit Perth. I've never been here before."

They walked for a few more minutes before Binh said, "How much do you know about Vietnam and the war?"

"Not much. Only that the war happened when I was a kid. Australians fought there, and it was brutal, jungle warfare."

He nodded. "It was brutal and—like most wars—it was complicated. The conflict dragged on for twenty years. The north was supported by communists. The south was supported by countries like Australia and the USA. Eventually the communists won and the Western allies pulled out."

They reached the Halls Head coastal path and turned south. There were walkers moving in both directions, some strolling and others powering along. The sea stretched out to the horizon, a smooth sheet of blue with the gentle murmur of waves on the beach.

"I lived in a small village in the south of Vietnam. Our situation was relatively peaceful until the mid-sixties. By the time the war came to us, I was married with two children."

They passed two walkers with matching border collies.

"Our family was a lot better off than people in the capital. The village was too small to matter, and we survived by growing our own vegetables and keeping quiet." He sighed as though the weight of all the evils of war was on his shoulders. "But we couldn't avoid war forever. A stray bomb dropped onto the local school. Mai's older brother was one of seventeen children killed."

Rachel drew in a hissing breath.

"After that, things got harder. We had more children, but our third child died young and the new baby wasn't doing well." Binh kept walking. "All we wanted was peace to live our lives. Peace to let our children grow up and give them the best we could. A chance to study and a chance to be healthy."

Things so easy to find in Australia, yet hard to find in too many countries around the world.

Someone behind them trilled a bicycle bell, and they moved to the edge of the path.

"Rumours swirled around our village. Terrible stories about

chemicals falling like rain from the skies. Of children being stolen to fight. We were terrified. Terrified to stay, terrified to move. Where could we go? Our whole country was devoured by war."

Once again, he lapsed into silence. The sun twinkled off the sea.

"Some talked about fleeing to surrounding countries like Thailand, but going by land was impossible. Too many war zones to cross, with no guarantees that Thailand would accept us."

Pete had told her they'd escaped by boat.

"The least dangerous option was by boat, but where were we to find a boat? Even if we did, where were we to get the money?"

"We didn't know Jesus, so we presented offerings and incense at the temple. I begged the gods for mercy, but they took no notice. I'd almost given up when my wife came and told me the gods had answered our prayers. We had boat tickets."

Binh walked over to the lookout platform. "I usually turn around here, if that's okay with you."

"Of course." Rachel leaned on the railing alongside Binh. A few puffy clouds clumped far out to sea, but the rest of the sky was a bright blue.

"Look," Binh said, pointing. A back and fin arched, then another. "I see dolphins several times a week."

"This is a stunning place to live."

Binh turned to her with a smile. "Sometimes I think Vietnam was another life."

He turned and started walking back along the path they'd come on.

"I believed the gods had done a miracle for us." He shook his head. "Took my wife at her word, sold our possessions and land to a relative, and packed our things together. We loaded Mai, our baby son and our bags onto a small cart, and filled the cart with fruit to sell. Then we pulled it two days to the coast."

She could picture their fear. Fear of the children crying at the wrong time, or getting caught in a bombing raid, or being stopped. Terrible. And the story couldn't have a happy ending.

"We had an address for a supposed relative in the fishing village." Binh shrugged. "We weren't stopped, and once again I assumed the gods were protecting us."

A gentle breeze blew, lifting Rachel's hair as they walked back towards Binh's home. She'd seen pictures of Vietnam and an occasional documentary on the war. The boat people had risked everything to leave all they'd ever known. Little money, few possessions, and not a word of English. Just a desire for a better life for themselves and their children.

"We managed to sell our load of bananas, and I handed the money over to my wife. She'd told me she was handling the payment for the boat." Binh spoke in a quiet monotone. "My wife was nervous, and the baby started to cry."

Rachel had checked with Pete last night about whether telling the story might be too much for Binh, but he'd said Binh was willing.

"I remember my wife rocking the baby to sleep and whispering to Mai. It irritated me at the time, because I wanted to nap in the shade." He shook his head. "If I'd known what was to happen, I'd have clung to her too."

A feeling of dread leaked into Rachel's gut. Their footsteps were loud on the silvery-grey weather-worn boardwalk, laid to protect the sand dunes from their feet.

"In the middle of the night, we abandoned the cart, picked up our few belongings, and set off for the tiny harbour."

Her imagination filled in the details of fear. Rachel fisted her hands. Obviously Binh and Mai had made it, but what had happened to his wife and the baby?

"There were others there, all trying to keep quiet. We'd given something to the baby to make him sleepy. My wife handed him to me. The boat men pushed us all on to the boat. It wasn't until we sat down that I realised my wife wasn't with us."

Binh turned his face away from Rachel and took some deep breaths.

"Binh, you don't have to tell me all the details."

He turned back to her. "It's important. Most Australians are sheltered from suffering. It does get easier every time I tell the story. Somehow God shines his light into the darkness and gradually eases the sting."

Rachel had found this to be true, too.

"I searched the boat, becoming more desperate with every second. Then one of the others tugged my arm and said, 'sit down' and pointed to the jetty. My wife was standing there, and a man was holding her arm. There were others there too, men and women." He swallowed noisily. "There'd been no miracle. My wife had sold the only thing she had to save the rest of us."

The tears ran down Rachel's cheeks. "Oh, Binh." Her voice cracked. "I'm so sorry."

"I still don't know what happened to her. Whether she's alive or dead."

Rachel wanted to ask questions but didn't know him well enough to dare. It would be like treading on his toes with steel-capped boots.

"I searched after the war, but it was hopeless. She was just one of thousands. The men who sold themselves were forced to fight or labour, but the women's fate was more varied." He stared out to sea. "My wife was very beautiful. I haven't dared to think about what happened to her."

Rachel had always assumed her nightmares were as bad as they got. Maybe not. With two children dying in Vietnam and his wife missing and maybe dead, Binh had enough trauma to fuel any number of nightmares.

"I would never have left my wife, but little Mai looked up at me, and I couldn't abandon the weakest members of my family. I couldn't let my wife's sacrifice be in vain." His voice dropped so low she almost missed it. "I've always wondered if I made the right choice."

A bird soared in front of them, pure white against the bright blue. *Why, Lord, why? Why are some people's lives smooth, and others, often through no fault of their own, have one day of searing pain after another?*

"It was terrible on the boat. Almost no shade and little to drink. The boat owners already had what they wanted, and it was easier for them if we died. Soon the weakest ones started to do so." He shuddered. "They just tossed the corpses over the side and ignored the wailing of the family members."

He sighed again as a couple jogged past, joking and laughing.

"The boat broke down, and we drifted for three days. More people died. They too were thrown overboard. We had already eaten most of our fruit, and I was scared to get the final two pieces out of our bag. How could we eat in front of people who had none? We lay there and prepared to die. My baby son died that morning." His voice shook. "I worried Mai was going to be next. She just lay there with her eyes closed."

Rachel reached out her hand and placed it on Binh's shoulder. "I am so very, very sorry."

"The woman next to us on the boat finally spoke to us. She said, 'Unless my God rescues us, we're all going to die.' I cursed the gods out loud, but she told me about the Creator who controlled the weather. She told me about Jesus, who calmed a storm and fed five thousand people with a few pieces of bread and fish."

"And what did you think, hearing these stories?"

"I thought it sounded crazy, but we were desperate. I didn't care who the god was. If he could help, I'd do anything. The lady prayed, asking the god who created the universe and cared for all the small birds and creatures he'd made, to look down and rescue us."

Rachel turned her head to look at Binh. "What happened?"

"Nothing—for a while. I assumed her God was just like any other god. Quite, quite useless. Someone who didn't care for people like us." He smiled. "I didn't yet know that this God was as different from the gods of my childhood as it is possible to be. He was already working."

Rachel almost grabbed his arm to demand the next part of the story.

"We didn't know, but the two men in charge of the boat had overheard the stories and prayer. They had already been battling with their consciences about several bunches of bananas. The hot weather had ripened them too fast and they couldn't eat them all. The woman's story convinced them to hand them out, so there was enough for everyone on the boat."

"What about the two pieces of fruit you had?"

Binh started to laugh.

"What are you laughing about?"

"Well, the story talked about the little boy who'd brought his picnic and shared it and Jesus turned it into lunch for everyone." He wiped his eyes. "Turns out that most of the people on the boat still had food, but everyone had been too fearful to bring it out in front of others. First, one admitted they had something to share, then others. Soon there was enough for another few tiny meals."

"Wow, that's incredible."

Binh nodded. "Once everyone started sharing, the boatmen admitted they had enough water if we were careful. Together we put up some shade cloth and even a sail."

Two black swans flew over with their clarinet-like calls.

"And the Christian woman led us in prayer for rain and rescue. One of the men said that if this God was going to send rain then we'd better be ready, so we set up the awnings to funnel water and found every container we could."

"And did it rain?"

Binh nodded. "About two hours later it poured. Not for long, but enough. Enough to fill every container twice over. We drank all we could and then saved the rest. The next morning, a boat spotted us and we were towed to the nearest island, which turned out to be part of Malaysia."

"Did Malaysia have refugee camps?"

"It didn't have much choice. Eventually they built camps, and there were others in Indonesia and Thailand and the Philippines. We were some of the first to arrive, and Malaysia wasn't prepared for the sheer number of us." He rubbed his head. "Pirates attacked some boats. Others broke down because they weren't suitable for long journeys. Some say a quarter of the refugees died at sea."

Rachel remembered seeing television reports of the boat people, but they'd only been sad or scared faces on her screen, never real people. Never people like Binh, who'd lost nearly all his family.

It didn't seem fair that she'd grown up in a place where peace was normal. Yes, she'd lost two family members, but neither had been due to the violent injustices of war.

"The camps were full of disease. My baby son would likely have died wherever we went. He was too young to cope with the conditions. Little Mai survived measles and dysentery. We were lucky to have been on an island. It was cooler and probably healthier than other places."

They turned away from the beach to walk along a cement footpath, past gardens which had never experienced anything more violent than a war on weeds.

"How long were you in Malaysia?"

"About fourteen months. Long enough for me to learn some English. I was determined to give Mai and myself the best possible chance of a new life."

Pete had told her that once they'd arrived in Australia, Binh had ended up stacking shelves in a supermarket rather than something more suitable for his obvious intelligence. Prejudice had blocked him from better jobs.

They were nearly back at Binh's home. Rachel still had heaps of questions, but she'd ask them at breakfast. She wanted to hear how Binh had become a Christian and how he'd learned to forgive—because he must have learned to forgive. He couldn't be the man he was without having shed the burden of guilt, anger, and bitterness.

CHAPTER 40

*P*ete mowed the lawn while Rachel and Binh were out. It was the least he could do, and it would be too hot later.

He wanted to talk to Binh too, but it might not be possible with Rachel around.

By the time they returned, the lawn was mowed, the mower was back in the shed, and he'd showered and dressed. He had just finished laying out the breakfast things when they walked in the door, and each headed upstairs to shower and change.

Pete waited until he heard the second shower turn off before he turned on the gas for the frying pan. By the time they were ready for breakfast, the scrambled eggs would be done. Rachel might want muesli, but Binh still preferred a cooked breakfast.

Binh and Rachel arrived at the table at the same time. Rachel's hair still wet, but neatly combed. She wore a casual skirt and blouse, and looked summery. He wasn't going to say anything, though. She'd once told him how much she hated those sorts of comments from men.

"We saw dolphins," she said, taking a seat. "And heaps of black swans."

"It was a perfect morning for a walk," Binh said. "You should visit more often." He held out his plate for some eggs, and Pete served him straight from the pan.

Pete took a piece of wholegrain toast out of the toaster and sat down with his eggs. "Did Binh tell you his story?"

"We got as far as the Malaysian refugee camp." Rachel poured milk onto her muesli.

Mai had once told Pete that she remembered little of their boat trip from Vietnam to Malaysia, but the trip to Darwin had been clearer in her mind. She'd described her bewilderment at arriving in a totally alien place surrounded by white people who jabbered at them with too-fast English.

"Binh, were you going to tell Rachel how you became a Christian?" Pete asked as he put some salt on his eggs.

Rachel swallowed her mouthful. "It's not too much for you?"

Binh shook his head. "I've told you the hardest part of the story. It was much easier once we arrived here and met Jesus."

"Did you ever see the lady who told you about Jesus again?" Rachel asked.

Binh smiled. "Yes, she and her daughter became our good friends in the camp. They told us lots of Bible stories."

"But they didn't come to Australia with you?"

Binh shook his head. "They had relatives in France." He shrugged. "We never had their address so we couldn't write to them."

Binh had once told Pete he'd chosen Perth to escape his past. It had paid off in terms of language acquisition, but it must have been tough for the first couple of years. Especially not having people around who understood anything of his past life.

"The last thing our friend said to us was that she'd be praying God would guide us to real Christians who'd look after us."

Rachel leaned forward. "And did God answer that prayer?"

Binh finished his last mouthful of egg. "The person who was

assigned to help us settle knew Jesus. She not only helped us fill in all the paperwork and taught us how to find second-hand clothes, but took us to church with her that first Sunday."

Rachel held up the teapot. "Tea for anyone?"

Binh declined but Pete handed her his cup.

"Mrs Jennings organised a place for us to stay that first year and helped me with banking and enrolling Mai in school." Binh paused. "Helped with everything, really. She also found us a church." He chuckled. "We were the only non-white faces there, but they eventually got used to us."

It made sense to Pete that Binh would later help other migrants to settle. He'd never forgotten what it had felt like to be welcomed.

"My grandmother was involved in welcoming migrants. She said it was a task that Christians were uniquely able to do," Rachel said.

"She's right." Binh sipped his tea. "We'd already seen God's hand at work, so it didn't take long for us to become Christians. Mrs Jennings found someone to read the Bible with us. We read in Vietnamese, they read in English, and we discussed it as best we could."

Rachel nibbled her lip. She seemed nervous, but Pete had no idea why.

She shifted backwards in her seat. There was definitely something on her mind.

"Binh." She leaned forward. "I appreciate hearing your story. I know it must be difficult to share, but I have one question. I've been struggling with forgiving someone ..." She flushed. "But when I hear your story, you've had so much more to forgive. How did you do it?"

"I didn't," Binh said.

Rachel's eyes widened, and Pete started praying.

"It didn't happen quickly. There was too much to forgive. My fellow countrymen, the Americans, my wife, God, and even myself."

Lord, help Binh's words to connect with Rachel.

"About a year after I became a Christian, I went through a terrible few months. The pastor had been talking about how God is in control of all history." Binh held out his cup for more tea. "I walked out and locked myself in the toilets." He chuckled. "The pastor came and found me."

"What did he say?" Rachel asked.

Binh laughed. "I can't even remember. He spent the next few weeks listening to me and praying. He wasn't afraid of my anger or doubts."

Pete put down his cutlery. "Is that where you learned to encourage people to talk out their feelings?"

Binh nodded. "I guess so. That's why I purposely came to see you a few weeks after Mai and the children's funeral. He'd shown me that Christians don't have to have all the answers. It's more important to be with people and let them talk. He taught me not to be afraid of tears."

"I think I've been afraid my emotions would shock people." Rachel's voice cracked and she covered her eyes with her hand.

If it was a simple matter of shouldering her burdens, Pete would do it in an instant. But this was something between her and God. As a child he'd once tried to help a butterfly out of its chrysalis. He mustn't do the same for Rachel. The struggle was part of the journey.

"I'm grateful God provided Gina and Dirk." Rachel pointed at Pete with her chin. "And Pete."

His heart soared. *Progress.*

"I can't really explain how I came to forgive," Binh said. "It was step by painful step, and I often had to forgive the same people over and over again. The more I got to know Jesus, the more I trusted him, and the more he led me to lay down my burdens of bitterness."

"Burdens of bitterness," Rachel murmured. "Yes, that is what it feels like."

"One of the things I found really helpful was doing a Bible study on forgiveness. I looked at every story or verse on the subject that I could and wrote notes on it."

"That sounds like something I could do," Rachel said, reaching out to gather the empty plates in front of her. "Thank you for trusting me with your story." She stood up. "Pete has been dying to talk to you. Why don't I do the dishes and give you two a chance to catch up."

CHAPTER 41

*R*achel sat at the desk in her room back in Perth. Binh had given her a list of Bible stories about forgiveness—both God forgiving people and people choosing to forgive others. Already she was finding it helpful, but she was also going to do one more practical thing.

She took out a sheet of A4 paper and picked up her pen. She wrote a single word.

DEAR

She stopped. Nibbled her pen. The second word was problematic. She didn't want to call him 'Dad', but 'Father' seemed so formal. She still sometimes called him 'William' in her mind, but she couldn't write it. There was no use starting the reconciliation process by upsetting him on the second word. *Lord, give me wisdom.*

She decided on 'Father,' and paused. What to write next? The truth would be best.

I FIND THIS LETTER ALMOST IMPOSSIBLE TO WRITE, LIKE TRYING TO CROSS THE HARBOUR BRIDGE IN A SINGLE LEAP. I'M CHOOSING TO WRITE AS A FIRST STEP. I DON'T PROMISE THAT THIS WILL BE EASY OR THAT I'LL BE DELIGHTED TO SEE YOU THE DAY AFTER CHRISTMAS.

Her hand shook and she laid down the pen. Christmas. Families did Christmas together, but it would be better if her parents would give her more time to adjust to everything. Christmas was only a month away. Last Christmas they'd still had Esther and Gran.

GOD HAS MADE IT CLEAR TO ME THAT I CAN'T CLAIM TO FOLLOW HIM AND LIVE WITH ANGER IN MY HEART. OTHERS HAVE MUCH MORE TO FORGIVE THAN I DO. THEIR EXAMPLE HAS SHOWN ME FORGIVENESS IS NOT ONLY POSSIBLE, IT'S A NECESSITY. NOT JUST BECAUSE JESUS BOTH COMMANDED AND DEMONSTRATED IT, BUT BECAUSE MY HEART NEEDS TO BE SET FREE.

On the way out of Mandurah, she'd asked Pete to stop at a newsagent. She'd bought a journal and that evening had written out her discussion with Binh. Esther's journals had obviously helped her process her life. Maybe journalling would help Rachel, too.

MY GOAL IS TO WRITE TO YOU EACH WEEK BETWEEN NOW AND WHEN YOU RETURN. NOTHING FANCY. JUST WHAT'S ON MY HEART AND THINGS I'M DOING.

THIS WEEK I'M IN PERTH WATCHING JOSH'S SOCCER GAMES AS HE REPRESENTS NEW SOUTH WALES. I HOPE YOU MEET HIM

It would have been a good test to see how her father related to Josh if they met, but her mother had probably already told him about Josh. The old William would have walked to the other side of the road to avoid anyone with a disability.

If William was really a new creation as he seemed to be, then he would make an effort with Josh. He'd better. Her friends were a non-negotiable. Esther's diaries had recorded how William had wrecked several of her previous relationships, including one with someone William deemed unsuitable. At that point, Esther hadn't had the courage to stand up and do what was right. Cancer had been the inciting factor in her journey, the change that not only gave her the ability to stand against their father but also a heart big enough to forgive him.

Rachel looked back over what she'd written. She didn't know what else to write. Hopefully, it would get easier over the coming weeks. Since she was here watching soccer, she'd write about soccer.

JOSH IS PLAYING IN THE SPECIAL OLYMPICS. NSW LOST THE SEMI
AND WILL BATTLE IT OUT FOR THIRD PLACE.

William probably had no interest in soccer, but she had to fill the letter somehow.

We've also been cycling around Perth, and we drove down to Mandurah. Lots of unusual plants which seem to like sandy soil. Have you ever been here?

Rachel wrote a few more lines, wrestled with how to sign off the letter, and ended up writing:

Sincerely, Rachel.

The letter was sincere, so that was an appropriate way to end.

Now she'd wait and pray and see how her father responded. If he had truly changed, she'd hear from him soon.

CHAPTER 42

*B*ack in Sydney the following Tuesday night, Rachel picked up the mesh bag of soccer balls, draped it over her shoulder, and headed towards the car park with Pete. She opened her car and slung the balls in the back.

"Wasn't it great having Josh back?" Pete said. "All cock-a-hoop about his medal."

"And not at all upset that it was only a bronze."

Pete handed her the stack of plastic cones and she added them to the pile of equipment. He then propped himself against the side of her car.

"Ian and Lyn were more excited with his sportsmanship award," Rachel said, attempting to keep the conversation going.

Pete had seemed distracted all evening. She'd had to nudge him several times when it was his turn to do things. One of the players had said loudly that he must have a girlfriend. She hoped not. She couldn't handle any more heartache at the moment.

"Rachel?"

"Yes?" She tried not to sound too eager to prolong the conversation—any conversation.

"Have you heard back from your father yet?"

She'd told Pete she'd written, and he'd said he'd pray with her.

"No, but I'm sure he'll write back as soon as he receives my letter. I'm not sure how long the mail takes to and from Lord Howe. I might get a reply by the end of this week."

She'd only been doing her Bible study on forgiveness a few days, and she'd also begun to pray regularly for her father, but already she was convinced this was the right thing to be doing. She was content whether they remained at a polite distance or God did a miracle and she ended up with a real father. God could be trusted. He'd brought her this far, and he wasn't going to abandon her now.

"I'm praying often." Pete's voice was as gentle as a butterfly kiss.

Rachel turned her head away as the heat of a blush warmed her neck and cheeks. *Oh, Lord, you know the desires of my heart.* She no longer wanted to just be friends, although it would be easier in many ways. She now wanted to unsay her words after Josh's birthday party. The Perth trip had shown her even more of Pete's qualities. In her experience it was rare for a man to remain such good friends with a woman who had rejected him.

"—that's what I'd like, more than anything," Pete said.

Horrors. She'd missed something important. Pete was looking at her with a mix of expectancy and something else. Anxiety?

"Pete, I'm sorry. I was preoccupied and missed most of what you said."

He coughed. "I hope that isn't a sign of things to come."

"Truly, I am sorry. I do want to listen to what you have to say." Had she missed the words she most wanted to hear?

Pete cracked his knuckles and took a deep breath. "I was asking if you thought there was any hope of a future for us?" His Adam's apple bobbed. "As a couple, I mean."

"Yes," she blurted. Her face heated. "My mind seems to have changed over the last few weeks. N-not my mind exactly, but my decision ..." Her voice trailed off. She sounded like a teenager instead of a woman in her forties.

A smile twitched at the corner of Pete's mouth. "Are you saying yes to exploring whether we try to make it as a couple?"

She nodded. "I wanted to before, but thought I wasn't nearly good enough for you. I still think that ..." All the fears in her mind surged out like ants disturbed from their nest. Tension knotted in her neck.

Pete beamed at her. "Let's get this straight right from the beginning. It has nothing to do with being good enough or not. God wants his children to follow him and honour him. Let's put that as our priority and see where he leads." He peeled himself off her car. "Neither of us have felt we deserved to be happy. We've both been nodding our heads in time with the music of Satan's lies."

"But we have made progress."

"It's only since Dad told me about using God's word as a sword to fight that I realised how often I believe Satan's lies. Every day. Several times a day, actually. It's scary." He touched her elbow. "Let's walk to the end of the street and back."

They hadn't even started this relationship, and yet she was going to have to set a boundary. A boundary her old acquaintances would never understand. But, if this relationship was going to be about honouring God from day one, it had to be done. "Pete, there's something I need to say."

He turned towards her with a flash of a smile. "I wonder if it's the same thing I want to say, and which is making me feel just as ill at ease."

She felt nervous as well, but this was Pete. Her friend. The person who'd been most like a brother. There was nothing to fear. She took a deep breath, her stomach fluttering. "I feel we need to go slowly. Not because you make me feel uncomfortable." She laughed dryly. "Rather the opposite, but I've made too many mistakes in the past, and I don't want to do that again."

He laughed, a warm sound that put her at ease. "I was going to suggest the same thing."

They reached the end of the street and turned around. Above them, a shy sliver of silvery moon peered through a patchy smattering of clouds.

"If we're going to go slow, we better stop walking in the darkness on such a beautiful night."

Rachel laughed. "Uh-huh." Nights like this were made for holding hands and sharing long kisses.

"Josh is going to be delighted with our news."

Pete chuckled. "He'll probably try and take credit for setting us up."

They walked back into the well-lit car park and Pete winked at her. "Miss Rachel Macdonald, will you do me the honour of having dinner with me tomorrow evening?"

Her heart sank. "I can't do tomorrow evening, and Thursday is soccer training."

"Well, Friday then."

"Friday is all yours."

Pete cleared his throat. "We'd better not make it too formal. If I see you again in the dress you wore at the annual party, I'll lose my head and trample over our guidelines."

"Was that what happened at the party? I couldn't work out why you avoided me."

He rubbed his eyebrow. "I wasn't expecting to see a vision of beauty in the nursery after months of boots and work clothes. That evening woke me up from my long slumber." He cleared his throat. "I was afraid everyone would notice my change of heart."

She wanted to do cartwheels round the car park, but at this stage of life she'd do herself an injury. She contented herself with unlocking her car door while grinning like a Cheshire cat.

Pete opened it for her. "See you tomorrow, Rachel."

She blinked. He'd never said her name with such warmth

before. She'd see him tomorrow and the day after, and the day after that. She hugged the thought to herself.

She put the key in the ignition and started the car.

Gina had moved into Rachel's house the previous weekend. Poor Gina was going to have to cope with a housemate who was drunk on emotion and probably incoherent.

Hip, hip, hooray!

EPILOGUE

*E*ighteen months later

Pete looked on as the technician ran the ultrasound wand over Rachel's belly. "There's the baby, no—just a minute." The woman moved the wand around and peered more closely at the screen.

Rachel gripped Pete's hand and looked at him with large frightened eyes.

Pete stroked his thumb over her hand. Pregnancy had unsettled her. Maybe it was the hormones. Lately, she'd found it easier to listen to her fears rather than the quiet voice of truth. She and Pete were having to take those fears to God once again, fighting with their spiritual sword, and learning to trust. Every single day.

"No, I was wrong. Not one baby, but two," the woman said, beaming up at him as though she'd produced a rabbit out of a hat.

"What?" Pete choked mid-breath.

"You're expecting twins," the woman said.

Tears ran down Rachel's face and she grabbed Pete's hand. "I can't believe it."

He leaned down and kissed her enthusiastically.

"We'll have to believe it." He gestured at the screen. "I'd say that proves it."

Rachel looked up at him, her eyes shimmering with tears. For some reason she'd been convinced she'd never have a baby. She had even warned him before they were married, but he had told her it didn't matter. He wasn't sure how he'd feel about being a father again anyway.

But God had known him better than he knew himself. Known he'd want fatherhood more than anything once given the chance, and now—Pete kissed Rachel again—now they'd be parents twice over.

He couldn't wait to tell the soon-to-be grandparents. He and Rachel hadn't said anything to them until now. They hadn't wanted to raise anyone's hopes, not when the baby would be the first and probably only grandchild on both sides of the family.

Rachel had been nervous from the minute she found out. Worried she'd miscarry, worried her previous abortion, or her age, would lead to complications. All her old fears that God would punish her for her past had reared their ugly heads. She said she knew God didn't work like this, but somehow fear clouded her thinking.

She and Pete had finally attended some counselling, separately and together, and that had given them new perspectives.

"Congratulations to you both." The technician handed Rachel some tissues. "It's easier if you wipe the gel off yourself." She pointed out the rubbish bin.

Pete's heart glowed with pride. It had taken him a while to convince Rachel he loved her, but things had moved rapidly once she finally believed him.

He'd been so proud of her on the day they were married. William might not have been a major part of the service, but he was there. Rachel had insisted he must be invited. She said Naomi would have wanted it.

Of course, things weren't yet perfect between Rachel and her father, but William and Blanche came over regularly for dinner, and the relationship was moving in the right direction.

Rachel rearranged her clothes and peered in the mirror to check her hair. She'd let it grow out after an earlier haircut, and he loved the way it framed her face. He loved lots of things about Rachel.

He reached out his hand. "Ready to go home?"

She smiled the smile that always made his heart stop and took his hand. "Sure am."

His eyes moistened as they walked out the door. *Twins.*

He restrained himself from bugling the news to the other parents-to-be in the waiting room and contented himself with a proud going-to-be-a-father smile.

First, a special celebratory lunch. Then, they could look forward to telling all the family, including Binh. They were going to be one large group of doting grandparents.

He kissed Rachel's hand and tucked her arm under his.

He used to think he was a strong man, until he'd been overwhelmed by losses he thought he'd never get over. Now he was overwhelmed again.

Overwhelmed by joy and the extraordinary grace of second chances.

ENJOYED GRACE IN THE DESERT?

Reviews sell books.

This book is independently published which means the only way it will be discovered is if readers tell others. Online reviews are a concrete way of helping authors.

How to write a review – easy as 1-2-3

1. A few sentences about why you liked the book or what kind of readers might enjoy this book. Even one word turns a mere star rating into a review.
2. Upload your review - the same review can be copied and pasted to each site. The priority sites are Amazon (you need to be a regular customer), Goodreads, BookBub, Koorong (for Australians), Kobo ...
3. If you loved the book please also share your review on your personal social media. Anywhere you can spread the word is appreciated.

A book can never have too many reviews.

STORYTELLER FRIENDS

Becoming a **storyteller friend** (http://subscribe.storytellerchris-tine.com/) will ensure you don't miss out on new books, deals and behind the scenes book news. Once you're signed up, check your junk mail or the 'promotions' folder (gmail addresses) for the confirmation email. This two-stage process ensures only true storyteller friends can join.

Facebook: As well as a public author page, I also have a VIP group which you need to ask permission to join.

BookBub - allows you to see my top book recommendations and be alerted to any new releases and special deals. It is free to join.

NON-FICTION BY CHRISTINE DILLON

1-2-1 Discipleship: Helping One Another Grow Spiritually
(Christian Focus, Ross-shire, Scotland, 2009).

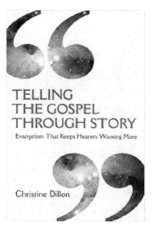

Telling the Gospel Through Story: Evangelism That Keeps Hearers Wanting More (IVP, Downer's Grove, Illinois, 2012).

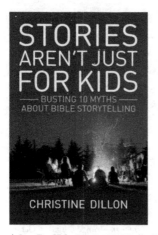

Stories Aren't Just For Kids: Busting 10 Myths About Bible Storytelling (2017).

This book is free for subscribers. It's a 'taster' book and includes many testimonies to get you excited about the potential of Bible storying. All these books have also been translated into Chinese.

FICTION - GRACE SERIES

Book 1 - Grace in Strange Disguise (October, 2017)

Book 2 - Grace in the Shadows (July, 2018)

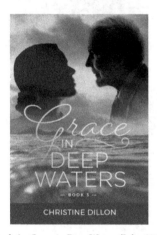

Book 3 - Grace in Deep Waters (July, 2019)

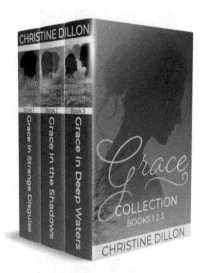

Box Set - Books 1-3

The digital novels + audio for books 1-2 can be bought directly from the author (https://payhip.com/ChristineDillon). You need a PayPal account to make your payment.

AUTHOR'S NOTES

Readers often ask authors how much of the story is based on fact or where we get our story ideas. My characters are not based on particular people, although some of the things they say or do might be based on real incidents. The snake incident was inspired by an event that happened last year to a family member. When I heard about their experience, I immediately saw its usefulness to this book.

With regards to setting: The first book mentions places I knew and loved but I didn't specify the place in case I changed details to suit the story. In the second book, I started to name the places and for book three, I consciously started to showcase different areas of my beautiful county. The fourth book highlights Kangaroo Valley which is an amazing place to visit. I had intended to go kayaking on the trip that is mentioned in the book but devastating bushfires closed off the area. The final two books in the series will be set in other areas of Australia. This also allows me to use these settings as the visuals for the book trailers (search for them on Youtube).

Along the way, I've learned a little about quilting, woodwork and more. Book 4 allowed me to learn about Special Olympics.

A COMPANION BOOK

Sword Fighting: Applying God's word to win the battle for our mind
(July, 2020)

The topic of 'Sword Fighting' is mentioned several times in *Grace in the Desert*. This non-fiction book allows the topic to be dealt with more fully and applies the principles to anger, doubt, guilt, low self-esteem, fear …

ACKNOWLEDGMENTS

Each time a book is published, I stand back amazed at what God has done. I am so thankful for the many people who pray. God uses your prayers.

2020 has been a big year with a Dutch translation of the first novel, a boxed set (ebook only), this novel, and also a non-fiction book to accompany the fourth story. Along the way we've also had major changes with the Covid-19 situation. It's another miracle that the book will be released on time since many of those involved were working with more distractions than usual.

A novel is not the place to explain fully what is meant by something like 'Sword fighting' in the Biblical sense of applying God's word to win the battle for our mind. The original non-fiction booklet on the topic has been around since 2008, but I never published it. If people brought up the subject I would send them the manuscript. The catalyst for finally publishing the non-fiction book was that two friends wrote and asked me to do so and it just so happened (I don't believe this was a coincidence) the subject was raised in this novel. The non-fiction should be published about a month after the novel.

One thing I've noticed this time, is how smooth the teamwork of publishing has become. I'm more confident about what help I'm requesting and how to manage the process. My beta readers (they read the book before it is professionally edited and make suggestions about big issues like story, character, and dialogue) and the proofreaders have grown in confidence. We now know who is best with grammar or commas … Thank you to Kate B., Jane C., Sarah L., Jane P., Lizzie R., Suzanne R., Laura T., Claire U., and Kim W. After everyone else finished proofreading, Annie Douglas Lima did another read through. Annie writes young adult, action and adventure, and fantasy novels.

Continued thanks to my editors, Cecily Paterson and Iola Goulton (we've done this four times now) and cover designer, Joy Lankshear (four novels and two non-fiction books).

Discussion Guide

There are discussion guides for each of the novels on my website.

www. storytellerchristine.com.

ABOUT THE AUTHOR

 Christine has worked in Taiwan, with OMF International, since 1999.

It's best not to ask Christine, "Where are you from?" She's a missionary kid who isn't sure if she should say her passport country (Australia) or her Dad's country (New Zealand) or where she's spent most of her life (Asia - Taiwan, Malaysia and the Philippines).

Christine used to be a physiotherapist, but now writes 'storyteller' on airport forms. She spends most of her time either telling Bible stories or training others to do so.

In her spare time, Christine loves all things active – hiking, cycling, swimming, snorkelling. But she also likes reading and genealogical research.

Connect with Christine
www.storytellerchristine.com/

facebook.com/storytellerchristine
instagram.com/christinedillonstoryteller
pinterest.com/storytellerchristine